I1033034

3  23
STRAND PRICE
5 00

# HOLLYWOOD FOREVER

For Pat &
Sylvan,

# HOLLYWOOD FOREVER

## SUSAN GOLDSTEIN

**FIVE STAR**

*A part of Gale, Cengage Learning*

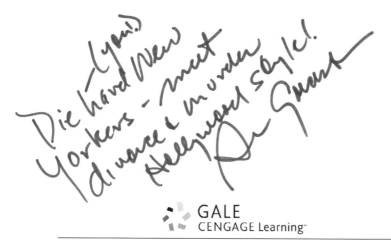

Die hard New
Yorkers - meet
divorce & murder
Hollywood style!.

**GALE**
CENGAGE Learning™

Detroit • New York • San Francisco • New Haven, Conn • Waterville, Maine • London

GALE
CENGAGE Learning™

Copyright © 2011 by Susan Goldstein.
Five Star Publishing, a part of Gale, Cengage Learning.

**ALL RIGHTS RESERVED**
This novel is a work of fiction. Names, characters, places and incidents are either the product of the author's imagination, or, if real, used fictiously.
No part of this work covered by the copyright herein may be reproduced, transmitted, stored, or used in any form or by any means graphic, electronic, or mechanical, including but not limited to photocopying, recording, scanning, digitizing, taping, Web distribution, information networks, or information storage and retrieval systems, except as permitted under Section 107 or 108 of the 1976 United States Copyright Act, without the prior written permission of the publisher.
The publisher bears no responsibility for the quality of information provided through author or third-party websites and does not have any control over, nor assume any responsibility for, information contained in these sites. Providing these sites should not be construed as an endorsement or approval by the publisher of these organizations or of the positions they may take on various issues.
Set in 11 pt. Plantin.

**LIBRARY OF CONGRESS CATALOGING-IN-PUBLICATION DATA**

Goldstein, Susan T.
  Hollywood forever / Susan Goldstein. — 1st ed.
    p. cm.
  ISBN-13: 978-1-59414-933-7 (hardcover)
  ISBN-10: 1-59414-933-X (hardcover)
    1. Divorce—Fiction. 2. Murder—Fiction. 3. Hollywood (Los Angeles, Calif.)—Fiction. I. Title.
  PS3607.O4857H65 2011
  813'.6—dc22                           2010041862

Published in 2011 in conjunction with Tekno Books and Ed Gorman.

Printed in Mexico
3 4 5 6 7 15 14 13 12 11

To my father, Frank Goldstein, who always inspired me to believe that I could make anything happen. Every step I take, you will always be with me.

And to Denise Dietz, a great editor, cheerleader, and inspiration—but more importantly, a great friend.

# ACKNOWLEDGMENTS

Thank you Jean and the crew of Jean V. Naggar Literary Agency who have believed in me and believed in me. It took a while. My gratitude and thanks to Sheila Brant. I wouldn't have been able to get near the computer—but for you. Thank you to every client and family law attorney who asked, "When will there be a book?" If ever there was a motivating question, that was it. And thank you to some others—you know who you are.

# CHAPTER ONE

I can't exactly pinpoint when I started getting weird. Anyway, weird is relative. And this is Los Angeles.

Maybe it was when I figured out that my husband was cheating on me. Maybe, more likely, it was before that. Maybe, just maybe, it was when my favorite pastime became taking daily walks at Hollywood Forever Cemetery instead of the Beverly Hills flats. Maybe it was when I realized that visiting my "friends" at the cemetery was the best part of my day.

My friends at Hollywood Forever are dead.

They're good listeners. Their troubles are over. And they had real troubles, too. William Desmond Taylor, the infamous Paramount movie director, was murdered. His killer was never caught. He has a crypt at the Cathedral Mausoleum but rests there under the name William Deane Tanner. A complicated story. This is Hollywood.

My other friend is Benjamin Siegel, aka Bugsy. He was murdered, too. It was a mob murder. But what's the difference? Dead is dead. Dead soon stinks, whether it's a car accident or a mob hit. He's buried in the Beth Olam Mausoleum.

Usually, I visit Bugsy and Bill. It's not too long a walk from one to the other. Sometimes I start with Bill. It depends on my mood and who I think will be a better listener that day.

A year ago I started growing roses so that I'd have something nice to bring the boys when I visit.

George Washington, our first president, was a rose breeder. I figure if he could make the time to tend roses, what excuse do I have? I have lots of time. My husband, Benjamin Crowley, yes *the* Benjamin Crowley, is rarely home. I used to think he was working. A lot.

Now I know the truth. It isn't that I'm naive or gullible. Or maybe I am. Maybe I was. It just seemed impossible that my life could be reduced to the plotline of a dime store novel. Not me. I couldn't be living a Lana Turner, Barbara Stanwyck, Bette Davis, 1940s tearjerker. This was me. The tumor had to be benign. The phone call in the middle of the night had to be a wrong number. The plane crash was the flight that took off just before mine. The canyon fire ravishing homes was one canyon away from my house.

I had been raised to believe in happy endings.

And they all lived happily ever after.

Right. Tell that to William Desmond Taylor and Bugsy Siegel.

# CHAPTER TWO

When you exit the Beth Olam Mausoleum, you're looking right at the famous Hollywood sign. It's quite a sight. The mausoleum is to my back, with hundreds of dead Jewish folks resting in peace. In front, headstones pop up like boiling potatoes rising to the surface. The mausoleum is nestled in between swaying palm trees. Overhead, the sun beats down on the headstones like Buddy Rich pounding without pause.

The air is so still that I strain and try to hear any sound. A few leaves quiver softly and I pretend to hear laughter, though I don't. Instead, I think I hear the echoes of mournful sighs from another time. It's all part of my overeager and underused imagination. I laugh at myself, out loud, and the sound I make wraps around the still tombs.

Dead ahead, the Hollywood sign presides over me and the flock.

The ultimate Messiah.

Within seconds of that thought, I think: *Now I've done it. Sacrilegious, irreverent, blasphemous.*

Heaven—is there one? Well, it won't want any part of me. And why should it? I wish my husband was dead. No, better yet, I wish Hunter McCall was dead. And I want to be the person who kills him.

You can learn a lot about death when taking daily walks around a cemetery.

Am I weird? Perhaps. Morbid? Slightly spooky? Deliciously

dangerous? Yeah, dangerous. I like the way dangerous sounds. I should talk to Bugsy about danger. He's probably the cemetery's resident expert on danger. Here's the thing, I would rather be dangerous than complacent.

Am I starting to lose my mind? A little bit. But only a little bit. I'm still able to run the house, attend charity lunches, get the household help paid timely, shop with my friends. In the world where I live, this means I'm sane. But I don't feel the same as I used to feel. Everything has changed.

It is painful to think that a lousy marriage is moving me closer to that fine line, a teetering seesaw between sanity and not.

I hate to think that I, Samantha Crowley, of Beverly Hills, California, formerly Samantha Feldman, of Queens, New York, allowed myself to become everything I hated and despised—a woman whose identity is so integrally intertwined with her spouse that she ceases to exist when he exits. How could I have let this happen?

When did it happen? It wasn't this way before.

Before what? Before we had money? Before Benjamin Crowley became a household name?

Before Benjamin Crowley, the celebrity?

Does life get complicated because of money or because the people we love become treacherous?

Or do the people we love become treacherous because of money? Impossible to figure out where it begins. Definitely impossible to know where it will end.

A few years ago I would have told anyone who asked that my life was perfect. The illusion created by not looking too closely was fabulous. These days I hardly take a breath that's not filled with a combination of self-pity and self-loathing. The illusions kept me afloat and now I'm sinking.

I've tried to explain this to my best friend, my best *alive* friend, Ren. She doesn't get it. She doesn't want to get it. She chain-smokes another Marlboro, rolls her head so that her lustrous dark red hair makes a sensuous half circle, and continues to believe in her immortality. She sails on her illusions and she has no intention of allowing me to disturb her balmy breezes.

I look at the graves and it frightens me that I envy their occupants. After a while my body feels heavy, lead weighted. Ren, at forty, looks as good as a perfect twenty-year-old. She is lithe, graceful, ethereal. A modern-day Juliet Prowse.

Neither of us is healthy. But Ren is happy.

I'm a mess. Yesterday I came up with a new angle on how to get rich in Los Angeles. Start a twelve-step program for the unhappy Beverly Hills babes. Rent the Rose Bowl for the first meeting. Promise them free spa passes and discounted therapy.

Focus. For days I've been commanding myself to focus. I need a plan and now I have one. It came to me in the way that all good ideas do. Cast yourself in a mindless, distracting task and the brain is free to create. In this case, I was tending to my roses. Deep watering. Wondering how much water erupting from my hose comprised four to five gallons. Watching what I hoped was my deep-root system enjoy the generous drink they were receiving on an unseasonably hot April day. The glimmering of the plan came and slowly soaked into my brain like the rose roots lapping the water with dehydrated tendrils.

Armed with the knowledge of my plan, I feel empowered. Ren keeps telling me that I need a good divorce lawyer. I know better. What I needed was a plan. I haven't shared it with anyone except Bugsy Siegel and Bill Taylor. They like it. My plan has high drama for Bill and edgy poetic justice for Bugsy.

Keeping a secret from Ren has been strange. Until recently I shared everything with her. But not this. Not yet.

This morning I got to the cemetery before sunrise. I had an

early morning walk before the sun's heat embraced Los Angeles in a claustrophobic cocoon, and now I have an almost electric buzz. Like a beer buzz with legs. Thinking about my plan makes me vibrate. As I drive back to Beverly Hills, along Santa Monica Boulevard, I finally get what that girl, Sheryl Crow, is singing about.

I drive home and watch the sun come up over Santa Monica Boulevard.

# CHAPTER THREE

It is the twenty-third day in a row I have paced through my living room and tried to imagine life without the Chagall, Matisse, and the very small Picasso. Very small Picasso because the cheap son of a bitch, as I now refer to him, had said "Enough with the artwork already" after my second Sotheby's auction. I had begged and pleaded for a Picasso and he had said, "All right. But just a small one."

Yes, Master. Yessir. Yes, your lordship. Yes, asshole.

And now he will probably want to take one or two in the divorce. Maybe he will decide he wants all three.

I look at the Chippendale armoire we had shipped from the sleepy, quaint Vermont town where we journeyed to "get away from it all." He can have it. He's always liked the old stuff.

Thought it gave him an air of old world respectability. God forbid anyone should think of us as nouveau riche. Even though that's what we are. How come I never saw what a snob Benjamin is? How controlling he is. I let him talk me into leaving college, never writing my book, never having children, never this, never that. How come? Lots of questions. Pointless questions.

I'm turning into a whining divorcee. Which means I'm becoming a bore. It's one thing to whine to Bugsy and Bill, quite another thing to be whining to my living friends. Such and few as they are.

Snap out of it. That's what Ren told me yesterday.

Easy for her to say. Things come easily to Ren. For me, life is

15

more of an effort. It has taken all of my thirty-nine years to tame my shoulder-length, chestnut-brown hair. But the frizz is finally gone. And sure, staying slender came easily for me, but it wasn't as if I've ever had a figure that stopped men in their tracks. The exclamation to describe Ren is WOW! The adjectives are exotic, flamboyant, gorgeous. Adrienne Martel is a sculptress. Not just a sculptress. An extraordinarily talented sculptress. I am painfully in awe of my best friend. That's so much nicer and easier to say than jealous.

Is envy a better choice of words? Who am I kidding? Envy is nothing more than a word created by the jealous.

I have no talents. Zero. Nada. Good old Benjamin, the son of a bitch, has seen to that. This marriage was about *his* talent.

Boring, balding with weird fuzzy gray hair exploding out of his scalp like dirty microwave popcorn, and a workaholic is how I would describe Ren's husband, Stephen, a successful life insurance broker. Rumor has it that he is frightfully dishonest. And my husband is alarmingly handsome and successful. And a cheater. And a son of a bitch.

Ren and Stephen have a son, Blake. I'm not resentful. It's just another place where the cheater cheated me.

Stephen and Adrienne Martel are thrilled to announce a new addition to their happy home: Blake Martel, lucky seven ounces, born—when was Blake born? I think he's fifteen now. I remember the birth announcement like it was yesterday. Ren actually had the printer use the word "thrilled." He insisted it wasn't done that way and she insisted it was, this time.

That's Ren. My friend the trailblazer. My friend the artist. My friend who was always so much more interesting, better-looking, and talented than I. Now, do I sound resentful?

I always wanted to write The Great American Novel. But my husband was the author and I was the wife. Those were our labels. Carved in stone. Like one of Ren's works of art.

By the time Benjamin's third book hit the bestseller list, he could command an advance that would have allowed us to move anywhere in Los Angeles. I wasn't sure where we should move, but when Ren phoned and told me that a perfect house one door down from her house was on the market, indecision became decision. Coldwater Canyon. Beverly Hills nirvana. It had been listed for 2.9 million but Ren knew they were going through a divorce and we could steal it for 2.6 million.

And now we were going through a divorce and someone could steal it from us. Living in Los Angeles is all about timing your next move around someone else's misfortune.

Opportunity in Los Angeles is that interesting German word for which there is no English equivalent. *Schaenfreude.* The feeling of well-being from the tragedy of others.

I'm barefoot. Our floor is cold, hard, beautiful, expensive marble. Sometimes at the cemetery, I take off my sneakers and run the cool, lush, beautiful grass through my toes. It's funny what pleasures cost nothing.

Under the dining room table is our most prized rug. We paid a small fortune for it when Benjamin and I traveled to Tokyo on a book signing tour for his sixth, or it might have been his seventh, book. He wouldn't even let the translator, who traveled with us at the publisher's expense, barter on our behalf. It doesn't look good, he told me. This coming from the man who bargained with cigar-chomping Moe of Moe's Furniture for Less to get a $165 sofa for $115. The sofa was on the curb in front of the store, but that was another lifetime.

In the last twelve years, Benjamin has forbade me to tell that story. He also demands that I stop calling him Ben or Benny like I used to when we were first married. Like I used to when we were in love. That was a name for the unpublished.

I have to stop thinking. I need an OFF button. I look out the stained beveled windows of our dining room. The specially designed windows cost more than three gardeners—on my street—earn in one year. Combined.

Indulgent. Extravagant. Unnecessary. Our life in three words.

In front of my house I watch a tall, slender, barefooted black man, dressed from his neck down to his ankles in black spandex, hold a silent boom box over his head as he dances and twirls on my sidewalk. Well, not actually my sidewalk. The City of Beverly Hills sidewalk, directly in front of my home.

It's always a strange sight to see a street person in this city of the rich and famous. I wonder if the boom box works. I hear no sound coming from it. He is dancing to a tune playing in his head. Good for him. We should all dance to our own tunes.

If I walk out to the sidewalk and start dancing with Dancing Man, will my neighbors think I am crazy? Will they run to their telephones to spread the word that Samantha Crowley, wife of prominent author Benjamin Crowley, has gone out of her mind because her husband left her? Or might they say, "Look at Sam, that free spirit, whirling and twirling in the street with the common man"? Nah.

I run upstairs to throw on a pair of pants and shoes. I'll go out in the street and move and shake with the dancing man.

I have a wardrobe that would put the second floor of Bloomingdale's to shame. The gray linen pants look good with the white cotton Fred Segal T-shirt I purchased for $55. Ren laughed and told me she could get the same T-shirt at K-Mart for $8. She's probably right. Now that I am getting divorced, maybe I should think about such things. I will. But that's tomorrow. Another day.

Scarlett O'Hara postponed bigger decisions.

By the time I get out the front door, the Dancing Man is gone. Isn't that always the story? One tiny delay for a wardrobe change and opportunity vanishes.

I look up and down my street, but there is no sign of Dancing Man. As if he had never been here.

As if he had been a hallucination. Even worse, a foreboding of things to come. Was I going to end up out on the street with nothing? Would I be poor after my divorce? Homeless?

Now I am truly hallucinating. Benjamin and I have a net worth of more than twenty million dollars, with a constant flow of money coming in on a daily basis from his novels, television serializations and adaptations, movies made from books, computer games, toy and comic book deals, and Internet sites.

Nike wanted Benjamin for a commercial. The closest Benjamin's been to a basketball or baseball since we met is watching ESPN at a party once a year. I have to stop thinking this way. We have plenty of money.

I look up and down our palm tree–lined street and watch the flapping green fronds cut into a perfect royal blue sky as smoothly as a knife cutting through a Boston crème pie. Each house is different. Each beautiful in its own unique way.

The house next door to me on the south side is a magnificent Mediterranean limestone, a small castle, although fortress might be the better word. Ren lives on the other side of that house and, in the past year, neither she nor I have ever heard a sound from that house, never seen a person enter or leave. No deliveries, housekeeper, not even the pizza man ringing the bell.

But someone does live there. Lights go on and off. The postman brings mail. Someone mysteriously retrieves the mail, even though Ren and I have never caught a glimpse of him or her.

Ren's girlfriend, Bea, who works for the biggest realty company in Beverly Hills, ran the title on the house. The former owners, an elderly couple, sold the home for 3.1 million dollars to a corporation known as "Ghosts and Such." As if the whole damn thing wasn't mysterious enough.

Maybe Bugsy or Bill's ghost took a shine to me and rose from the grave to buy the house next door.

*Keep it up, Samantha!* When I think this way I know I'm wobbling on the sanity tightrope.

Ren and I love the idea that we have our very own Boo Radley. Who doesn't love *To Kill a Mockingbird*? Who wouldn't love to live next door to Boo?

We joke about it a lot. Almost always ending our conversation with the words "Boo, who?"

Benjamin told me Ren and I are juvenile, and it was no wonder that our neighbor had chosen anonymity when faced with the prospect of being befriended by two such bothersome women.

And that's one of Benjamin's kinder comments.

Benjamin left me. *He* left me. Why had I stayed with this man?

My phone is ringing. I run inside the house, knowing that contact with any living human is better than being alone with my present thoughts. I do not have one healthy preoccupation.

It's Ren. Thank goodness. A sane, loving shoulder and brain. We used to talk five times a day, but I have become distant, removed, and I sense she feels me slipping away.

"What were you doing for the last ten minutes, standing on your front lawn?" Ren pulls no punches.

"You were watching me?" Even odder than me standing on my lawn doing nothing was the idea that Ren had been watching. She couldn't possibly have seen me from any window in her house, so she, too, would have had to be standing outside.

Who's more crazy, the watcher or the watchee?

"Not exactly watching," she says. "I took a letter to my box for the postman to pick up and I saw you. I was going to call out but I figured I'd telephone. I waited a couple of minutes and then popped outside to make sure you were back inside, and there you were, still standing on the lawn. Then I checked every few minutes."

"Why didn't you call out to me?"

"I don't know."

No one in the world loves telephones more than Ren. We live 250 feet away from one another, but she would prefer to talk on the phone. My ear gets tired. Ren has a cell phone in her car, her home, her handbag, her art studio, her gym bag. She is never away from a phone. Maybe yet another illness that requires a twelve-step program.

"I was just thinking," I say, a non-answer to two questions back.

"About what?"

"I don't know . . . our street, Boo, my life, my divorce, becoming a homeless person."

"Okay, stop this right now. Enough! You need to retain the best lawyer Benjamin's money can buy. I was just talking to my friend, Lou Ann, and her best friend just hired—"

"Stop. Please. I don't care. Really."

"Don't be a fool. That's all you should be caring about."

I hear Ren's sharp intake of breath, which means she just lit a cigarette. It doesn't matter what the surgeon general or anyone says. It is *her* life.

"Ren, we've been through this. The bag lady thing is a joke. Just me being melodramatic and feeling sorry for myself. You and I both know the law. We've been through this with Diane and Cassie and Janet . . ."

When I start thinking about all of our divorced friends, I wonder how I ever thought my marriage was invincible. In Beverly Hills, kryptonite comes in the form of a flawless, twenty-four-year-old babe who gets confused between cellulite and cellular. Benjamin's babe, so the rumor mill tells me, is a predictable form of kryptonite.

I pick up where I cut myself off. "And we know the law. It's fifty-fifty."

Ren takes a deep drag. "Right. So why do I get the feeling there's more going on here."

That's why I love Ren so much. I never meant to sound like I didn't. She can read me perfectly.

Definitely a hell of a lot better than my husband of more than eighteen years.

"Fifty-fifty is just not going to be good enough." I've muffled my voice. Maybe Ren won't hear me.

Ren chuckles softly, the sound tinged with conspiracy. How *does* she make that sound?

"More. You want more than fifty percent, Sam. I think we need to look into Beth's lawyer. He was the one who—"

"No!" I didn't mean to shout. At least, I didn't mean to shout at Ren.

I intended to keep the plan a secret between Bugsy, Bill, and me. But Ren is my best friend. My reality. I need to talk and hear talk back occasionally. At times I can be infuriatingly female. I need to tell someone. Even if it's against my better judgment. Without an ounce of menace in my voice, I tell Ren the essence of my plan. All I have is essence. The details will follow in time.

"He's got to die," I say, "and I'm going to do it."

Ren gasps. She doesn't fluster easily and it had not been my intention to unnerve her. "Oh my God! Forget the lawyer. You need the name of Beth's therapist."

"Ren, calm down. I don't need either."

"I've resumed breathing. I'm in control. I'm listening." Ren shares my flair for melodrama. "I thought you were talking about real dead. Like needing a hit man, a killer, whatever they're called."

"Exactly. But different, of course."

"Sam, I'm getting nervous again and I'm not following you. Usually I do."

"It's simple. Take me *literally*. He's got to die. If he's not mine, then he's going to belong to no one."

"Honey, I know you love Benjamin, or at least I know you once loved Benjamin, but—"

"Benjamin? Ren, you've got this all wrong."

There is no response. I hear Ren inhale and can visualize her cigarette burning.

"I'm talking about Hunter McCall. I have no intention of allowing him to live. Hunter McCall must die."

# Chapter Four

"That's what you're going to wear?" Ren is giving me her most disapproving look but I don't care. The new me.

"Why not? I don't have to impress him. He has to impress me."

Ren is taking me to a Beverly Hills divorce lawyer. She has corrected me three times already. In California, they are called family law attorneys. In my mind, the use of the word "family" for a lawyer who is going to end your marriage makes no sense.

For this most auspicious occasion I don old, beat-up sneakers, black leggings that unequivocally prove I am no longer built like a twenty-year-old ingénue, and a wine-colored, mid-thigh-length, chenille sweater. I look like I am ready for freshman English 101. I feel like I am ready for a plot at Hollywood Forever Cemetery. This morning I missed my sunrise walk for the first time in months. No matter how much I look like a college freshman, this morning I feel ancient.

"Fine," Ren says "If that's what you want to wear, it doesn't matter, but let's get going. Your appointment is at eleven."

It is 10:30 A.M. and we are driving there in the new Hummer that Stephen just purchased for Ren. We will be there in five minutes.

Driving with red-headed Ren in her open-topped Hummer makes me feel like I am with Maureen O'Hara on her way to rescue John Wayne from some uprising in a tropical forest. It is a nicer image, far more exotic, than two perimenopausal Beverly

Hills ladies off to see a divorce lawyer. We're off to see the wizard. Hah.

Ren is wearing a high fashion–looking Versace summer dress with matching shoes. Her version of fatigues.

Bright orange and green is usually a fairly abominable combination but smashing on Ren.

"You look better for the part than I do, Ren. Let's switch identities. You say you're me and I'll be the supportive friend."

Ren sneers.

We get to lawyer Denny Brillstein's office fifteen minutes early. His reception area is almost as large as my too-large living room. The artwork equals or bests mine. The furniture is Italian, like mine, and I can't help wondering if Beverly Hills family law attorneys have to wait five months for deliveries.

Ren and I walk up to the receptionist, who I'm sure is waiting for a call from either Paramount or Warner Brothers. She is a cutie. Wouldn't it be too funny if the divorce lawyer's receptionist is Benjamin's new babe? I'm working myself into a slow, quiet rage. It happens that way sometimes. It pops out of nowhere, starts like a small harmless fire at a campsite, and flares into a full-scale conflagration.

I tug on Ren's dress sleeve and whisper loud enough for Miss November to hear, "Ren, this isn't a good idea. We should leave."

She gives me an upraised eyebrow and tells the receptionist my name.

"Now." I say the one-syllable word more than audibly.

She gives me another look and I sit down quietly and turn my attention to last month's *Vanity Fair*. If I hadn't married Benjamin, they would probably be doing an article about me. It doesn't cost to fantasize. Twenty minutes later, we are escorted into Denny Brillstein's office.

For the next three minutes we are bombarded with offers of coffee, soft drinks, espresso, muffins—both fat and non-fat—

and Perrier or Pellegrino. Denny assures us that we should call him Denny. I wonder if it is short for Dennis or Denzel. I have a thirty-second fantasy about Denzel Washington and then return to earth. It is fantasy day. We are introduced to Brillstein's secretary, far too young and good-looking to have been his faithful sidekick for much longer than the last three days. Her name is Mindy or Cindy or Windy. It's all a haze. I always mix up consonants.

Ren and I are given a choice of chairs or sofa. We are given the choice of how much light we would like to have filter through the mahogany louvers. Before exiting, Mindy/Cindy/Windy discreetly places a box of tissues near Ren's chair.

They have almost everything down to a science, but are still stuck with those 50/50 Vegas odds of messing up on which one of us is actually the client. Neither Ren nor I utter one word while the dog and pony show plays out. I am perfectly content to sit back in the well-cushioned chair and sip my Diet Coke and watch.

When we finally do formal introductions, I detect Denny's furtive glance at the tissue box, as if he could maybe, through sheer willpower, make it move next to me. I promise myself that if Denny is able to display telekinetic powers, I will hire him as my attorney.

The tissue box doesn't move. Things are not looking good for Denny.

"So you're the wife of the famous Benjamin Crowley." Denny chuckles. When he laughs, his nose wrinkles in an unattractive way. Denny is getting too much sun. He needs some tanning pointers from George Hamilton.

Has someone said something funny? I don't like him. It's not just the chuckle. There is something about his perfectly black, slicked-back hair, with a face so clean-shaven it looks as if he must take a razor to it once an hour. Or maybe it's the navy blue Armani suit that fits so perfectly. Or maybe the tie I recognize from a Neiman Marcus catalogue. It costs $350. Maybe I just don't like his tasseled gray Gucci loafers. Or maybe it's his teeth. How could they be so white and perfect?

Maybe it's because his office is decorated better than my home, which I have always considered to be close to perfect. Or maybe it's because I wanted Diet Pepsi and all he had was Diet Coke. Who knows?

Now that Denny Brillstein has me identified, I wait for his next play.

He looks at Ren and says, "And you're . . ." He leaves it hanging.

I suspect Ren is as unimpressed as I when she succinctly answers, "The best friend."

Denny nods in his imitation of sage.

He puts his fingertips together to make a small steeple. His diamond pinky ring twinkles. I don't notice a wedding band but I do notice him noticing me notice.

He nods in his imitation of commiseration.

"Yes, I've been this route myself," he says. "I'm a single man now. Of course, that means I don't have commitments in the evening that prevent me from being at your service whenever needed."

He speaks the words to me but is mentally undressing Ren. I happen to know Ren is strongly opposed to being mind-raped.

Half an hour has passed, which I calculate to mean at the hourly rate of $750, $375 has been spent for a Diet Coke and the opportunity to see a really beautiful office, to watch Denny lust after my best friend, to see Windy/Cindy/Mindy audition for secretary, or whatever, and to work myself into a rage by imagining my husband getting it on with someone very similar.

I want to click my sneakers together and go home.

"You must have a rather substantial estate," Denny says.

I don't respond, as he has failed to give the last two words of his sentence the higher-pitched inflection that denotes a question.

Denny says, "He's filed?"

I nod yes. Two can play the nodding game.

Denny says, "He can't change any insurance after he files."

My thought is *so what,* but I say nothing.

"Did you and Mr. Crowley have a prenuptial agreement?"

I shake my head.

Short, sweet, and to the point. Denny now knows what he needed to know. With no prenuptial agreement, we are talking about a lucrative divorce where Denny could make mega-bucks. For the next fifteen minutes Ren and I listen to numerous war stories about various Famous People he has represented. In each case he has not only been victorious but cunningly creative, a family law maverick and, though he hates to use the word, he has been told more than once that he is "remarkable."

"You know what's remarkable Mr. Brillstein—"

"No, no, please call me Denny."

I hate when my punch line is trampled.

"You know what's remarkable, Denny? That I've actually stayed here this long." I make the move one makes when exiting a room is imminent. I stand up.

"Were you under the impression that we were here to talk about you?" Ren has figuratively—and literally—risen to my level. She, too, is standing, and she looks as angry as I feel.

Her face has taken on some of the orange flame of her dress.

Denny Brillstein is flustered. *His* face has turned beet red, his suit has wilted, and he looks like a two-day-old salad.

"I think you ladies have completely misunderstood," he says. "If you'll just let me explain, I think we can get this straightened out."

Ren and I exchange a look. She nods. I love it. Our signal to conclude the meeting. I wonder if Denny loses his cool this easily in court or only when he is about to lose a fat retainer.

His words trail after us as the door to his suite *whooshes* shut: "You know we haven't talked about anything substantive and you haven't paid me, so if your husband decides to . . ."

In the elevator, I look at Ren. "We need to get our priorities straight."

She understands completely. "You're right. Where should we go for lunch?"

"You decide. Just pick a place where we can sit as long as we want without interruption."

Ren selects an Italian restaurant in Beverly Hills that is off the beaten track. One winds through a narrow alley to get there. If it is possible for anything in Beverly Hills to cry out FOR LOCALS ONLY, this is the place.

Standing outside the restaurant, within six feet of valet parking, is a street person. He wears blue jeans that give new meaning to "lived in," a tattered black T-shirt, and sneakers that have been cut away in the front to allow his toes to flap freely. His toes, hair, and beard look as though they haven't been washed since the last time my housekeeper scoured the top of my refrigerator.

Like a mantra, he repeats to each person who passes the same words: "Could you loan me $1.83?"

The Valet parking costs $4.00. Where did he come up with $1.83?

I look in my purse and find two singles. Who carries money anymore? Will he accept two dollars? Do I get seventeen cents change?

Am I a complete or only partial idiot to be pondering this?

I hand the man two singles as he asks me, "Could you loan me $1.83?" He takes the money, squints in a way that may be a smile or the glare of sun in his eyes, and asks Ren, "Could you loan me $1.83?"

As the waiter takes our drink orders, Ren's cell phone chirps. Up to now, we'd been on the verge of a Ren record—one full hour with no phone calls. I remind the waiter as he walks away that I want no ice in my diet soda. Ren reminds him to keep the white wine spritzers coming. Whoever she is talking to doesn't seem to care if she has two or three other things happening on her end of the conversation.

I dip a piece of the freshly baked bread into olive oil and I am about to land the delicious combination in the center of my mouth when Bea, the real estate agent, appears at our table. We've never been friends socially but we have frequented the same parties and, in Beverly Hills fashion, have been introduced and reintroduced countless times.

Bea is wearing too much makeup, her hair has been colored too blonde for what I estimate to be her sixty years, and her stylish business suit is too tight and definitely too short for the extra thirty pounds she carries. Other than that, she looks great.

"Hi, Bea. You look great."

Though her mouth is stuffed with bread, Ren manages to greet Bea and continue nodding into the cell phone. I wonder if the person on the receiving end of Ren's call can somehow sense the nods.

"Darling, I've heard your dreadful news," Bea says. "Is there anything I can do?"

I have to pause for a moment and do a quick mental check. Aha. The divorce. The family law matter. I decide to take the same approach I took with the non-telekinetic Denny. Keep it short, simple, and to the point.

"No."

Bea looks as if someone has fed her bad fish. No doubt she anticipated a more protracted response or, at the very least, some soap opera–ish morsels of gossip.

She says, "Would you like me to come out to the house?"

I want to answer "no, not unless you clean refrigerator tops," but decide against easily misconstrued hostility.

"What for?" I ask as Ren continues nodding away on the phone.

"To figure out the right price for a listing. To see what work should be done before it's listed." Bea turns to me. "Darling, I don't want you to feel stressed about this. You can just put everything in my hands and I'll take care of whatever needs to be done. You poor thing. Bea will take care of you."

As far as I can tell, all we have established is that Bea knows her own name but is vague about mine. And the fact that Bea is prepared to trade her first born for the listing on my house.

"Bea, darling, do you really want to help?"

I get the kind of eager nod that would make most sixteen-year-old boys pee in their pants.

"Absolutely. Anything."

"Great. Would you kill Hunter McCall for me?"

There is now no doubt about it. Ren can listen to two conversations at the same time because, almost choking on the luscious brushetta, she ends her call and shoots me a filthy look.

I say the only thing I can think of. "What?"

# CHAPTER FIVE

The rest of lunch does not improve. I am accosted by Jim, the stockbroker. We met a few years ago at a neighbor's party. He wants to know who I have retained to handle my investments. He gives me his email address, website, home and work phone numbers, fax and cell phone numbers, and another that may be his pied-a-terre. All this crammed on one lavender business card. Jim assures me he is familiar with the particular needs of divorcees. From the leer on his face and the pink-flush stain that creeps along his balding scalp, I'm not sure if he is suggesting a solution to my financial woes or my sex life.

A man I have never seen before angles his way to our table. He introduces himself as Dr. Dan, the plastic surgeon who took care of Cassie's "chin problem." Before I can speak, he assures me that with a slight breast enlargement and tummy tuck, I'll be ready to tackle singles life with new zest. There is something scary about the way he says the word "zest." Dr. Dan winks and tells me he'll throw in sucking my thighs for free.

Dr. Dan looks a little like a cross between Bela Lugosi and Bob Newhart. Just perfect since I don't know whether to scream or laugh.

Before I have a chance to do either, he is angling his way to another table while his business card slowly drifts onto my lap.

A man dressed entirely in royal blue, who looks surprisingly like Bette Midler, is strutting across the patio in our direction. I give Ren a questioning look and then realize I am looking at the famous hairdresser, Jupiter. You, too, can have your hair colored and cut for a mere $375.

Jupiter, a complete stranger, actually runs his fingers through my hair while making what sounds like a disgusted gurgle. There is something decidedly creepy about his tentacle-like fingers assaulting my scalp without invitation. Bad goosebumps are traveling down my back.

Jupiter says, "Darling, Diane told me the gory, gory details. She is such a love that she wanted you to know that you can have her regular Thursday appointment. You'll feel oh so much better if we put a different color and texture and style in your . . ." Jupiter is searching for a word, as apparently what rests atop my head does not merit the label hair. "Locks. Call the salon if you're available. Ta."

I never said a word; he never took a breath.

While Jupiter is distracting me, a stocky man with a handlebar moustache pulls up a chair to the table and is studying Ren's breasts. When Jupiter scoots away, the man turns to me and speaks with the enthusiasm of a car salesman. Which is precisely what he is.

"Hi babe, remember me? Bob Kirby. I sold your husband the Mercedes."

I nod in the negative but Bob is obliviously talking away, not the least bit interested or concerned about my response.

"I'm at Lexus now. Here in Beverly Hills. And you'll love the car. Put a little zing back in your life." He too has mastered the one-breath approach and is able to coordinate that with reaching into his breast pocket to hand me a business card.

"I don't need a car, Mr. Kirby." Though judging from today's reviews, I need a lot more zest and zing.

"Call me Bob. You may change your mind. Call me when you do."

He gives Ren and me his best smile. There is a small gap

between his two lower front teeth that makes me think of a comedian I once saw at The Improv. In many ways Bob is funnier.

Ren has watched the parade in silence. I try to smile but all my mouth can do is twitch. I remember what my Mom always said. You smile with your eyes. My eyes are not smiling. "Think it's safe to take a bite?" I ask Ren.

She says, "We go at the count of three."

"It's a plan. One, two . . ."

Wrong again. A woman is smiling and nodding at me from across the room, and though I can't place the face, the smile is familiar. I know it from somewhere. How can one recognize a smile independent of the rest of the face?

"Who is that woman nodding at me like one of those dolls with the bobbing heads?" I ask Ren.

The fork approaching her mouth stops. "Oh my goodness. That's what's her name."

"Ren, it would help if you could be more specific?"

"Right. Let me think a moment." She pauses. "I got it. Dr. Lana Green, the radio psychologist. You know who I mean. She's on the radio from, I think, ten to two every day."

"So what is she doing here now? And why is she nodding at me like an idiot?"

"I couldn't say. Did you ever meet?"

I would have answered no, but before I can, Dr. Lana has descended upon us. It is official. I have become part of some Beverly Hills professionals' feeding frenzy. Hovering over me is the emaciated face of one of the most beloved and famous therapists on talk radio in the United States.

The temptation to crawl under the table is overwhelming.

"Ms. Crowley, it's so nice to see you out and about. I think it's a dreadful idea for one to stay secluded in their home when going through a difficult time."

"Not their home. It's her home or his home." I even stun myself with this snotty, rude correcting retort. On the other hand, I have to confess I find some real, nasty pleasure in cleaning up her grammar. With three published books, the least she can do is learn to speak the language properly.

With a mild air of confusion she says, "I beg your pardon?" Only momentarily daunted by my silence and her inability to grasp the situation, Dr. Lana continues. "I wanted to tell you that I have all sorts of meditation and calming exercises for depression. And if those don't work, there's remarkable medication today with minimal side effects."

I have to put an end to this. Now. So I ask, "Do we know each other?"

"Of course. Don't you remember? We met at the Beverly Hilton lunch given by Writers World of Southern California. You were there with your husband and we were talking about our rose gardens."

Now that she's jogged my memory, I do remember the lunch, one of scores of lunches Benjamin and I routinely attended. At the lunch, Dr. Lana and I had a thirty-second conversation as I checked out her most recent cradle-robbing conquest, whom she introduced as a "dear significant friend."

Based on that thirty-second encounter and the shared experience of a wilted chicken Caesar salad lunch, Dr. Lana apparently feels fully qualified to render an opinion on my mental state and needs.

So I just say what I think. "I remember now. You're Dr. Lana. Based on our thirty-second encounter and an afternoon of wilted chicken Caesar salad, do you feel qualified to render an opinion about my mental state and needs?"

Dr. Lana takes two steps back. "There's no need to be rude. I have some private patients and just thought I might be able to get you in."

I catch her eyeing with disapproval my black leggings and oversized sweater. Perhaps she fears divorce has warped my fashion choices.

"So tell me, Dr. Lana, are you still dating that luscious child hunk you brought to the lunch? He was sort of a cross between Tom Cruise and the Little Rascals."

Dr. Lana looks shocked. Ren looks like the Bolognese may explode out of her mouth. I feel great.

"Well, it's pretty obvious you're in denial and not ready to handle some sound advice to help you move on," Dr. Lana says.

"Tell you what, why don't you move on?" My rudeness gives me a rush. It feels so good.

With that, petite Dr. Lana Green takes her ninety pounds and stalks away from our table in a manner that looks very much like a huff. You need a little more bulk to pull off a good huff.

Ren is staring at me. Bug-eyed.

"I was too terrible, wasn't I?" I say the words but I don't really care.

"Too terrible but also too funny. I loved it. She had it coming. They all have it coming. What a bunch of vultures."

I couldn't have said it better.

"Ren, what am I going to do? It feels like my life is under a microscope. I don't have it in me to be gracious to interfering people who haven't been asked."

Ren takes my hand and holds it. "We'll get this sorted out. It's just going to take a little time."

"I don't know if I can do this. I made him and if he can't belong to me, he should be killed. It doesn't matter what any lawyer tells me, I don't care about the law. I'm not going to change my mind and I need someone who can help me. I won't be happy until he's dead."

The pitch of my tone rises with each sentence. Ren's

complexion visibly pales. I feel slightly hysterical. I probably look mad as a hatter. Ren looks as white as Dracula in need of a transfusion.

"You're back on this again? Sam, you're making me really nervous. To whom are you referring, exactly?"

Ren's use of *whom* makes me grin. "Made you a little self-conscious about your grammar, didn't I? My reading the riot act to Dr. Lana hit home, I see. Of course, the better wording might have been: 'Exactly to whom are you referring?' But no matter."

Now Ren is becoming slightly hysterical. "No matter is right. What are you talking about?"

"Same as before. Hunter McCall."

There, I have said his name again. The name that haunts my days, my nights, and even my sleep. Hunter McCall, whom I know better than anyone on earth.

"Are you out of your mind? You do know that Hunter Mc-Call is a fictional character. A make-believe character who popped out of your husband's brain."

I wince at her words. Too painful. Ren doesn't understand.

I say, "Not true, I'm afraid."

"What do you mean?"

"I was always a supportive wife."

Ren is finally scooping some Bolognese into her mouth and my non-revelatory response is not going to further deter her enjoyment of lunch. She nods.

"Actually, Ren, I was supportive in ways that I've never discussed with you." This more oblique statement merits a grunt while she chews her food and makes a hand motion, which I know means continue.

"You see, Benjamin could spin a fairly good yarn but the personality he lacks was also missing from the characters he tried to create. They were blah."

Ren puts down her fork and is listening intently. Listening with her ears and eyes. The way my Mom said good listeners listen.

"You know what I mean, blah, blah, blah. Nothing. Zero. Not interesting. He needed a character creation, Ren, that's what we're talking about. Creation. What he really needed was for his wife to birth him a child, only not one of flesh and blood. He needed for me to birth him a protagonist for his books. Someone who could live the stories he liked to imagine."

Ren's cell phone rings and she pushes some mysterious button that transfers it to voicemail. She scoops my hands into hers. I look at her long tapered fingers and beautifully manicured nails painted with some unusual colored polish. It looks as if it might be in the yellow family and I think, not for the first time, that if I could look half as good as Ren I would happily die young. A stupid, morbid thought, but at the moment I am consumed with feeling sorry for myself. I should never miss my daily walk in the cemetery. Talking to my dead friends is therapeutic. If I gave it up, I'd need Dr. Lana.

As Ren leans forward to ask me a question in a more hushed tone, half the men in the restaurant turn their heads to stare at her freckled cleavage. With her movement, each freckle takes on a life of its own. Ren says, almost reverentially, "Wait just one minute here. Are you telling me that you created Hunter Mc-Call?"

I bow my head slightly in humble acknowledgment and give her a half smile. I feel like Hercule Poirot modestly admitting to his discovery of the pivotal clue. If I had a moustache, I would have given it a twirl. "What do you think of your old friend now?" I resist saying *mon ami.*

"Well, I don't know. I'm at a loss."

A first for Ren. I'm not at a loss. I want to tell her everything. "He wrote more drafts than I care to remember of Hunter's first foray into crime. Only it wasn't Hunter. In one version it was a dashing, obnoxious ladies' man who was supposed to be like James Bond but was too dumb. When he smartened him up in the next draft, the protagonist was a Nero Wolfe type. This, of course, did not suit Benjamin who wanted his character getting some female action in at least every other chapter. So then he did a third draft and tried to put some charm and humor back into the character, who ended up something like Lew Archer meets Columbo. Hard-boiled humor that wasn't tough or funny. It was a truly dreadful combination."

"I never knew any of this," Ren says. "I thought Benjamin just went into his office and plugged away at the computer six hours a day and came up with this mesmerizing character who had all these adventures."

"Right. That's what he wanted everyone to believe. Benjamin doesn't know Dorothy Sayers from Dashiel Hammett, Frederick Forsyth from Elmore Leonard. When he decided to write these adventure-slash-mystery books he went out and rented sixty videos. For one solid month we watched two movies a day while Benjamin took notes. For Benjamin, the VCR was the greatest invention of the twentieth century. He could pause a movie for as long as he wanted while he took his notes. It's calling ripping off the great writers of the twentieth century."

"I don't believe what I'm hearing."

"Believe it. The movies were great. Quick vehicles to give him ideas about plotting and pacing and dialogue—"

"Wouldn't reading the actual books have been better?"

"Better yes, faster no. Benjamin was in a big hurry and he figured it wasn't about quality. It was about getting the hang of what kind of stories and characters worked."

Ren's phone rings again. She answers it and says, "Not now."

"And he did get the hang of it," I say. "Ben's a fast study. Only he couldn't come up with the right leading man. He needed a protagonist whom his readers would love. He needed a winner with the right balance of brains and suave. Try as he might, each character fell flat."

Ren looks confused. "If you didn't write the books, how did you create the character?"

"It started with me writing a six-page personality profile of Hunter McCall. I created a character that I thought would be original and fit with the entanglements Ben envisioned for him. Before each new book, I'd update the profile to flesh him out, age him, mature him, and give him some new quirks and perspectives. As Ben wrote, he'd ask me what Hunter would do if faced with various different scenarios."

Ren gasps. She's beginning to understand. Anything less than a gasp, I would not have believed she understood. She lights her first cigarette since I started speaking. Ren is riveted. She has forgotten to smoke and is not on the phone.

"I birthed Hunter," I continued. "Ben believed I knew Hunter better than anyone. He didn't trust his instincts for Hunter. At least not as much as he trusted mine."

"Unbelievable. I mean, what you're saying. Unbelievable. This went on through the last book?"

"No. For the last two books he wanted no input from me. He told me not to bother with profile sheets. He never asked me once what I thought Hunter might do in a particular situation. He never discussed the books at all. In the past, I'd get briefings at dinner on the progress of the current chapter. He has a top editor now." I shrug. "Who knows how he uses her."

Ren drags deeply on her cigarette. I can tell she is stalling.

"Spit it out, Ren."

The beautiful fingers on her right hand fiddle with the cigarette pack while the fabulous nails on her left hand softly drum the table. "He must have known pretty far ahead of time that he wanted to end the marriage. He needed to wean himself from your input and was making sure he could wean himself and still write a successful book."

"A-plus, my friend. That's exactly how I see it. That's why, since no court will award me Hunter McCall, he's going to have to die. I created him. And I have the right to kill him."

# CHAPTER SIX

Jack Sharrow's favorite Hollywood story was the one where Douglas Fairbanks and Charlie Chaplin once raced each other on horseback down Hollywood Boulevard. The winner's prize was dinner at Musso and Frank's Grill. Jack didn't know if the story was true but he liked it.

He liked to picture the swashbuckling Fairbanks and the comical Chaplin on horseback, racing down a street now lined with hookers, addicts, and the homeless, each actor intent on beating the other. Hollywood then and now. It wasn't about the dinner. Jack was sure of that. It was about the glory. The glory of being the victor.

People still raced down Hollywood Boulevard. Only not on horses. Musso and Frank's Grill had celebrated its 80th anniversary. But no longer were the red leather booths occupied by the likes of F. Scott Fitzgerald, Dashiell Hammett, William Saroyan, and William Faulkner. Things change, but men still make silly wagers and men still want to be victorious.

Jack didn't think about victories anymore. He took one day at a time, hoped for the best, and expected the worst. Now he looked at his face in the rearview mirror of his truck. Once he had been a good-looking guy, but it had been quite some time since he'd taken care of himself. He needed a shave. He needed sleep. He needed exercise. He needed to feel good again, but that wasn't going to happen.

At the moment his most pressing need was to find Grant.

He'd keep driving, even if it took the entire night. Grant was somewhere between Hollywood and downtown, and Jack had to make sure that Grant stayed out of trouble. If he didn't do something soon, Grant would wind up in jail.

It was 11:30 P.M. and the action on Hollywood Boulevard had started to pick up. Jack turned left and headed south. Maybe Grant was on Sunset Boulevard. Maybe Grant was home tonight, watching reruns of sitcoms on late-night TV—but Jack didn't think so.

Not for the first time, he wondered what had motivated their mother to name her sons after U.S. presidents. Jack—full name Jackson—suspected she had big dreams for her boys. She always saw the glass as half full.

She had certainly tried to instill that optimism in her sons. If she had lived, maybe Jack and his brother could have made her proud. But she hadn't, and Jack was glad she couldn't see what they had become. As far as Jack could tell, he and Grant were no better than two empty glasses.

Empty glasses made him think of that Frank Sinatra song. The one where he says that it's a quarter to three and there's no one left but him and Joe. The storyteller's objective is to get his glass filled.

So set 'em up, Joe. If only it was that simple.

# CHAPTER SEVEN

The sun shines differently in Beverly Hills.

If you think I'm making it up, ask anyone who lives here. The morning after my visit to the lawyer, the sun wakes me from a deep, dreamless sleep. Through the pine window slats, the sun batters my face until it sees my eyes open. Then it laughs and moves on to another victim. It's only 6:05.

Never too early to start a morning mental checklist of things to do. Well, maybe a little too early.

I don't want to think about how puffy my eyes must look. I yawn and, for no reason, think about the farmer's life. The little I know about farmers is what I've seen in movies. Movies never show farmers' wives with puffy eyes. Why is that?

I look at my bedroom, larger than some entire apartments, and think: *I'm spoiled*. Spoiled and humiliated. An interesting cocktail of a bad attribute and pointless emotion. My life is filled with contradictions. Self-pity mingled with self-righteousness. All less than winning combinations. I need to get up and drive to my walk at the cemetery. Such an L.A. concept. Driving to one's walk each morning. I haven't told Ren about where I walk. She's never asked. Ren doesn't rise with the farmers' wives. She sculpts until late into the night. Ren's morning starts at lunch.

If I want to do my divorce the right way, what I should do is list my house for sale, tuck my tummy, enlarge my breasts, change my hairstyle, invest my money, buy a new car, start therapy, and hire the best family law lawyer in town. But, for me, there is only one right way. Kill Hunter McCall. I have set a difficult goal. I know what I want to do. Now I just have to figure out how to do it.

I live in the land of glitz, glamour, and gossip. Disseminating information is the lifeblood of Los Angeles. Disseminating innuendo and inaccuracies is what keeps this town pumping and jumping.

Media to spread information is for hire everywhere. Newspapers, radio, television, Internet, skywriting. They can announce Hunter McCall's death, but that won't actually kill him. I haven't completely flipped. I know an assassin is useless against a fictional character.

My goal is unambiguous. Kill Hunter McCall. But how? I refuse to believe it can't be done. As insane as it sounds, there has to be a way. I need to clear my head. It will come to me when the time is right. Focus elsewhere. My peach silk pajamas make me feel yummy. I used to sleep nude when Benjamin and I were in love, but when that stopped, I figured what was the point? A girl should take advantage of the lovely sleepwear on the market.

How to kill Hunter McCall? I love my peach pajamas. Watch the faucet turn on and off. This is how easily a woman can distract herself. I hate and love that ability I possess to interrupt myself without missing a beat. To switch gears in a beat. I'm a traitor to feminism. I can meander from yummy to self-hate in less than five seconds.

Barefoot, I take my schizophrenic ego, puffy eyes, and peach pajamas and trundle down the stairs.

Benjamin always hated my walking barefoot. It made me like doing it even more. In a fit of unearned glee, I hop, like a five-year-old, down seven marble steps. Something good is going to happen today.

Something good has to happen today.

A high-priced decorator suffocated every room of my house with excruciatingly expensive good taste, except the library, which is my designated room to do with as I please. Because the room was never intended for anyone's use but mine, it has only one chair. The chair is like a hippopotamus, huge, battered, stained, ugly, overstuffed, and instantaneously commanding of respect. It is exactly like one of those chairs sought out by college freshman for a finals all-nighter. You don't sit in it, you descend into it. It's not just a seat, it's a visit. It isn't a chair Benjamin will seek in the divorce. He probably doesn't know it still exists. It's our last surviving piece from Moe's Furniture for Less.

On the chair lies the gray sweatpants and navy T-shirt I wore two days ago for my walk at the cemetery. I do a guy thing. I pick up the pants and shirt, tentatively sniff at strategic spots, and determine it will not be too gross to wear again for this morning's walk.

If it means wearing unlaundered clothes to reinvent myself, so be it. I must change, not my clothes. I have to become someone new. I need something better than a plastic surgeon. I need a miracle.

My Nikes are pushed under the chair. If I don't go upstairs for underwear and socks, I can be dressed and out the door in under a minute. Unthinkable to the old me, which is precisely why I reach for my sneakers and decide not to go upstairs.

Stabs of genius always seem to come at the most unlikely moments. I am tying my shoelaces when I have the epiphany.

Here I am, in my room, surrounded by the things I love the most—my books. Hundreds of them. Everything from Charles Dickens to Charles Willeford. From Donald Westlake to Don DeLillo. In those pages are hundreds of my friends.

It is all right there, under my nose, or in front of my eyes.

How does one go about killing a fictional character? With another fictional character. Of course. Instead of groaning about never having written The Great American Novel, I can now not only write the book but also kill two birds with one stone. I can write my book and have my protagonist kill Hunter McCall.

It's a great idea. A stroke of genius. *Samantha, take a bow.* I knew today was going to be good. I'll go to the cemetery and walk and create. I'll spend my walk plotting out the story and I know as surely as Bea would take the listing on this house and Dr. Dan would happily cut my body and Jupiter would give me a hairdo that makes the other planets rock 'n roll, that I will have my core storyline figured out in the hour and a half I spend in the cemetery.

The book is there. In my head. Bouncing and kicking like a newborn screaming to get out. I feel as though I have been writing this book since the first day of my marriage, eighteen years ago.

I grab my keys and race out the door. Bugsy and Bill will love this news. As I get into my car, I think about paper and pencil. Then I shrug off the thought. Today is a day for thinking and plotting.

Completely cerebral.

In all the years we have been together, the hundreds of dinners and lunches, never once has Benjamin shared with me how he goes about actually writing a book. I don't know if he makes outlines or plans the whole book in his head or just sits at the computer and lets the spirit move him.

It is frightening how much I don't know about my husband. What kind of music he likes. Does he know how to cook? Does he like 1940s screwball comedies? Does he prefer New York or Chicago?

Look how long it took to find out he didn't like me. Look how long it has taken for me to find out I never liked him.

Here is one thing I do know, after spending a lot of time with writers. There is no one right way to do it. So I'll do it my way. And my way will be to plot the book out in my head, then sit down and put it on paper. It's something I have to do.

There is no other way to kill Hunter McCall.

The drive is fast. Coldwater Canyon becomes Beverly Boulevard as you pass the Beverly Hills Hotel. I drive into Beverly Hills. No one gets to work in Beverly Hills at 6:15 A.M. On Santa Monica Boulevard, I turn left and pass Beverly Hills City Hall, library, and the jogging park on the north side of the street.

Even the joggers aren't up yet. The jogging park is a minute from my house, but I still drive to Hollywood each morning.

Beverly Hills. Anyone can knock it, be a reverse snob and say it's nothing, no more special than anywhere else. But that's not true. It has a serene, regal quality. Still, I drive to Hollywood.

There's no mistaking when you leave Beverly Hills. Quite abruptly the majestic homes end. I've always wondered who lives in the last house that serves as the demarcation line between the two worlds. On its most westerly perimeter, West Hollywood starts with good restaurants. A few blocks east, the stores and restaurants become more funky, flamboyant, and sexually diverse. Keep traveling east and entertainment becomes adult directed—the euphemism for something to satisfy any sexual orientation or taste.

Travel further east and the boulevard diversifies in yet other ways. Light industrial, a movie studio, trendy restaurants next to pet grooming stores, two solid blocks of small theaters for the struggling actor/bartender and actress/waitress to use as forums to flex their talent muscles and to dream of discovery.

Keep going east and there it is: Hollywood Forever. A cemetery for which you pay in advance and if you don't like what you get, it's too late to fight, too late to make the familiar

L.A. threat of a lawsuit. But this is Los Angeles, where the impossible often happens. Here, even the dead find a way to sue.

Because there is no traffic, I arrive in twenty minutes.

There are no cars in the cemetery lot. There is a morning stillness here that I like very much. Muted, gentle sounds come from the small animals and birds. The air smells clean. The air is cool but not cold. When I walk, small droplets of sweat that form on my forehead and behind my knees evaporate instantly. Right now the cemetery belongs to me and me only. There are no gardeners, no mourners, no tourists, no maintenance crews working on ongoing renovations.

Usually I want to clear my head when I walk. Not think about the years ahead. Not think about the years I had been betrayed. But today is different. Today I am going to think and think hard. Plot out my book so that tonight I can start writing.

There is an immediacy in this task that has never existed for anything else I have ever done in my life.

I park and get out of the car. I don't stretch, twist, or turn before I start my walk. I've noticed that people turn the slightest form of exercise into a ritual. My grandmother used to walk for hours to do her shopping in a variety of small food stalls in Brussels. I seriously doubt she needed bottled water and a pre-walk stretch to get her shopping done. Neither did she need $225 walking sneakers or sweatbands or legwarmers. The times, they have changed, and not necessarily for the better.

So instead of solely enjoying the landscape today, instead of pouring out my complaints to Bugsy and Bill, I have a project. I need to think out the plot of my book so that my protagonist will, for good reason, kill the legendary Hunter McCall. After all, it is not my intention to create a homicidal maniac to kill the heroic heartthrob of adoring readers. The infallible Hunter McCall has to goof. He has to make a serious and irreparable mistake so that my hero, maybe heroine, will be justified in taking him out.

Thirty-six minutes into the walk, I have a storyline. It works. I like it. Readers will like it. Dare I jinx it by thinking filmmakers will like it, too? I want to tell someone. Bill, the movie man, seems the best choice, though Bugsy, the gangster, would really get it. I look to see who is closer. Bugsy. I head toward the Beth Olam Mausoleum.

I pass the plot with the little park bench. A person could sit and mourn for hours, days. I don't know if I want anyone to get comfortable for too long at my gravesite. I hope anyone visiting me has something better to do. Come for a few minutes, fill me in on the gossip, and leave.

Someone has been visiting Bugsy and has left him white lilies. They are very lovely, though far too many for the small cup on the perimeter of his crypt. She should have shared some with Bugsy's neighbors.

I can't imagine Bugsy having anyone but a female visitor.

I tell Bugsy I hope she was pretty. I give him a wink and like to think he winked back. I tell him I am writing a book. I tell him that Hunter McCall is going to die. He approves.

My visits are never long. Today's is five minutes. My footsteps in the mausoleum sound lonely and muffled. Bugsy's mausoleum is much warmer than Bill's. I can feel my sweatpants starting to stick to my skin. I still want to walk for another half hour. It's going to be hotter today than yesterday.

I can feel blisters starting on the back of my ankles and curse my laziness in not taking the extra minute to grab my socks. Sweat is trickling down my cleavage. I look at the navy blue T-shirt and see that sweat stains have formed on my neck, cleavage, and armpits. Those parts of the shirt now look almost black. Something about being this hot, sweaty, and smelly makes me feel young and I like the feeling a lot. I remember when I was ten years old and managed to get away with showering only five times during an entire summer at camp. Accomplishments came more easily at the age of ten.

I remember my name being sewn into all of my clothes. I remember how blisters at camp hardened and callused and I never needed a bandage. I remember sleeping on top of the sheets so it would be easier to make the bed in the morning. I am among the dead reflecting on my childhood. It is strange, yet comforting.

Maybe that's why I like the cemetery. For some perverse reason it makes me feel like I felt in summer camp. Inexplicably, it makes me feel young.

Then I shudder as if suddenly chilled. When I was a kid we used to say that meant someone had walked on our grave. I look up and see the Hollywood sign. Below it, I see a man standing among the tombstones. It is as if one of the graves has gifted a body back to the mortal world. I don't know him, but I know there is no reason for him to be in the cemetery. I know with a certainty that puzzles me that he is not a mourner, or a tourist, or a gardener, or a maintenance man, or a walker. That is what he is not.

What he is, is handsome. Very handsome in an unconventional way. A nose that has been broken, maybe more than once. A hairline that is receding and thinning, combed back in a way that makes me think of a second-grade boy on his first day of school. He has a little more meat on his bones than is absolutely necessary. Tired brown puppy eyes match his brown hair. A face that needs a shave, but looks fine without it. Maybe a little older than I. The expression on his face isn't close to a smile. I can see that in his eyes. Eyes that are smug, smart, and questioning. And not smiling.

I look at my watch. It is 7:25 and he doesn't belong here. Maybe he is thinking the same about me.

He is watching me with similar intensity. We don't exchange the meaningless smiles reserved for strangers or greet one another with an equally meaningless cordial good morning. We just stare, silently.

The quiet of the cemetery feels different. I am not alone with its memories and stories. A stranger has joined us.

There is something else I know. Instinctively. I know he is angry. His expression never changes. It isn't unpleasant. But I know, in my gut, something is not right.

I wonder what he's thinking. His dark, stubbly face is impossible to read. In yet another instinctive flash I know what he is thinking: *She's not wearing any underwear.*

The new me hates the old me for blushing.

# CHAPTER EIGHT

*Braless.* That was Jack's first thought. The second thought was: *She's not wearing any underwear.* It looked like all the body parts were jiggling a little, but not too much. He liked that. He let his imagination do a little tap dance, soft shoe, waltz and hustle, and then turned the fantasy faucet to the off switch. He needed to get back to business.

Was this woman the business that had brought him to the cemetery? If not, there could be worse ways to start a Thursday morning. She wasn't hard to look at.

His left hand felt the roughness of his face. His body ached with fatigue. He tried to remember the last time he'd had a good night's sleep and a shave. And now he was waiting to rendezvous with a low life in a cemetery. What could be worse than blackmail? Death? Maybe, though he thought it was a close call. The last remnants of being civilized was all that stopped him from thinking about what he really should do. Kill the bitch.

The woman had telephoned and said to meet her at 7:00 A.M. at the plot with a park bench just a short distance away from the Beth Olam Mausoleum. So here he was, and the only person he had seen in the last hour was this cute gal with the jiggling body parts. Jack looked at his watch again. But this gal hadn't spoken a word to him. She must not be the one. He'd wait another twenty minutes and then leave.

Maybe it was all a hoax, a stupid prank. Hard to imagine.

The woman had been painfully specific.

She knew about the emptied-out dog food bag scam. The one where you bought the dog food, removed the food, took the empty bag back to the market, refilled it with hundreds of dollars of groceries, resealed the bag and checked it through as dog food. She knew about the bank fraud scam. The one where you opened a new account, got temporary checks and instructions to use the blank counter deposit slips. No one notices if you walk away with twenty or so of those slips. Then you encode the deposit slips with your new account number with magnetic ink and return them to the bank counter for other customers to use. So on any one day, each deposit made with a counter deposit slip goes directly into your account.

Unless someone is lucky to pull a deposit slip not encoded with your account number.

Jack knew the woman wasn't just guessing when she told him about the drug deal con. In the drug deal con, a person was approached to invest in a purchase of illegal drugs. After the "wholesale" purchase, the drugs would be sold for the street price and the investor would make a nice tax-free profit. Later the investor was told that the dealer was busted and the drugs and money confiscated. What was the investor going to do? Complain to the police that he was defrauded in connection with a dope deal? The people willing to take that kind of chance were not the sort to go to the cops. But this woman knew exactly who they were.

The woman knew too much. Entirely too much. Thinking that way made Jack conscious of the gun tucked into his pants and covered by his shirt. It would not be good to get busted. What had he thought he would do with the gun? The woman had to be someone who knew him and Grant, but no person came to mind. A stranger would never have figured out all the cons.

The woman on the phone had sounded menacing. That was one thing the really deranged had in common. You could hear it in the voice.

Jack didn't think she'd be impressed with, or even care, that the stolen food had gone to the poor and homeless. Or the money from the bank scam had gone to the poor and homeless. And that the money taken from people willing to sell drugs on the street had gone to the poor and homeless.

The rigidity in the woman's voice reminded him of cops he had known. Could she be a cop? It wasn't inconceivable that a cop had figured it out and was now shaking him and Grant down. Jack could tell from the woman's voice that she wasn't the type to care about the poor and homeless.

He could tell from the woman's voice that she had probably never been enchanted with the story of Robin Hood.

# CHAPTER NINE

On the drive home I remember Peter Perkal. I am starting to think like a writer. I have my plot and now I need a publicist.

Peter Perkal, a famous L.A. publicist, is a mover and shaker in Hollywood. When Patsy Woods wanted to get the Academy Award nomination and everyone knew she didn't have a snowball's chance in hell, who made it happen? Peter Perkal.

He planted a story in the tabloids subtly suggesting that Patsy's daughter had a rare blood disease that might destroy the chance of her having a long, happy life. Sympathetic stories, especially those related to children, make people remember an actor's performance more favorably and more kindly.

She didn't win but just getting the nomination helped her score two lucrative movie deals. By that time everyone had forgotten about Patsy's eleven-year-old daughter who, in fact, had been diagnosed with a mild case of anemia and put on iron pill supplements for six months. I know the true story because Ren's son, Blake, goes to the same pediatrician. Winona Woods's medical records had apparently been on the doctor's desk during his meeting with Ren and she took some minor liberties when he stepped away to check on a semi-hysterical patient.

The Internet has changed everything. We have redefined the concept of privacy in our new world, so Ren didn't hesitate to snoop. Even if it was the old-fashioned way.

The Patsy Woods story was only the tip of the iceberg of what Peter is capable of doing. I've heard enough stories about him to fill a four-night miniseries. Did you ever notice how closely miniseries and miseries resemble one another?

Peter Perkal's office is in Century City. It's not really a city. Just another Los Angeles concoction. Two white monoliths piercing the Los Angeles sky serve as the beacon that you have arrived in Century City. His office is in the more westerly of the two identical buildings. Century City is a concrete jungle in which movie theaters, restaurants, stores, and the offices of many of Southern California's power brokers are housed.

The first mistake I make is treating my call as though I am phoning for a dental appointment. I completely forgot what I am. A nobody. Somehow I had the delusion I would phone and he would see me. In this town, it is only easy to see the people you don't want to see.

I am about as successful getting past the receptionist as enticing a Buckingham Palace guard to let me take a quick look at the queen's undergarments. After minutes of verbal foreplay, I conclude that the best I am going to accomplish is scheduling a telephone appointment to speak with Perkal's assistant some time in the distant future. At that rate, I will be a very old woman before Peter and I meet.

I hate what I do next but it's the only way I can think of to get the job done. I say to the receptionist, "Please tell Mr. Perkal that I'm Mrs. Benjamin Crowley."

Magic. Peter's assistant, now identified as Missy, immediately picks up the phone and wants to know how she can help me. If I tell her it will be all over.

"Missy, this is a rather delicate matter for the telephone, dear. I really need to meet with Peter." I think using his first name will make me sound more like a player.

"Oh, Mrs. Crowley, I do understand," Missy continues in this extraordinarily breathless voice that is, no doubt, the other reason she got this job. "It would just be so helpful if I might tell him what this is about. You understand."

I understand. She doesn't. Under the circumstances it seems appropriate to take on a more matronly tone. After all, at the ripe old age of 39, matronly isn't such a stretch.

"I do understand, dear, but this is just a wee bit too confidential to discuss over the phone. You do understand, darling, don't you?"

One more *dear* or *darling* or *understand* and I will puke.

What is she going to say? No? Not likely. She says just what I hoped to hear. "Could you hold a moment, Mrs. Crowley?"

I know the next voice I hear will belong to the infamous Peter Perkal. I try not to become too crazy over the fact that but for Benjamin's name I would never have gotten past the receptionist.

"Hello, is this Samantha Crowley?"

Peter Perkal's voice booms and soothes simultaneously.

When you've got the gift, you've got the gift.

I say, "It is."

Short, simple, noncommittal. Let him ask the questions. A psychologist once told me it's a good way to reverse roles. Short answers make the one who's asking feel more vulnerable.

"I understand from Missy that you have a confidential matter to discuss with me. What can I do for you? Is this about your husband?"

I let his last question slide through the cracks. "Could we meet?" Wrong, wrong, wrong. I change the tone of my voice. I add an element of what I hope has the ring of authority. "I'd like to meet. I don't want to do this on the phone."

"I see." I can hear him flipping through pages. Lots of pages.

"Mr. Perkal, this is a pressing matter and, frankly, I'd like to meet with you soon. Soon as in tomorrow. I know this is short notice but that's just how it is."

"Samantha, may I call you Samantha?" He continues without

waiting for an answer, "This is a bit sudden and mysterious. Don't you think?"

I need to make him hungrier. "Suit yourself, Mr. Perkal. It's tomorrow or let's pass and I'll find someone else."

I hear a noise in his throat. I can't identify the noise but I have a good feeling. I can almost hear him thinking.

"Hold on a moment, Mrs. Crowley." What happened to Samantha? Why are we back to the formal *Mrs.?* And for the record, *Ms.* would be more politically correct in this city of political incorrectness.

"How about if we meet at the Peninsula Hotel for lunch at one o'clock tomorrow? Will that work for you?"

"Absolutely, Mr. Perkal. I'll see you then."

Black magic.

Here I am, the future Ms. Nobody, about to meet the popular, pompous publicist, Peter Perkal, at the Peninsula. His life is an alliteration. He could have been a pepper picker or a poultry plucker or Paris painter. It still would have worked. But he is Peter Perkal, publicist.

I walk out the front door of my house, my mausoleum, and give the world a smile. Spandex Dancing Man, barefoot and serious, is holding his boom box high and again dancing in front of my house. Other than my dancing friend, no one else is in sight. I go back inside the house, close the door, reopen the door, and walk out again. He is gone.

Was he really there? Am I having street people hallucinations? With only a little less enthusiasm, I smile for my absent friend.

So now all I have to do is decide what I should wear to meet Peter, Peter, pumpkin eater.

# CHAPTER TEN

Breakfast always made Jack sleepy. After the hard-ass mystery woman didn't show up, he had gone to a breakfast joint to have the $3.95 breakfast special. If you forgave runny eggs, over-cooked bacon, and over-buttered toast, it was pretty good. If you didn't meditate too long on high cholesterol, heart disease, and hardening of the arteries, it was great.

Jack thought about how big breakfasts were touted as the way to start one's day. As far as he was concerned, a big breakfast made you want to go back to bed and that was exactly where he was headed.

He drove, half asleep, until he reached the winding, narrow path that took him to his small but comfortable home in the Hollywood Hills.

Depending on where you were in the climb, you could catch a glimpse of a vowel or consonant in the Hollywood sign. He had bought here long before it became prohibitively expensive. He could have sold his home on numerous occasions for ten times the purchase price, but what was the point? He had no desire to move. No desire to live anywhere else. Nowhere to go.

Home was sanctuary. The places he could call sanctuary, the people he could trust, the number of things he believed in, could no longer be counted on more than one hand. It made him sad but it was a fact. He tried not to think about it. He wore sad like Londoners wear raincoats. A constant companion.

The phone call from the woman was the first time he had felt anger in a long time. The intensity of the feeling scared him. It brought back everything he'd rather forget. When he was a cop, he had been used to feeling angry. The ugly, stupid things people did to one another left him either numb or filled with rage. Rage got the adrenaline pumping. The pumping made him feel fearless. Fearless made him reckless. And reckless made him a great crime fighter.

A great crime fighter right out of the comic books. Because comic books were the only places where one could catch bullets with bare hands and swoop down to save the day in the nick of time.

In real life it was all over when he got there and the bullets had killed.

Four years ago, at his mother's house, it was real life when he arrived with backup. Too late. In a robbery for a mere fifty dollars, a bullet had killed his mother. His seventeen-year-old brother, Grant, had watched, helpless, as a stranger stole from him life as he knew it. Except for the memory of what he'd witnessed, Grant was left unharmed.

Unharmed. It depends on how you define it. The guy would have done both Jack and Grant a favor if he had killed Grant, too. Memory can be as potent as a bullet.

But even in the midst of the horror, Grant was the kid brother of a cop. He gave Jack an accurate description of the car and driver. The perp. That's what Grant had said to him that late afternoon, not quite twilight, when the temperature was cool, not cold, and the air smelled like green.

That's what Grant called it when he was a kid. On days when the gardener came and cut the grass, Grant would walk around sniffing the air in an exaggerated way and announce, "The air smells green today."

That not-quite-twilight day that smelled green, as their mother lay dead in the driveway of her home, Grant said the perp was around thirty, white, tall, balding, and driving an old, beat-up black Mustang convertible.

That was the exact description of the perp Jack shot and killed twenty minutes later.

Fortunately, the perp was still armed, which made the outcome of the police investigation easier for Jack. If he had cared. Within thirty seconds of shooting and killing the man who had murdered his mother, Jack knew he'd be resigning from the force, if he wasn't asked to leave. His career in law enforcement was history. He didn't believe in the good guys anymore. They couldn't catch bullets in their bare hands. They didn't arrive in the nick of time.

So now here he was, ten o'clock in the morning, ready to go back to bed. Ready to crawl under the covers and try to pretend that the last two days had been a dream. Hey, if you're gonna dream, dream big. How about that the last four years had been a dream?

Jack worried that sleep wouldn't come. An underestimation of the heavy effect an unusually large breakfast might have on his system. When the telephone rang, it woke him out of a deep, mercifully dreamless sleep. He thought he must have been sleeping for hours, but when he looked at the bedside clock he saw it was only fifteen minutes.

There was no hello. No greeting. Only the same voice, hard, cold, and very annoyed.

"So tough guy, what happened to you today?"

The training from his old police days was still there. Jack was instantly awake, not groggy or unfocused. His puzzled response stemmed from true bewilderment, not from being awakened.

"I don't understand. What do you mean 'what happened'?. I was there. Where were you?"

"Just where I said I'd be. You were looking right at me."

It couldn't be. Was she saying that she was the gal he had

seen? The one with no bra? The one he had thought was kind of cute? He had been positive the girl was there to jog or walk. That she had nothing to do with this mess. Why even call it a mess? Blackmail. This voice, this evil, belonged to that girl?

Maybe he had been away from the force too long. In the past he had always felt confidence in his judgment. He was rarely, if ever, wrong. Well, it seemed like he had been on a wrong streak for four years, so why should he be surprised?

Why had they not connected? He didn't understand.

"Why didn't you say anything to me?"

"I wanted you to speak first."

That answer didn't make sense. What had she been waiting for? They weren't there for a social conversation or a stroll. Something didn't feel right. Nothing about this woman felt right.

"I don't understand and I don't want to play games with you. Why don't you just tell me what's going on?"

"Okay, I will. I think you were armed and I think you intended to kill me."

How did she expect him to respond? How did she want him to respond? He had been armed. Had he intended to kill her? Probably not. He may have wanted to kill her but he came to the cemetery to hear what she had to say. To assess the situation.

He needed to understand what was going on. His head was starting to hurt. He hoped it wouldn't be one of those blinding headaches.

"I didn't intend to kill you. That's nuts. You made some threats. You claim to have some information. You suggested we talk. So that's what I thought we were going to do."

"I know more about you than you think. You didn't arrive in time to save your mother. You protect your little brother. I know you don't want any harm to come to him. I don't think I'm reading you wrong. You had a gun and you wanted to kill me."

Of course she was guessing, but was she right? He wasn't going to kill her. This was crazy. Jack didn't answer. Let her keep talking.

"Forget about talking. You know what I know. I already told you. And you know it's not a fishing expedition. It's accurate. I know hard facts. So I think the part we're up to is my demand. Right? Wouldn't you say that's where we're at?"

Her voice was so cold it sounded like an over-coached actress trying out for the part of Ma Barker. Demand? The idea was almost amusing. Petty cons. Stolen groceries. What did she want? A piece of the haul? Salami sandwiches and pickles.

"All right, I'll pitch. What do you want?"

"For me not to make your and your brother's life a living hell, let's say two hundred and fifty thousand dollars."

Jack stifled an involuntary noise that she'd probably think was alarm, but was really a snort. "I hope you're kidding because there's no money like that around here. If you really know what's going on, you'd know that you're way off base."

She made no effort to hide her ugliness. "I know what's going on and I know you'll do what it takes to protect Grant. Otherwise, he's going to jail. Won't be so nice there for an unhappy boy like him, don't you agree? I think a resourceful guy like you can find the money. And if not, Grant goes to jail or you kill me." She laughed lightly, as if it were just an easygoing joke between friends.

"So, Jack, I'll see you tomorrow morning, seven o'clock, at the cemetery. You know me now, so I don't have to give you a location. You'll see me. You can give me a down payment and tell me when you'll have the balance. Okay, sweetie pie? I'll see ya tomorrow."

She hung up before he could respond. Just as well. What possible response could he have given her?

Jack thought about the man he had killed four years ago. A person doesn't kill another person over something like this. Jack suspected there was much more going on than a blackmail scheme. He had no idea what it could be, but something was terribly wrong.

It was almost as if she *wanted* him to kill her.

# Chapter Eleven

It is an unusually warm morning. I am feeling a little fashion challenged for my walk. I hate to wear shorts. Talk about feeling like you're back in summer camp. Once you hit thirty-five you really should give serious thought as to whether shorts are a smart look. It is too hot for sweatpants. Leggings will work but do I really feel secure enough to let a bunch of dead folks see my ripples of cellulite?

In the end, I compromise. The solution to most fashion problems. I take one of my oversized pink T-shirts, cut off the sleeves, and wear it over black leggings. Six months ago the idea of using a pair of scissors on my clothing would have been unthinkable. Today, converting my T-shirt into a tank top is a liberating experience. Welcome to the new Samantha. A decisive woman of action.

More importantly, the T-shirt will hide the more offensive bumps and ripples and now I will be comfortable. I strap a fanny pack around my waist.

I feel cool, unencumbered, and look forward to my visit with Bill and Bugsy. I am ready to do some serious walking. Come on boots, start walking.

The previous night I worked on the book and ignored three phone messages from Ren. I let my answering machine do the talking for me. "Hi, this is Sam. If I'm not picking up it's because I don't want to speak. Leave a message."

The old me would never have recorded a message like that.

The old me could never have ignored a ringing phone. The new me did so with difficulty. Given time, everything gets easier. Deconstructing T-shirts, not answering telephones, who knows what's next for me. Fly me to the moon and I'll play among the stars. So this is what all those people I labeled quacks meant by empowered.

And I am getting closer to killing off Hunter McCall. The writing is going well. My muse is not off vacationing at some desert spa.

Santa Monica Boulevard moves quickly this morning. My windows are rolled down and I enjoy the drive. On hot days in Los Angeles, the air is usually a smoggy, polluted air that makes owning white towels an unwise choice. But today the air feels clean. It is hot with no haze.

You can see it is a city surrounded by mountains, not just a city on the ocean like many people think.

Most mornings I have the cemetery to myself. Will such a glorious morning attract joggers from the Hollywood area? No matter. It might be nice to nod and smile at strangers today. I park the car, see no others in the lot, and revel in a sensation that I can only think to describe as ridiculously optimistic.

Maybe it is good vibes about my lunch later today with Peter Perkal. Maybe it is the progress I am making with the book. Maybe it is because I feel like my life is going to start over. Maybe it is the thought that I am going to accomplish what had looked like the impossible.

I am going to kill Hunter McCall.

Unless I am killed first. Which is a possibility I had never considered.

The attractive man from yesterday is here again. He still needs a shave. He still isn't smiling. He is still intently watching me.

There is one big difference. Unless there is someone standing behind me, he is pointing a gun directly at me.

I look over my left shoulder. No one there. The gun is pointed at me. It is so unbelievable I forget to be scared, but only for five seconds. Then I get scared. Very scared. Too scared to speak. Too scared not to speak. No longer empowered.

My mouth opens to scream. I didn't know I was going to do that. The scream isn't bad. Loud, throaty, frightened. It's my audience that leaves something to be desired. Contrary to the Wes Craven school of thought, dead folks don't hustle out of graves. The dead aren't rising to aid this damsel in distress. I am screaming for an unresponsive group.

What do you do when confronted with a homicidal maniac? Should I continue to scream until my voice disappears? Should I strip off my clothes and offer my body in exchange for my life? Should I pretend to faint? Should I offer to drive to the bank and withdraw all my money and give it to him? Should I try to run away? Can I possibly outrun a man like this? Will he chase me?

If I had played guess-what's-going-to-happen-to-you-today, this wouldn't have made the first thousand guesses. This type of thing doesn't happen, at least not to me. Certainly not in broad daylight. On a beautiful day. On a day when the air smells good. On a day when I feel empowered. On a day when I embrace abstract, blind optimism.

In the end I reject all my ideas, blink away tears that aren't going to help, feel my heart pounding like it will explode, and in a voice barely audible, even to me, I ask, "What do you want? Why are you doing this?"

Then I start crying.

Women's liberation be damned. I am scared. Maybe he'll feel sorry for me if he sees me crying. Maybe, somewhere in his maniacal malevolent heart, he has a soul.

I wish I hadn't cut the sleeves off my T-shirt. It's as if there is no sun. Just cold. I shiver and sob and wonder if I will be dead soon. I have a fleeting thought that Hunter McCall would probably face death with more dignity. I make a mental note to make sure he does, in case I live to finish the book. My pink T-shirt is stained with tears and becoming transparent. Something about me and this man. When I first saw him I wasn't wearing any underwear and now my bra is framed against my wet T-shirt. Everything about my death is going to be undignified.

Shouldn't a person about to die be thinking about something significant? Isn't this the time to finally have deep thoughts? On the throes of death, my life boils down to lamenting an underwear crisis.

The man is looking at me as if I am crazy.

He says, "What do you mean what do I want? This is about what you want, not me. Why are you crying, anyway? All of a sudden you're not Ms. Tough Guy?"

He is walking toward me. The gun is gone. I didn't see him slip it into his pants or a pocket. For a brief second I wonder if I was hallucinating.

"You're pretty bold telling someone to do something and if he doesn't like it to kill you. It's not fun looking down the barrel of a Colt .45, is it?" he says, dispelling any hope about hallucinations.

He is now standing no further than three feet away and looking more pompous than threatening. I don't have any idea what he is talking about. But he's no longer pointing a gun at me, which makes me feel we've made significant progress.

I decide to proceed gently. For some reason this man thinks we've spoken. Who knows how little it would take to provoke him into pulling the gun again. So in a calm, second-grade teacher voice, I say, "We've never met. We've never spoken. Why are you saying these things to me? I know you were here yesterday when I was walking, but we didn't speak. Don't you remember?"

Like a cloud swiftly moving past the sun, the angry look on his face turns quizzical, almost concerned. The maniacal psychopath of two minutes ago now looks like a man with whom you'd want to snuggle, perhaps run your fingers over his brow to unfurrow the pensive frown. Maybe I am losing my mind.

I feel lightheaded and hungry. I am no longer afraid. How very inconvenient to have hunger replace fear. Life is so frequently a no-win situation. I need to sit. One of the grave-sites right next to us has a bench. It is intended for the elders of the departed families to have a comfortable place to sit while visiting. I'm sure the poor soul resting in peace, only a few inches away, will forgive me. Maybe even understand.

You always hear that you shouldn't make any sudden moves with these criminal types. The smart protocol is to ask permission.

"Look, I'm feeling a little faint. Would you mind if I sat down on the bench here?" I point to the bench no more than three feet away.

The man looks embarrassed. "Of . . . of course," he stammers. "You don't have to ask permission. Please sit if you want. Can I do anything to help you?"

I must look terrible. Now we are both embarrassed. This is stupid. He is acting normal. There is no gun in sight. I sit down. It helps. My blood starts circulating everywhere it should. I decide to tackle the situation.

I ask, "Are you no longer threatening me?"

The answer to that question will more or less set the tone for the rest of this encounter.

"It depends. Are you no longer threatening me?"

"How have I threatened you?" I try not to shriek. Shrieking is neither my most attractive feature, nor one that men usually warm to on any occasion. I say, "I don't know you. We've never spoken before."

Now the man looks genuinely unhappy.

"You're going to make me explain what you know? Okay. Fine. If that's the way you want to play it. You called me the other day and told me to meet you at seven A.M. at the cemetery. I was here and so were you, but you're right, we didn't speak. You called me again yesterday and told me to meet you at seven A.M. today. And here you are and here I am."

"Why in the world would you think I called you? I'm here almost every day at seven, for my walk. You spoke to someone else. Not me. Why would you even think it was me?"

"Do you see anyone else here?"

He has a point. There's just the two of us. Only I know I didn't call him.

"I see your point. But it doesn't change anything. I don't know you and I didn't call you and I never arranged to meet you, or anyone else."

"Who are you?"

"I'm Samantha Crowley." I start feeling braver. "Who are you?"

As if he never pulled a gun on me, he steps up to my bench, extends his hand to shake mine, and says, "I'm Jack Sharrow and I think I owe you an explanation."

You know what men need? A best friend. Because if they had one, they wouldn't confide so freely in strangers. Which is exactly what Jack Sharrow proceeds to do.

I hear his story with a combination of fascination and bewilderment. I hear about the tragedy of his mother. I hear how he arrived too late to save her. I hear how his brother has, overnight, turned into a thief, a reaction to the nightmare he witnessed. A thief who keeps nothing for himself and steals for the poor. And then there is Jack, a shattered man, who is trying to help his brother. Only now, a woman is trying to blackmail them. And, finally, why he thought I'm that woman.

The sun feels hot again. My fear has evaporated, unlike my sweat. I know I look dreadful. Sweat is trickling down my neck and arms, spotting my shirt. My hair is probably frizzed on one side and flat on the other. Very attractive.

In light of what I am hearing, shame on me for being preoccupied with my appearance. But what can I say? This Jack Sharrow is an attractive man and it has been a long time since an attractive man has talked to me, let alone confided in me.

So maybe I need to overlook that he killed a man, has a con man for a brother, has drifted through the last four years of his life, and is angry and lost. Maybe I need to ignore the fact that he pulled a gun on me, is in the middle of some kind of blackmail crisis, and seems to have misplaced his entire moral core.

A girl can't have everything.

His story told, I say nothing, and we agree by a long silence to part. Jack suggests we exchange phone numbers. It's as if we just had a traffic accident. It seems the right thing to do. For me, the prospect that he might call and suggest lunch or dinner makes the exchange an attractive idea. I could use a night out with a good-looking man. Even a good-looking man who comes with a grocery cart full of problems.

Or maybe it is I, not Jack, who has problems. When I think about his story carefully, I agree with him. It almost sounds as if the caller was provoking Jack to kill.

And when he got to the cemetery the only woman to kill was me. Something stinks here. If Bugsy Siegel were alive, I would have gone to him for advice. Where is a good wise guy when you need one?

# CHAPTER TWELVE

Old baggy cotton print pants with a red T-shirt to match the little red balloons on the pants. The pants had cost $12 at Venice Beach. That's what I decide to wear. I don't know why. My mother would have killed me. My husband would have divorced me. Except, he's already doing that.

Maybe I'm experiencing a new rebellious phase. Maybe I've become the reverse snob my Dad always accused me of being. Maybe it's just the act and art of reprioritizing.

In any event, it's not the sort of outfit one typically sees at the Beverly Hills Peninsula Hotel restaurant. The place where gazillion-dollar movie deals are made while tabloid reporters hide behind potted palms. To hell with the world!

I turn down the street known as Little Santa Monica Boulevard, not to be mistaken with the other Santa Monica Boulevard it parallels. These are the things you learn when you live in paradise. If you don't, you're sent back to towns with street names like Main and Front.

I am surprised to see Ren's son, Blake Martel, walking hurriedly toward Wilshire Boulevard. He attends Beverly Hills High School, which is only a few blocks from the hotel, so I guess he could be going home or to lunch. Neither seems likely. He looks rushed and flustered. He doesn't see me and I don't make myself seen.

Crossing my car's path as I pull into the hotel driveway is the oddest street person. It's unusual to see a street person in

Beverly Hills and this one is a whopper. A plant has taken up residence on top of his head. A three-foot plant, almost tree-like in appearance, seems to be sprouting directly out of the top of the man's head. His raggedy pants and shirt are forest green and in his own bizarre way, he is more color coordinated than I am.

The Plant Man stops in front of my car and smiles a toothless grin at me. It is sweet and scary at the same time.

Contradictions abound. Like Chinese food. Sweet and sour. What would Confucius make of all this?

I redirect my attention when I see the price of valet parking. I wonder what my dad could have bought with eighteen dollars when he was young. A car instead of a parking space for one? I wonder if they expect a tip over and above the eighteen dollars. Probably.

The valet parking man gives me the look as I drive up. Everyone knows that look. The one that suggests perhaps Madam has come to the wrong place. I pull down the visor and look in the mirror that every self-respecting female driver has clipped on. I am a mess. No question about it. Not thoroughly blow drying my hair has resulted in an abundance of frizz and curls my head hasn't seen since college.

My failure to apply even minimal makeup gives me that refreshing washed-out look. Basically, it is now a face that says I know how to suffer with the best of them.

My clothes, basic beachcomber, are the finishing touch for this valet guy as I exit the car. He exchanges a look with one of his co-workers. I would bet all of Benjamin's money that these guys are either writing screenplays or waiting to land movie parts. In either case, I have been sized up and discarded. I can be of no help to them, nor do I have the requisite sex appeal to command respect, even if I am a nobody.

Maybe they are right. How does it go? You're nobody till

somebody loves you. And no one is loving this somebody lately. I give him a bright smile but no eyes, and he and I both know what it means. I'm here. I'm going into the hotel now; take my car and stuff it.

In Altoona, Pennsylvania, you meet someone at the local hotel and if you lunch there, it's eating. In Beverly Hills, California, you meet someone at the local hotel and if you lunch there, it's dining.

Tablecloths, crystal, maitre d', real flowers, the whole works. I recognize Peter Perkal from his many television interviews. He is bloated in a way to which either you are born or cultivate after too many business lunches.

His face has a squished look at if someone took a rolling pin and gently moved it back and forth over his features until they were all of equal protrusion. I study his face and try to figure out how his chin, nose, and brow can be so perfectly aligned.

As I approach, he rises to greet me and tries to hide his shock. I would have respected him more if he had simply said whatever he was thinking about my appearance, but no matter. I want this man's help in my effort to kill Hunter McCall. We don't need to become lifelong friends.

I should have dressed better. Bad Sam.

"Mrs. Crowley. Such a pleasure."

"Thank you, Peter. May I call you Peter? And please call me Sam."

"Of course, Samantha."

For the next ten minutes we play the who-do-we-both-know game and he beams while I regale him with flattery. I know how it's done and to get what I want I am willing to play.

He picks at a Chinese chicken salad and drinks three glasses of iced tea. Thirsty guy. Thirsty or nervous. I sip at my Diet Pepsi and heartily gobble a Cobb salad sans avocado. Who needs those calories from a fruit that has the same texture as one of your body organs?

I can see Peter is getting restless. The rules of etiquette are such that he can't suggest we get to the point until near the end of the meal. I have to assume he is hoping I want to talk to him about doing public relations for Benjamin. Why else would he have agreed to our meeting?

"Peter, you are so delightful to talk to but I bet you would like to know why I suggested we meet."

On his squished face he raises an inquisitive eyebrow.

"You know, of course, my husband Benjamin." He starts grinning and nodding so vigorously it's a good thing he doesn't have a plant precariously attached to his head. "And that we're separated?"

The grin disappears in less than a second. I guess he didn't know.

"So the reason I wanted to meet with you is because I've had some thoughts about killing . . ."

I pause as every bit of blood drains from his already pale, squished face.

". . . Hunter McCall," I finish.

His mouth is empty but it sounds like it's bulging with bread when he mumbles, "I don't understand. What in the world do you mean?"

I smile, I hope brightly, and say, "I mean that there's no reason why the character he created with my input and that actually I created and by that I mean . . ."

Again I pause. Because I'm getting a little flustered and sidetracked, mostly because Peter now appears to be looking for something under the table, although it is a distinct possibility that he is trying to hide. Glancing around the room, I determine he is not in the line of sniper fire. That leaves me as the object to be avoided.

"Killed." He actually hisses the word. A hard thing to do with a word starting with K. "Hunter McCall is a fictional character. What do you have in mind and why in the world would I be a party to it?"

"It will be the publicity coup of the decade, Peter. Don't you see? I've found out that in the divorce Benjamin retains McCall and I want to right the wrong. The law can't do it so I had to find another way. I thought you might have some clever ideas. That's why I came to you. You're the best." An encouraging smile and stroking words, what more did this idiot need?

"Are you mad? Consult a lawyer. I'm sure you're entitled to some financial interest in the books he's written. Why have you brought me here?" He starts looking around in the paranoid fashion of Los Angelinos who fear they will be recognized as having been in the company of a has-been or a loser or the *persona non grata* of the month.

I start to protest and explain. I have seen an attorney. This isn't about the books. It is about the character. I stop talking when he is two tables away. Moving as fast as his Gucci loafers will carry him.

I'm not stupid. I knew this was a long shot. I close my mouth, which I sense more than know is still agape. One of those childhood flashes comes. My mother glaring and saying, "Close your mouth. It looks like you're trying to catch flies."

I don't know why I had my mouth open as a kid. As an adult, I feel inclined to open it again after the waiter swooshes by and drops the check on the table. The price would feed a family of eight in Altoona.

Peter the Great has stuck me with the check.

# CHAPTER THIRTEEN

I think I heard it on the *Today* show during some serious banter between Meredith and Matt. But I was blow-drying my hair and that could affect the ability to hear a Rolling Stones concert. I know for sure I heard it on the radio when I was fixing myself dry cereal and a banana.

Some time yesterday, after our lunch, Peter Perkal was killed instantly by a hit-and-run driver.

Apparently, he was crossing big and little Santa Monica Boulevards from his office in Century City, heading toward Marco's Pizza. I guess after picking at his salad and leaving me with the bill, little piggy Peter decided he wanted a doughy, cheesy lunch experience. Marco's isn't "dining," but it has great pizza.

What an awfully strange place for someone to be hit by a car, let alone killed. And then for the driver to leave the scene—well, that takes nerve of a different nature.

I think about what an odd coincidence it is, but mostly I wonder if he'd be alive had he stayed with me and eaten his entire salad. That goes to the core of a different philosophical debate. Are our futures predetermined or do we really have the capacity to make our own luck?

The ringing phone sets my heart racing. I have no idea why. The news of Peter's death has made the day take on an ominous quality.

When I hear Ren's voice, I feel better. She is cheerful, smart, focused. All the things I need in this exact microsecond.

"Hey, sweetie, I haven't spoken to you in twenty-four, make that closer to thirty hours. What's going on?"

"Nothing really." For some reason I don't want to tell her about my meeting with Peter. I just want a little female bonding

Ren says, "Why don't you come over for lunch and we'll sit in the gazebo, let some rays try to find us, and gossip about friends."

"Sounds good. I'll see you at one o'clock?"

She hangs up. Ren's way of agreeing.

I pick up four days' worth of mail, in a stack, all unopened. My compulsive persona is slipping away. I flip through the bills, ads, the solicitations. In this age of computers there are no more letters. The fine art of letter writing is dead. Love letters via email.

In the middle of the stack is an envelope addressed to Benjamin from his agent, Carol Haber. One person who has not received his change of address.

I open it. Let him cry federal offense and file a lawsuit. I dare him. It's a boilerplate letter telling all her West Coast clients when she will be in Los Angeles. She is staying at the Beverly Hilton Hotel. Based on the dates, she is here in L.A. right now.

The Hollywood-invented light bulb that goes off over someone's head goes off over mine. Bingo. Serendipity. I have an idea. A good one. I might have said it has been staring at me all along from the keys of my portable upright. But in the age of computers, a writer is not bonded in that same Raymond Chandler–like way with the mechanism that gives life to his stories, taps out the words to create the rhythm of the dance.

When my protagonist kills Benjamin Crowley's protagonist, Hunter McCall, Benjamin Crowley's agent explodes the book to the publishing world. I close my eyes and have a bidding-war fantasy.

Carol Haber will love it. She will represent me and we will sail on to a type of fame, fortune and controversy that only happens with genuine trailblazers.

I get the number of the Beverly Hilton. I want to set up a meeting as soon as possible. If she hasn't gotten Ben's change of address, there is a good chance she doesn't know about our separation.

Maurice, her guy Friday, takes my call. It would be misleading to call him Carol's homosexual assistant. To be fair, he is no sexual, a third alternative in our ever-expanding universe.

Maurice may be the most neutered human being I've ever met. His voice is soft but not feminine. Or masculine, either. He has no facial hair and wears his almost silken-looking straight brown hair in a side part. He is constantly shrugging nonexistent bangs out of his eyes. His wire-framed glasses intensify green eyes that are so lovely no woman would ever use makeup to enhance them. His nose is perfect but not in a nose-job way, and his lips are full but not too full.

Maurice never leaves Carol's side. He never sleeps further than one room or one floor away from her. I heard that he purchased a small studio in Carol's trendy and expensive Upper East Side co-op so that he would be near to her whenever she beckoned, which I understand to be often. I even heard that he is in the process of trying to get a studio on a higher floor so that it will take less elevator time to get to Carol's penthouse.

It is so absurd and beyond comprehension I long ago ceased trying to understand or figure it out. The bottom line is that one has to go through Maurice to get to Carol. So that makes the little man, of indeterminate sexual proclivities, a very important person.

After reasoning, pleading, and ultimately demanding, I get Maurice to agree that Carol will see me at five P.M. for drinks at the bar of The Regent Beverly Wilshire. This way she will only be three blocks from her dinner destination, Spago. Maurice makes normal inquiries about Benjamin. I am right. They have no clue Ben and I are separated. Once again, the use of his name has gotten me where I want to be. It makes my blood chill.

I have to keep reminding myself that my ends are what justify my means.

The day turns warm and the cloudless sky makes me think of the blue pajamas I recently sent from Saks Fifth Avenue to Ren's cousin, Marylou, in Duncan, Oklahoma, as a gift for her new baby boy. I figured she'd be impressed.

Now that I am going through the big D, I had better come to grips with what an insufferable snob I've become. The big D is changing me but I should have changed irregardless. Is it redundant putting "ir" in front of regardless? I scoot down the stairs two at a time and run into the library, where I pull my dictionary off the shelf and check. Lo and behold, the dictionary says that using it is poor style but, nonetheless, it does creep into the speech of the well spoken. Perhaps to give greater emphasis, my faithful dictionary suggests. Is the dictionary making excuses for people like me? Like I?

I'm getting silly with excitement. How can Carol resist such a great idea? At 12:55 P.M. I lock my front door and walk two houses down the block to Ren.

She is waiting on her doorstep, like a puppy in training. Her cell phone is glued to her right ear, her head is nodding, and she has her neck pulled back so that the sun beats down, full force, on her upturned face. A cigarette hangs loosely in her right hand, the ashes very close to falling off from their accumulating weight. She looks, as always, quite beautiful. Her red hair, radiant, sparkles like the sun flashing off a red snapper diving in and out of the ocean. Today she reminds me of Rita

Hayworth. I wonder again how her listeners are able to intuit the nods.

She terminates her call as I walk up the path, and gives me her full attention. "Sam, what are you wearing and what have you done to your hair?"

I am wearing twelve-dollar baggy Venice Beach pants. This pair has little gray elephants instead of little red balloons. It seemed inspired when I bought them. My gray Ann Taylor T-shirt cost $62. What's wrong with this picture? My hair, which I so meticulously blow-dried, is pulled back with a black barrette into a low ponytail. No more college courses for me. I am headed right back to high school.

So I guess she has a point, only I say, "Never mind."

With all the stuff happening in my life, how much time and attention should I really be expected to give to my appearance?

"With all the stuff happening in my life, how much time do you expect me to spend on hair and clothes?"

"And makeup?" Ren's last dig.

I look at her and my look says stop and she does.

Always adept at shifting gears, Ren rattles on as we walk along the side path that leads to the backyard. "If you would just hire a good lawyer, all of this stuff you're angsting about would evaporate."

"Poof." I say it quietly, but with a certain amount of venom.

"Gosh, Sam, you know what I mean. I'm just trying to get you to—"

"Here's the deal. We don't talk about me, my divorce, or related issues this afternoon. We just have a nice girl's lunch without a care in the world."

Ren turns and gives me a dirty look but says, "Fine."

As we approach the gazebo I can see that Ren has prepared a nice spread for us. Fruit salad, pasta salad, slices of delicious, exotic cheeses, and a sampling of different breads. My ultimate weakness, bread.

"Ren, this is really nice. What kind of breads?"

"One is olive, one is potato and herb, and the other is rosemary and olive oil. I got them at the Farmers' Market."

And then for no reason in the world it hits me. My best friend is having an affair. She no longer leaves the lingering aroma of expensive perfume in her wake. There is something more lemon-lime about her smell. Cool, natural, clean, happy. I don't know how I know, I don't know why the bread makes me certain, but as sure as my name was Samantha Feldman, my beautiful, red-headed, vixen-like friend is cheating on her husband.

The Ren of four weeks ago stirred up memories of Juliet Prowse. Today she is Rita Hayworth. Simmering lust and passion. It is palpable.

I'm not going to say a word. Will she bring it up? Now that I think about it, I haven't responded to Ren's protest that she hasn't heard from me by saying "right back at you." I haven't heard from her, either, and she's the telephone freak. I recall how quickly she ended her call today as I came up the path.

What was that all about? Since when does Ren end a call just because I arrive?

Maybe I am being overly suspicious because of my own circumstances. Maybe, because I am keeping secrets from my best friend, I think she's doing the same. Why don't I want to tell her about the book I'm writing? Why did I keep my meeting with Peter Perkal a secret? Why am I going to keep my appointment tonight with Carol Haber a secret?

I've never told her about my morning walks at Hollywood Forever. Certainly not about Jack Sharrow. Why not? That is precisely the type of drama one shares with a best friend. On the friendship meter, my rating has plummeted. The person in this glass house should stop throwing stones, even if they are imaginary.

As if she is strolling through my thoughts, Ren pops four seedless green grapes into her mouth. Then she says, "Wasn't Peter Perkal Ben's publicist at one time? Did you read about the hit and run in the paper?"

"No. I didn't read it, but I heard it on the radio." I am answering as if I'm in court instead of lunching with a friend.

"Just terrible. I never heard about anything like that happening over there near Century City. I mean, sure people get hit by cars, but this one just took off. And it sounds like he was run over twice. As if to make sure he was dead. Trés bizarre."

I am wolfing down watermelon and cantaloupe slices as if I have a sudden need to replace bodily fluids. "Not so strange when you think about it. If you hit someone and kill them, I mean kill him, would you want to stick around to have a conversation with the police? What if you're charged with manslaughter or worse? And, if you've killed him, there's no chance he can identify you or the car."

Who am I, Perry Mason? Actually, I sound more like the villain in the piece. Why am I sounding so defensive? If I sound that way to myself, what must Ren think?

"Sam, what are you saying?" Ren actually sounds horrified. "Are you suggesting that if you hit a pedestrian, you should drive away from the scene of the accident as fast as possible?"

The watermelon slice I'm steering toward my mouth slips between my fingers and makes a soft, swooshing splatter noise as it hits the gazebo decking. I don't mean to be acting odd. I can't seem to control myself. I need to pull myself together.

"If you have an accident, you stop. Of course. I guess this person got scared. Why are you making it so complicated? Maybe some woman looked down at her grocery list, took her eyes off the road for one split second, and splat. She's supposed to pick up her husband's dry cleaning and her kid at school or she can call her husband from the Beverly Hills Police Station and say 'Hi, honey, by the way, can you come and post bail because I seem to have killed a man while I was debating whether I should go to the supermarket and pick up a filet mignon I was going to barbecue for your dinner tonight?' Why is it so hard to imagine she might keep driving?"

Where was my off switch? Why am I acting guilty? There, I've finally said the word. Well, at least said it in my head. I've done nothing wrong. I had lunch with the man. I didn't kill him.

And then we both see a flash, extremely bright, from the upstairs bedroom at Boo's house. Ren looks startled, then pale, then alarmed. I watch her iced tea and wonder if it's peppered with gin as it goes flying off the table. Ren's body seems to tilt as suddenly as a sail that has just caught the wind.

Not more than two seconds later we hear a sharp report that sounds like a gun. Then, silence. I am confused. "Was that a gun, Ren? It's the same as thunder and lightning, right? The flash comes before the sound of the gun?"

Ren looks calmer now. She rights her glass, puckers her lips in a way to equally spread the lipstick, and says, "You're confused. The noise always precedes the flash."

We are having our strangest conversation of all time. And I am positive that she is wrong and positive that she knows she is wrong.

"Ren, something just happened at Boo's house. Do you think someone was shot? It sounded like a gun? Should we call the police? Should we do something?" She doesn't answer. "Ren, what do you think we should do?"

I'll be darned if Miss "How Can One Drive Away from the Scene of an Accident" doesn't just shrug her shoulders as if to say: *Who knows? Don't worry, be happy.*

# CHAPTER FOURTEEN

With a passing nod to *Cosmo*, I transform myself from Venice beach gal to Beverly Hills babe.

For my meeting with Carol Haber, I put on a black silk Donna Karan suit with an exquisite Evan Picone canary-yellow silk blouse and black-and-yellow Stuart Weitzman shoes. I do my nails in a warm cream color. No rings. Matching gold bracelet and necklace, care of Cartier. Gold and onyx earrings, courtesy of Tiffany's. I look drop dead. Makeup, hair, and nails to perfection. The whole nine yards.

I give the car to valet parking and this time don't think about the charge. These valet guys don't look like struggling screenwriters anyway. Maybe they have families to support and this is a real job.

Sitting on a bench in front of the hotel, a bench I assume is there for guests to comfortably wait for taxis and their cars, is the most extraordinary street person. Her jet black hair, peeking out from a colorful scarf, belies her wizened face. Her glorious colors give her an exotic Eastern European aura. Her clothes are a gypsy sort of outfit, but there is little you can see of her clothes as she is covered everywhere in buttons. The Button Lady.

The buttons are as diverse as "Mickey Mouse" and "I Love Reading" and "I Like Ike." Hundreds of buttons cover almost every inch of her clothes. They cover the scarf wrapped around her head and much of her face. Some of the buttons look like they go back sixty years. The little Button Lady may be worth more than some of the guests at the hotel if she ever peels the buttons off her tattered clothes and gets them appraised.

She is mumbling to herself as if trying to remember the words of some long-forgotten song.

I am so absorbed with watching her, I don't hear Ren's son, Blake Martel, say hello to me until he repeats it a second or maybe a third time. His proximity startles me. I ask him what he's doing here.

He has the casual, unruffled confidence endemic to being fifteen. A confidence that either erodes or escalates with time and experience. I look at him and want to say, *never grow up*. But I don't. Grownups are not supposed to reveal that grownup secret.

His jeans look pressed and his hair is slicked back neatly. He is applying for a busboy job at the hotel restaurant. I say that his mom hadn't told me and he shrugs and says he has to get going because he doesn't want to be late.

Will Blake mention seeing me? I have not told Ren about this meeting. She will have questions if Blake tells her. What should I say? Why not the truth? Why am I making my life more complicated?

I am fifteen minutes early. It would be good discipline for me to sit patiently at the bar and sort out my thoughts for a few minutes. We're always running away from getting bored by ourselves. I sit down at the bar and start my wait.

A man I once would have referred to as older starts a conversation with me. He looks to be in his late sixties, pleasant-looking with an admirable tuft of white hair and a glistening, clean-shaven face that cries out Irish.

It takes less than three minutes for me to figure out that he thinks I am a hooker. I don't get it. I guess it's like all professions. You tailor your look to the clientele. After all, here I am all dressed up and out of my baggy Venice Beach pants in order to impress Carol Haber. And in the process I appear to have impressed this wild Irish rogue.

I put my hand on his arm, give him what I think and hope is a provocative wink, and say in a hushed voice, "Gotta run. Tonight is already committed."

Am I flattering myself or does he look disappointed? I sit down at a table near the bar, take small sips of my Diet Pepsi, and patiently study the eclectic artwork and my manicure while I wait for Carol.

Carol Haber and boy wonder, Maurice, appear promptly at five. Carol looks nice in an anorexic sort of way. Like an older, wiser Karen Carpenter. Boy Wonder looks smashing in a navy blue suit. A Tanya Brown romance novel is tucked under his arm. He smells like almonds.

Carol's kiss misses my face by two inches. Maurice grins and holds up his hand in a wave. Agent and her right-hand boy are staying antiseptic tonight.

"Sam, darling, it's so good to see you. It's been ages. And where is Benjamin? Couldn't he join us?"

Carol's words are gushy, but she doesn't gush. She speaks in a calm, even relaxed way. Unfortunately, the question I hoped to divert, at least for a short while, has arisen in the first ten seconds. Should I tell the truth, lie, or be evasive? When in doubt, evade.

"No, he couldn't make it. But that's all right because what I wanted to talk to you about only indirectly concerns him."

"How do you mean, darling?"

Maurice hasn't spoken a word but extracts from his Louis Vuitton bag a Gucci notepad to take copious notes in the event I should let a pearl slip out by accident.

Carol looks at her watch. She can't be bored yet, I don't think.

A waiter comes by looking very starched and proper and asks if he can take drink orders. Maurice waves him off in a distant friendly way and I know this is going to be a short meeting unless I say something terribly interesting, terribly quickly.

"Carol," I say. I turn smiling toward Maurice, reconsider my opening, and think it the better part of diplomacy to include him. "And Maurice, I'm completing a book."

Before I can continue, Carol claps her hands together, Maurice grins harder, if that is possible, and she says, "Darling, how very quaint. Is Ben assisting you?"

This is going badly. I need to take the plunge and either go to the head of the class or go from bad to worse.

"The truth of the matter is that Ben and I are separated. He has nothing to do with this book with one big exception. My protagonist or some other character in the book is going to kill Hunter McCall. This book will break the bank, Carol. Off the charts, I just know it."

"Divorce," she says as she rises from her chair, "such an ugly thing. My darling, why would you even consider for one minute trying to kill the goose who's laying your golden eggs. Your book would be no more than a ripple. David hasn't toppled Goliath in quite some time, you know. Have you spoken to your attorney? Ben will have a restraining order of some sort, I'm sure, in no time at all." She shakes her head. "Not a good idea, Samantha."

I have been demoted from darling. I have a name again, a name in its formal and full-length version. Not a good sign with Carol. I don't want her to leave and she is leaving. Maurice has already taken two steps toward the door. I need a show stopper. Something to make her freeze in her tracks and listen to me.

"Whether you leave or stay, Carol, someone's going to die. I promise you that. With or without your help. And that's front-page stuff. Bestseller stuff."

It isn't exactly Bogart telling Louis it's the beginning of a long friendship, or Scarlett vowing she'll never be hungry again, but it does stop her, albeit only momentarily. I think she stops on the "someone's going to die" part and keeps walking on the "with or without your help." All I know is, I don't rate a good-bye.

A wave of heat rushes through me. I recognize it as panic. I feel my clothes start to cling. The hotel's hard-pumping air conditioner makes the sweat evaporate instantly, but my silk blouse is headed straight to the dry cleaners. I assumed Carol would be excited by my idea, that she would want to work with me. Happily. Until this moment, I hadn't considered that she might repeat to Ben what I told her. Stupid. Stupid. Stupid. That I am.

She is almost through the exit when I call her name. I am loud. I am beyond worrying who hears. My voice will catch up to her far faster than my legs hurriedly wobbling on Stuart Weitzman heels.

She turns, stops, and gives me a blank look.

Maurice does the same, except his look is not blank. More like mocking.

"Carol," I repeat, "you are going to keep our conversation confidential?"

I try to make the question sound like a demand, not a plea. It's doubtful I am succeeding.

"Whatever made you think that, darling? I'm not your doctor, lawyer, or priest." I think I hear her mutter, "Thank God."

She is gone before I can respond. But for the faint whiff of expensive perfume she leaves behind, it is as if she was never there. No trace of Maurice's almond aura. That leaves my wild Irish rogue. But when I check the bar he, too, is gone.

Valet parking retrieves my car in less than two minutes. It would make me feel better to give Button Lady a few bucks.

Two overly made-up teenage girls are now sitting on the bench, comparing their nail polish colors. They look rich, spoiled, and insipid. I hate them for no earthly reason. And Button Lady is nowhere to be found.

I think this is what they mean by batting zero.

# CHAPTER FIFTEEN

There are dreams that are so vivid and exhausting, they make you feel as if you never slept a moment the entire night. I have one of those dreams. I dream that Benjamin is in the house and we are talking and talking endlessly and though we never raise our voices, we are fighting.

The entire time he talks I listen, and wonder why I ever married him. When I try to respond, he takes a utility knife and begins slashing all the furniture and art in our home.

I guess we don't have to call in Dr. Freud for this dream analysis.

I hear the doorbell ring, look at the clock, see it is 9:00 A.M., and I don't want to get out of bed. I don't feel yummy. I don't even feel puffy. I feel numb.

I should be walking, but the thought of getting out of bed is paralyzing. I was up until four A.M., writing my great American novel. Writing like I never thought I could, and trying to block out what seems to be my unraveling grip on reality.

The bell rings again. Go away. Go away. Whoever you are I don't want to see you. But the person is now alternating between the huge iron knocker and the bell. It isn't close to music. It's noise. Of the worst kind.

Pulling on old green sweatpants and a matching sweatshirt, I troop barefoot down the stairs. It is still early enough for the cold marble to make my toes tingle. As the day heats up, so will my steps.

Without thinking, I open the door. Who does one fear at 9:00 A.M.?

The last person I expect to see standing on my doorstep is the star of last night's dream. But there he is, in the flesh. My body freezes in spite of the early morning sun. Benjamin looks about as happy to see me as I am to see him. But who would he have expected to answer the door? The downstairs maid? So much for failing to ask who's there. You only learn that when you're three years old.

I'm not in the mood to mince words. And I'm not in the mood for him at all.

"What do you want?"

Ben pushes through the door and walks into our large foyer. He glares at me, gives my bare feet a disdainful look, and generally mimes his disapproval of my appearance. So what else is new? In his right hand is a half-smoked cigar, still lit and lightly smoldering.

Before he can speak, I say, "Take that filthy thing out of my house."

My words make him smile in his absolutely cruelest way. Did he think I've forgotten that look or what it means? He walks to the front door, steps outside for a moment, and I watch him carefully place the cigar on the edge of one of the flowerboxes. His delicacy is out of consideration for the unfinished cigar, not the flowers. Of this I am certain.

He walks back in, still not speaking. He is acting this way to infuriate me. And he is succeeding.

"Benjamin, tell me what you want or get out. Better yet, why don't you just get out?"

Even Ben knows when to stop pushing. "I need to pick up a few things."

Nothing rings true. Ben has nothing remaining in the house of a personal nature and everything else will be divided later.

This trip to my front door doesn't make sense, so I ask, "What could I have here that you need?"

I hate the words as I speak them. How self-destructive am I? It's as if I'm setting myself up for his nastiness. Setting myself up for the scathing one-liner that is sure to follow. But he doesn't take the opening. He has a different agenda.

"Don't think for one minute that you're going to get away with writing anything that even remotely has to do with Hunter. I spoke to Carol and she told me about your idiotic idea. Give me the manuscript now."

He is demanding in the way that only a husband can be, and I don't think of him as my husband anymore.

"You can't talk to me that way, so forget about it."

Yeah, so forget about it. I sound like a New York comedienne, or a New York wiseguy. Or a New York comedienne imitating a wise guy.

"If that's the only thing you came for, leave now." I hope I sound strong.

"I want the Waterford pitcher we got in England."

I am going to say he can't have it. Then I think, I'll go fetch it, drop it on our beautiful marble floor, and watch it explode in a million lovely pieces. Probably not one of my better ideas.

"It's in the dining room on the teacart. Take it and get out."

I walk away, into the small den and flip on the television, hoping to block out the echo of his footsteps. The sounds of his shoes on the floor are enough to make me physically ill. The local news, the weather, a recitation of sports scores, anything is better than hearing him walk or breathe.

Holding the pitcher in both of his hands, he enters the den. Benjamin always reminds me of the actor John Gavin, the one who eventually became the U.S. ambassador to Mexico when his acting days ended. Gavin was tall, statuesque, classy. I hate, now, that Benjamin's exterior always makes me think of Gavin.

John Gavin had a quality. He always looked kind. I don't know if he was or wasn't. I know nothing about him, other than what I saw on the movie screen. I try to remember if there was ever a time when I associated Ben with the notion of kindness.

He looks like John Gavin now, only not at all kind and not nearly as good-looking. His face is distorted with a look of hatred that probably equals or betters mine. He says, "If you think, for one minute, that I'm going to let you get away with trying to do anything to hurt my career, you're not only wrong, you're crazy. I'll cut you down so fast you won't know what hit you."

This is how I like to see Ben—threatening and nasty. This is the kind of reinforcement that gets my juices flowing. Thank you, Ben. I am about to respond childishly, in a way that I'll later regret, but my attention is drawn away from Ben. His eyes have left my face and are widening. We are now both anchored to the television where the screen shows a large and seriously dated picture of Carol Haber.

Under her face is the year she was born with a hyphen followed by the current year. There is no mistaking what it means. Carol is dead.

Ben snaps, "Turn up the volume." This time I listen to him.

The newscaster's voice does nothing to change how silent the room feels. Carol's assistant found her dead in her hotel room. The assistant they refer to has to be Maurice. Apparently, he summoned security when she didn't respond to his phone calls or knock on her door. They had a plane to catch and he had been concerned about how late she was running. Only she wasn't running anywhere. Not anymore.

The police suspect foul play. Foul play always makes me think of baseball. Only this is nothing like baseball. Carol is dead. According to a local newsperson, an autopsy will be performed to determine cause of death. However, an investigation is underway as the police feel there is a strong probability that Carol was poisoned.

I don't suppose they suspect Wolfgang Puck even though she left our meeting to have dinner at Spago.

The news people must have gotten to the hotel immediately because there is a picture on the TV screen of a hysterical Maurice. I feel a wave of nausea as I imagine Maurice turning to the police and saying, "Oh, and just earlier this evening Samantha Crowley said to Carol, 'Someone's going to die, I promise you that.' "

Will he repeat what I said? Will he repeat it out of context? No one can seriously believe I'm involved. Do I have an alibi? Why do I need an alibi? And no, I don't have one. I was home alone, writing. I have the pages to prove it. Is that evidence? What am I worried about? Should I be worried?

I shift my gaze from the television to Ben. He doesn't look worried. Neither does he look particularly grief-stricken. What a cold asshole. He actually looks a bit bewildered.

*Dear Emily: What are the rules of etiquette for continuing to scream at one's estranged wife when you've just learned that your agent has been murdered?*

The newscaster moves onto another story and I push the remote and shut off the television.

It will be interesting to see who blinks first. Ben does. Of course, I have the home turf advantage.

"I can't understand how this happened? Who would have any reason to kill Carol?"

Ben's question isn't directed at me. He is wondering out loud. Perhaps he speaks to stop the thundering silence in the room.

Carol was an agent. She must have done lots of not very nice stuff to lots of people. There have to be people who wanted her dead. Though dead does seem extreme, even by Hollywood standards. But for me, that isn't the pressing question. For me, there is a bigger picture.

In the last seventy-two hours, two people have died within twelve hours of our conversation. Why? It has to be a terrible coincidence. But what a coincidence. This is one for the record books.

I don't want to respond to Ben's question. What I want is for him to leave.

"Ben, you've got the pitcher. Please leave. Now."

"You haven't responded to what I said. I want an answer before I leave."

Momentary confusion. Does Ben expect me to tell him who I think killed Carol? Then I realize that we are off the subject of Carol altogether. He wants me to address his outburst about my ruining his career. He wants me to acknowledge my understanding that he is going to cut me down. In other words, the topic of Carol's death is exhausted with his one sentence and, now, he is on to a more important subject, a subject that concerns Benjamin and only Benjamin.

Even if he doesn't feel drained by what we just heard, I do. Verbally jousting with him will be neither entertaining nor productive.

I say, "I don't want to talk to you."

He looks angry enough to strike me.

It is stupid to further enrage him so I say, "I'll give it some thought."

That slightly mollifies him, but not much. If he gives the Waterford pitcher just one more squeeze, it will burst into a million shards in his hands. The image of blood flowing from his hands makes me want to applaud. How will he be able to type all those golden words he spews each day?

Without another word, he turns and leaves the den. I follow to make sure he is leaving. He opens the front door and I walk out behind him. He heads straight for the flowerbox to retrieve his cigar.

The news of Carol's death does not make this man skip one beat. He puts the cigar back in his mouth.

I pray to the plant gods that a worm has crawled into the tobacco leaves.

He turns and sneers at me. Definitely not one of his John Gavin looks. "I know you saw Carol yesterday and the police will want to talk to you. I hope you've been a good girl, Sam."

I stare at him and say, "Get out of here before I kill you."

My words frighten me. Ben looks bored.

Except for the cacophony of birds chirping, a leaf blower whirring, and the distant sound of a lawnmower, the street is hushed and empty. Then I see movement and a man. It is that same strange street person who was in front of the Peninsula Hotel, the plant man. That strange, green, other-worldly individual with the plant growing out of the top of his head. He is standing in front of my house and looking directly at Benjamin and me.

# CHAPTER SIXTEEN

Ren inhales deeply and says, "He didn't get the job, but I don't think he really cares that much."

She is talking about Blake's job application for the busboy position at the hotel restaurant. On my being at the hotel, I have already been quizzed extensively. Before that, I was subjected to even more intense interrogation about what Ben's car was doing in front of my house.

I've been on the Ren hot seat for close to an hour. I think I did pretty well, all things considered.

Her call came within thirty seconds of Ben's red Jaguar pulling away. I wonder if Ren sits by the window and waits for life's events to unfold.

"It's so strange about Ben's agent, don't you think?" Ren doesn't want an answer. She needs to put words to the thoughts that have been cartwheeling in her head for the last half hour.

"Imagine, she comes here to L.A., is only here a few days and someone kills her. I mean if it's someone she knew you'd think they would have killed her in NYC where she lives and not followed her three thousand miles. Of course, it could have been someone here, but how many people could she have pissed off in Los Angeles?"

"I don't know." I think about what Ren's said and repeat, "I don't know."

"Sam, whatever is wrong with you?"

"Nothing."

Everything. I am becoming increasingly nervous about Peter and Carol both dying horrid, mysterious deaths. I am even more nervous about my reluctance to confide in my best friend.

Ren says, "Honey, you're not yourself. I sent some slides of my sculptures to a gallery in Santa Fe, New Mexico. They may be interested. Maybe, if they are, you and I can go there for a long weekend. Get away from all this."

Maybe one day I'll understand the logic. Spend three million dollars for a home and some astronomical sum to belong to a golf and tennis club and then conspire with your friends as to how to get away from it all. A new twelve-step program. The get-away-from-it-all program. The families in East L.A. trade homes with us for a week and we "get away" by living in their places and they "get away" by living in ours. Then expand the program, make it interstate. A Beverly Hills family can "get away" to Dixon, Iowa.

But all I respond is, "That might be nice."

"Sam, did you know there's a man in black spandex with a boom box on his head dancing in front of your house? Do you want me to call the police?"

"No, it's all right."

Where are all these street people coming from? Are they my guardian angels, or the devil definitely not in disguise?

I ask Ren, "Speaking of police, did you ever find out about that loud noise we heard coming from Boo's house yesterday afternoon?"

"It wasn't so loud."

This is an answer? I was there. It was loud. What's going on with Ren? All right, we'll do it her way. I say, "Well, no matter how loud it was or wasn't, did you find out anything?"

She shrugs off the question. "No. I don't think there was anything to find out. Let's have dinner tonight."

Ren can spend two hours grilling me to make sure I haven't

hidden from her any secret ingredient I put in my lasagna. She knows before I do who is walking up to my front door or dancing in front of my house. But there is nothing to find out about a possible gunshot coming from the house between us. At the very least, this is helping me understand some of my hesitancy about taking her into my confidence. Something weird is going on. But I am disinclined to confront her. I have secrets too, only now I am not certain which came first, my secrets or hers.

There, I have said the word, even if only to myself. *Secrets.*

I feel this need to keep everything secret.

"I can't do dinner. I'm going to this group meeting, 'Spit it Out,' at seven o'clock." I regret the words as I say them. I planned to keep this a secret as well.

Ren starts puffing away in muted excitement. "Isn't that the militant divorcee group? I know that group. At least three big movie stars' wives who got screwed royally belong, isn't that right?"

Wrong. Should I tell her? Should I tell her she is mixing up the writers' group "Spit It Out" with the divorced women's group "Spit Him Out"?

"Yup. That's the group." There, I did it. Lied for no reason to my best friend. I still deserve to live—but not happily.

"Listen, Sam, there's something I need to tell you that I shouldn't, but I have to because you're my best friend and that makes you an even closer friend, you know, than my husband. And though I hate to be devious and I really know I shouldn't have looked, I did and now I know and I think it's important I tell you, since you don't seem to be good at protecting your interests, though I have to admit that I feel so much better about everything now that I know you're going to the group tonight and I know they'd tell you—"

"Stop," I say it for her benefit as well as mine. Ren is verbally foaming. So not like her. What is going on, anyway? "Ren, you've just said half a dozen sentences, saying nothing. What are you talking about?" I feel immense guilt about her repeated references to our friendship. A person can stand only just so much.

"Here it is." Ren inhales deeply. I can visualize the smoke snaking down her throat and wafting up to her nostrils. On anyone else it looks obscene. On her it is nothing short of erotic. Ren should have been born in the forties, co-starring and smoking her way opposite a young, debonair Melvyn Douglas.

"I was in Stephen's file cabinet," she continues. "I was looking for something and I saw Ben's name and pulled out the file. Don't say it, I know I shouldn't have. Anyway, I'm not great at interpreting this insurance stuff, but it was pretty clear to me that Ben has a ten-million-dollar life insurance policy with you as the beneficiary. It was dated eight or nine years ago. You're the primary beneficiary. He hasn't changed it."

Let me think. Eight or nine years ago. Possible. Ben still liked me then. Love, I'm not certain, but my guess is he liked me well enough to let Stephen, super salesman, talk him into a policy before things like high blood pressure, cholesterol, and the like, became issues.

I say nothing. Ren says, "Do you remember the lawyer mentioned that once the case is filed, insurance is not supposed to be changed? That includes life insurance, don't you think?"

My mouth is dry, so suddenly that it feels as if I've been in the hot desert for days without a drink. The sun is beating on my marble steps and toasting my toes. I don't understand what she is getting at. All I feel is hot. I say, "I don't understand. What's your point?"

"Well, it's good to know. Don't you think?"

I sigh but not so Ren can hear me. "I suppose it's good to know, if he's dead, but he's not."

Ren pauses as if that never occurred to her. "Well, okay, I see what you mean. But just in case. After all, Carol Haber didn't expect to be dead today either, did she?"

Point. Game. Set. On that ambiguous note, we end the call.

It is certainly a good friend who noses through her husband's confidential files and discloses the product of her spying. A friend from whom I am hiding the fact that I plan to attend a writers group. That I am writing a book. That I just met with Peter and Carol. Shame on me.

Ren, on the other hand, is pretending there was no gunshot-sounding noise coming from the house between us. She has a lover, maybe, and hasn't told me. She is spying on her husband, going through his records, but for what reason? It wasn't to find out information about Ben. What was she looking for?

She has secrets, too. So what? Friends don't have to share everything.

The rest of the day I work on my book. No phone calls. No ringing doorbell. No street people nesting in front of my house. No interruptions. The book is cooking.

At about five-thirty I start getting hungry. What does one wear to the home of an individual hosting a writers' group? Will he serve food? I am disinclined to bring my ninety completed pages. I am writing at a phenomenal pace. It feels good. If I bring only the first few chapters, no one will know the book is about Hunter McCall. I have no idea what is expected.

I was invited to attend the group by Bicky Belinsky, the pastry chef at my favorite patisserie. She saw me hunched over one of her chocolate croissants, with my book notes, and casually asked if I was writing a book. It never occurred to me to keep the book a secret from her and, with overeager, school-girlish enthusiasm, I told her that I was writing my first novel.

Much to my surprise, she told me that she and her sister, Dicky, also a pastry chef but at a different patisserie across town, were writing a book that was a history of their family. Bicky and Dicky have lived together for the last thirty years, unmarried, childless, approaching the end of a sixth decade, and are the last of the Belinskys.

Do they honestly believe that anyone other than the two of them will be the slightest bit interested in their family history? Or maybe they have been driven to write their story for personal reasons, like I have. Bicky, short for Bernadette, is tiny and wrinkled, like a linen shirt just out of a hot dryer. She reminds me of a younger Granny from *The Beverly Hillbillies*.

I have only met her sister Dicky, short for Darnelle, once, and remember her as being of greater width than height. She is huge. Darnelle has eaten too many of her wonderful pastries and cookies. Her face is round and reminds me of the candy M&M faces kids make on big honey-colored cookies.

I only half listened when Bicky started chattering about the writers' group she and her sister joined. It wasn't until she mentioned the name Jonathon Harley that I listened with more interest. Only I wasn't sure why. Something about the name was familiar. Somehow I connected him with the book business, though her description of him did nothing to refresh my recollection.

From Bicky's description of Jonathon Harley, he could be David Niven. I wonder if maybe she doesn't have a crush on him. She told me he is British, very polite, proper, and distinguished.

Bicky whispered that he spoke the King's English and then confided to me, in an even more hushed tone, that she wasn't sure what that meant. His humor, she said, was very dry. He was retired from something but she didn't know what.

I could see Bicky let her imagination run wild. She probably thinks he's knighted and keeping it a secret. He walks erect and always wears a tie, she said. Bicky believes he's a widower, though she hadn't seen any pictures of a wife, living or deceased.

She was certain he isn't presently married but she didn't know why.

It isn't until Bicky tells me that you have to take a cable car to get to his Studio City home perched on one of the many lovely hillsides in L.A. that I decide to go. Maybe this Jonathon Harley can help me.

I have run out of people to call. Maybe he has connections. It sounds like he has some money. Of course everyone in L.A. creates that illusion and it's usually as real as believing tightly grasped sand in the palm of your hand will still be there when you unclench your fingers.

But who knows? Maybe he is for real. Maybe he is someone who can help me in my journey to kill Hunter McCall. It doesn't cost to hope.

# CHAPTER SEVENTEEN

Jonathon Harley's home is everything Bicky described and more. You hop into a four-seater cable car that transports you to his house in the sky. Floor-to-ceiling glass windows and doors open to decks wrapped around the house, overlooking more hillsides and the rolling blue skies of our mellow and occasionally ebullient city. That's the fun part of Los Angeles. People live in glass houses and do throw stones.

Bicky truly captured Jonathon in her description. It is like meeting a David Niven who wears small wire-framed glasses.

I'm glad I abandoned my Venice Beach grunge wear and donned a lovely David Dart print floor-length dress with a matching jacket. Casual, not fancy, but very pretty. The dress makes me look a little like a tropical fruit salad. The clerk described each swirling color on the abstract design as mango, banana, or avocado. I wish I looked good enough to eat. I would have loved some male attention.

But this is business and Bicky doesn't need to fear competition. Jonathon is all hers. Everyone is dressed nicely. Bicky and Dicky are dressed in what appear to be the same style, but different color, muumuus. Bicky wears a petite, pink version of her sister's blue tent. The wide sleeves and truckload of material can't hide Dicky's bulk. Bicky's muumuu looks like you can fit another person in there with her. On their laps rest trays holding an assortment of pastries and small cakes.

I am introduced to Paul O'Brien, whom I estimate to be

about thirty-five years old. He is conservative-looking with short brown hair and a small moustache. He's a little too much of the pocket protector type for my taste, but he has the aura of a guy who would love to have someone take care of him. Paul's face cries out: *I'm single, are you interested?*

It turns out Paul is a computer nerd, which doesn't surprise me one bit. I mean that in the kindest way. The computer is great, but the geek look could use some improvement. Bicky and Dicky fatten up the group, literally, but Paul is the one who makes it possible for them to write. Paul gives a free computer tutorial to everyone in the group.

Jonathon contributes his home for the meetings. Though very different in appearance, Jonathon and Paul seem to get on well. I watch them engage in a lively but quiet conversation shortly before the meeting is formally commenced by Jonathon, who appears to be the master of ceremonies.

"I think all of us have met Samantha Crowley. Bicky invited her to our group to see if she might be . . . interested."

I wonder if he is searching for the word *suitable*.

"Interested in replacing Hughie," Jonathon continues. "Who has, as I think all of us know, decided to take up tennis instead of writing. And, if I may add, I think made a very insightful choice inasmuch as I don't believe Hughie wrote more than five pages in the entire nine months he was part of our little group."

If page numbers is the decisive criterion for eligibility in this group, I should be in good shape with the speed at which my manuscript is progressing. Why am I worrying? I remind myself that I am here to find out if Jonathon Harley has connections to help me.

Jonathon says, "As we all know, Hughie's contribution to the group was the refreshments."

I conjure up a picture of high tea at a staid men's club.

Everyone in the group looks at me. At first I don't get it and then I do. The true decisive criterion for being in the group is volunteering to be the refreshment hostess. If I say yes, I am in.

I give a nervous cough, something I rarely do, and say, "With a little direction about what you like, I'd be delighted to take over the job of bringing refreshments."

Paul looks relieved. Bicky and Dicky are staring hungrily at the little cakes on their laps, and Jonathon, for the first time, gives me a smile.

"Excellent. I'm glad we have that resolved. Though it may vary on occasion, I think you'll find that generally Bernadette and Darnelle like lemonade, Paul has a preference for dark beer, I like my coffee very hot and very strong, and I provide my own little addition to the coffee from my private stock."

Jonathon sort of winks and gestures vaguely with his head to a room where I assume he keeps liquor and brandy and such.

I hear a faint noise and realize it is Dicky. She has very quietly said, "Pink." When I repeat the word to make sure I have heard her correctly, she adds, "That's the kind of lemonade we like."

I am beginning to get a clue why Hughie bailed. Jonathon lifts himself from what looks like a comfortable armchair, makes a *harrumph*ing type of noise I have only heard from colonels in nineteen-forties British films, waves an accusing finger at Bicky, and says, "I think it's time we started the business of our meeting and as all of you remember—" he gives me what seems to be a sympathetic look to mean all of us except the newcomer "—last time we met we agreed that Bernadette would read us some of the pages she and Darnelle have written."

Bicky looks as if she'd like to shrink into her oversized muumuu. "Couldn't we have Dicky read the pages? She so does enjoy reading aloud." Bicky gives Jonathon a look of pleading and unrequited love.

In a voice that makes me think of *Father Knows Best*, Jonathon says in a soothing but scolding fatherly tone, "Bernadette, we discussed this last time and agreed that it was time you got over this shyness about reading your work. We want to hear from you and I'm sure Darnelle agrees." Jonathon raises an eyebrow and gives Darnelle a look. If the look had been directed at anyone other than Dicky, I would have thought it was Jonathon's version of sexually suggestive. As the look is for Dicky, I assume it is a warning not to disagree.

For a small group there seems to be a great deal of subtle political dynamics. Or is it sexual dynamics? No way.

Dicky is nibbling at the corner of a small cake and looks as if she will agree to anything that will allow her to continue eating undisturbed.

Bicky stands up, makes slightly flirtatious eye contact with Jonathon, giggles nervously, and begins reading from a somewhat jumbled pile of papers she holds in her very thin, trembling hands.

Apparently the group has heard earlier portions of the Belinsky saga, and from what I understand, we seem to be picking up the thread some time near the turn of the twentieth century in what I assume is New York.

Bicky's description of the furniture, rugs, and artwork in the tiny apartment of her ancestors is taking longer to tell than a historical narrative of the furniture and art in the Hearst mansion. Bicky and Dicky have either found old family pictures, letters, and diaries or, alternatively, they have done excruciatingly detailed research. Whichever it is, it's impossible to endure the reading without constant yawning and fidgeting.

Jonathon sits erect and alert and appears to be absorbing each and every word. Paul adopts a clever posture that makes it impossible to tell if he is snoozing, concentrating on each stumbling word Bicky utters, or suffering from the most dreadful migraine. His right arm is raised and pulled completely across his face so that his hand comes to rest on his left ear. I want to tell him he'll never seduce a girl from this planet if he continues to sit in such a distorted, nerdy manner.

Dicky nods periodically, as if in agreement with her own words, and continues to stuff large crumbs from the little cakes into her ample mouth. I can see that the tray that previously contained ten small cakes now has only six.

I continue to do my best to remain polite, though after twenty minutes of almost nonstop reading, I may need to consider mimicking Paul's solution. The narrative is brutal. I thought the point of the book was her ancestors, not the household contents.

Abruptly, Bicky stops reading and sits down next to Dicky on a lovely two-seater couch that comfortably holds the one petite and one enlarged sister. I drift for a moment, but it seems that Bicky is, if not in midsentence, certainly in midthought when she suddenly stops reading.

If I wasn't entirely awake before, I am now as our small group breaks into polite applause. Bicky blushes gently. Dicky beams and offers her a cake.

"That was very nice, Bernadette. It was delightful of you to share your and your sister's work with our group."

Jonathon is certainly polite. I thought the objective of a group like this was to critique work. I wait to see if input is expected from any of us. When Dicky says "Shall we serve our refreshments now?" and Jonathon gently slaps his palms together and responds, "Splendid," I realize the group is about applause and eating, not serious writing.

Paul is craning his neck. When I ask if he is all right, he says, "I was just trying to figure out where the beer might be. Hughie used to bring a cooler to the meetings."

Bicky and Dicky have moved some objects off Jonathon's coffee table and are putting out doilies, paper plates, and little plastic forks, spoons, and knives. I watch with a combination of fascination and disbelief.

Bicky bats her eyes, which look like they may collapse under the weight of what I hope are false eyelashes, and says to Jonathon, "Is this okay with you, Jonathon, or would you like us to set the table differently?"

It seems as if Dicky gives Jonathon a conspiratorial wink, but I may be mistaken. Jonathon does his *harrumph*ing sound again and I realize that means we are all expected to take a seat around the coffee table.

Unless Jonathon Harley has some mighty great connections in the publishing world, I don't think attendance at another meeting is on my agenda. I wonder how to get the conversation focused on who Jonathon, or anyone else in the group, may know. I needn't have worried because the group has the same idea.

"So, Samantha, your name is Crowley. You wouldn't happen to be related to the famous author, Benjamin Crowley," Paul says as I watch Dicky shovel what looks like an entire small cake into her mouth.

No one knows about my relationship with Benjamin, not even Bicky, whom I have seen at her patisserie over the years. But there it is. Writing and Crowley. It isn't an unbelievable leap.

I try to think of how to avoid the question and then decide it would be easier to simply answer.

"He's my husband. Almost ex-husband. We're separated."

Paul has found beer and as he swallows, I am startled to hear him say, "Yeah, I thought so. He's dating this gal, Laura, who temped for a short while at the computer firm where I work."

I wince. Hopefully not visibly. At long last a name has been given to the abstraction. Do I want to probe? Is it worth it? It's unhealthy to obsess about this. The smart move is to ask no questions.

Paul takes another sip of beer. "Speaking of famous writers,

111

that famous publicist for writers, Peter Perkal, officed just down the hall from me. Isn't that something about what happened to him?"

I double wince. I am beginning to understand how it must feel to live in a small town.

I shouldn't have asked, but my tongue has a mind of its own. "What's she like?"

Bad, bad, bad. I hate myself for asking, caring, having an interest, wanting to know more, being human. But there it is. And there I am. Paul isn't the slightest bit confused by my reference to Laura, the topic that *preceded* his Peter Perkal remark.

"Well, I don't know. Let me see if I can remember. She's pretty, very pretty, slender, blonde with that kind of Greta Garbo pouty look. You know what I mean. Hazel eyes. She's smart and I think very ambitious. Kind of ruthless, which is odd for a temp. Hard. That's how I'd describe her. Soft on the outside, but hard on the inside. I wouldn't want to come up against her in a dark alley."

For a guy who is struggling to remember, her looks and personality appear seared into his brain. How does he describe women he doesn't remember?

My mood has deteriorated from boredom to depression. My guess is that Benjamin has been having affairs for years and Laura is the most recent of many. I hate how stupid I must appear to everyone. I feel like I should say something in my defense. Why do I need to defend myself to these people? Am I really that insecure?

What could I say, anyway? Yeah, I met someone too. He's good-looking and smart and used to be in law enforcement. Leave out the part that he's now a shell of his former self. Leave out that he's embittered, being blackmailed, and has a brother who is a Robin Hood con man. Leave out that we met when he pulled a gun on me and seriously toyed with the idea of killing me. Leave out that he never called and that we've never had a date.

What a pathetic mess I am. I shelve thoughts about Jack Sharrow and answer appropriately. "Thank you, Paul. I think I get the picture."

Paul smiles and nods. Bicky jumps up to get another napkin for Jonathon. Dicky is casting furtive glances at what looks to be an abstract painting hanging on the wall. I have to be misinterpreting her look but I don't think so.

Dicky's voice calls me out of a trance-like state. I am startled to hear her say, "So did any of you read in the paper about the terrible death of Carol Haber?"

Now how in the world do these people know Carol? Is it simply because Paul introduced the topic of death with his reference to Peter?

Everyone nods. I can no longer contain my curiosity. "Did you know her?" I ask no one in particular and everyone in general.

Bicky walks back in the room with the napkin she has retrieved for Jonathon and answers my question. "Yes, in a way. Dicky and I met with her once to see if she would be interested in representing us. Jonathon was kind enough to let us use his name as an introduction. It's very hard to get an appointment with her unless you know someone."

"Was hard. Not is. She's very much dead. So depending on how you look at it, it's even harder now or, looking at it another way, very easy to get an appointment." Dicky's comeback pounces on her sister. The chuckle after her statement is cold.

These Belinsky sisters are more complicated than they appear on the surface.

I say, "I guess you didn't hook up. I mean, she didn't end up representing you." I don't mean the question as any more than closure, though on this subject I wouldn't mind some elaboration. If they can describe a one-room apartment for twenty minutes, it may be interesting to hear five minutes on their meeting with Carol.

"No, she didn't," Dicky says and the topic ends.

Jonathon, without preamble, launches into a lengthy critique of the musical *Fosse*, which he has just seen. Interesting segue, and an odd choice of topics, as we are a writers' group and he is talking about a play with no script or dialogue, only music and dance.

When he takes a breath and sips his high-octane coffee, I take the opportunity to slip in my question. "Jonathon, when I heard your name I thought I recognized it. Was I right? Something to do with the literary world?"

"My darling girl, of course you were right."

There is a nervous laugh from everyone in the room, even Paul. How I love being the fool.

"I've written, let me think, it must be seven—"

"Oh no, Jonathon, it's eight books," Dicky quickly and helpfully contributes before either Paul or Bicky can get the words out of their already opened mouths.

Jonathon has a room full of fans. Maybe that's what these meetings are about. The Jonathon Harley fan club is now adjourned.

"My dear Samantha, I write my romance novels under the name Tanya Brown. I use that name but everyone knows it is I. I'm sure that's why you recognized my name."

Nice try but I'm not buying. I know his name for another reason and I had no idea he's Tanya Brown.

Not much later, the meeting winds down without reference to anyone's book or what will be discussed at the next meeting. I offer to stay and help clean up before Bicky or Dicky can make the same offer. I want a few moments alone with Jonathon. Maybe I can find out something more.

The sisters look disappointed when Jonathon tells them there is hardly enough mess to justify one person staying to help.

Jonathon turns the volume up on some classical music I don't recognize and tells me how much easier it is for him to write while listening to music.

I don't think I'm misreading signals when I get the impression he does not want to engage in conversation. I excuse myself to use the bathroom and on the way back, pop into his bedroom. I am snooping. I have no idea what I hope to discover.

On his dresser is a picture of Jonathon with Peter Perkal. I wonder why he said nothing when Paul mentioned that Peter "officed" down the hall from him.

Then each time I start to speak, Jonathon acts as if he hasn't heard me.

I leave the Harley residence no wiser and with a lot of questions. At the bottom of the cable car, not far from where my car is parked, I see Spandex Man bobbing and weaving to the sounds of his silent boom box.

"Curiouser and curiouser," as a *really* great author once wrote.

# CHAPTER EIGHTEEN

Now I know how *The Fugitive* felt. I haven't done anything wrong but two uniformed police officers are on my front doorstep, ringing the bell. Whatever they want, it can't be good.

Within three minutes I'll be the slice of gossip for today in Beverly Hills. They must have found out about my meetings with Carol and Peter. So what if they have? I didn't kill them. I haven't done anything wrong.

Can I just ignore the doorbell? How would they know I'm home? Later I can say that I was so intent in my writing, I didn't hear the bell. Or the pounding on the door. Or notice that they looked into each and every window, circled the house, and tried the back door, which I accidentally left open this morning when I returned from my walk in the cemetery.

The police are calling out to me from my kitchen. I can hear deep baritones, "Mrs. Crowley, Mrs. Crowley, are you here?"

Would they believe that I was so engrossed in my writing, I didn't hear their voices in my house?

I am wearing an old gray sweatsuit and my feet are bare. Not exactly what they expect from a rich Beverly Hills homemaker. I quietly exit my library, which I have converted into my writing room, and startle the two police officers standing half in my kitchen and half out my back door. That one foot out the door reminds me of the old television shows where you weren't allowed to show two people in one bed. At least one foot of one person had to be on the floor. One well-placed foot made it legal.

So, there are the cops, legal and startled.

They haven't heard my bare footsteps on the marble floors. When I say, "Officers, can I help you?", the younger one, very trim with a small moustache that looks like it will be fully grown within the next two years, lets out a yelp that causes his partner to give him a dirty look. The Beverly Hills police are supposed to have their act completely together. Each one on the force knows that it is only a matter of time before he or she will be discovered by a talent scout.

Judging from the looks of the older of the two officers, he is angling for a movie part. There are not too many men who display individual style when in uniform. But this guy pulls it off. He has slicked back, very Southern California blonde hair and intense, penetrating, Nick Nolte eyes.

Not every cop wants to be an actor. Some want to write screenplays. Some want to produce. Some just want to discover parents murdered by their sons and be part of the massive national media blitz and the biggest murder trial in California history. If you don't count O.J.

But my bet is that officer Blondie here wants to be a movie star, and that his barely mustachioed Sancho Panza–like partner has not been around long enough to have planned his career move.

So after the yelp from one, and a glaring stare from the other, Officer Blondie addresses me in his best, deep-throated, Bogart tough guy but underneath I promise there's an understanding human being, voice. "I presume you're Samantha Crowley."

I nod and wait.

"We rang and knocked on the front door and then decided to check around the back in case you hadn't heard us. Your back door was open. You know, ma'am, that's not a good idea. Even

117

here you should keep your doors locked at all times. You know you never know. You know?"

He does fine until the end when he lapses into a valley boy sing-song with that extra "you know." I assume the "even here" refers to Beverly Hills, the city of the privileged.

"And you are . . . and you're here because?"

These are cops. I don't feel any burning need to be at my most articulate.

"Of course. I'm Officer Johnson and this is Officer Perez." He points to "Sancho" who appears to be inordinately interested in the very expensive Cuisinart Benjamin insisted we buy, though neither of us had any idea how to use it or any intention of using it. It had just been another one of those Sunday afternoon strolls in Beverly Hills with someone Benjamin wanted to impress, a producer, a publisher. So when we passed William Sonoma he immediately had to buy the most expensive gadget that caught his eye.

From the lustful look in Sancho's eyes, perhaps I have misjudged the Beverly Hills Police Department. Maybe we have a fledgling Wolfgang Puck on the force. Forget making money in the movie business, the real way to money and power is through the stomach.

"We're here because we need to ask you a few questions about Jonathon Harley. You do know Mr. Harley. Am I correct?"

*What is this about? Am I allowed to ask?*

"Is something wrong? I wouldn't say I know him. Well, I mean I know him, but not very well. We just met. Can you tell me what's wrong?"

Officer Blondie looks about as interested in what I'm saying as I might be in reviewing his grocery list. There is a long silence. It is probably not more than twenty seconds, but it seems long. Is this something they teach in cop school?

"Well, I'm sorry to tell you this, Mrs. Crowley, but Mr. Harley is dead. He died last night and I understand you were with him last night."

Be still my pounding heart. Better to sit than to collapse is my motto, particularly in front of cops.

"I think we would be more comfortable sitting in my living room to talk. Why don't we just go in there." I hope my voice doesn't sound as strained to them as it does to me.

They follow me into the living room and sit. Officer Blondie picks Benjamin's favorite chair, the most expensive and comfortable one in the room. Why am I not surprised? Officer Sancho sits on the arm of the sofa. I wonder if that's why the sofa arms wear away sooner than the rest of the couch.

I don't want them to think I'm avoiding the question, so I start talking the second they are seated.

"Yes, I did see him last night but so did three other people in addition to me. We were having a writers' meeting at his house."

Cops in real life are not as stupid as the ones on television. These guys have at least done their preliminary homework. Officer Blondie says, "Yeah, we know about the writers' meeting. But everyone at the meeting says you stayed after they left to help Mr. Harley clean up. Is that accurate?"

This visit isn't a result of Benjamin walking out of my house angry and telephoning the police. It isn't a result of Maurice repeating to the police the dumb comment I made to Carol. It isn't because someone looked at Peter Perkal's lunch calendar. This visit is because I was the last person to see yet another recently departed. Now I understand.

*Died.* That is how the cops put it. Died says it all and tells you nothing. With police, died translates to murder. Someone is murdering everyone who crosses my path. I don't need to be a rocket scientist. No one has exactly said that Carol and Peter were murdered. But I know.

Should I ask the question everyone always asks on TV? Do I need to call my lawyer? Only I don't have a lawyer. Benjamin has lots of lawyers. But I don't. I don't even have a divorce lawyer. If I had followed Ren's advice, I'd at least have one of those.

I haven't done anything wrong. I keep harking back to that same tired internal whine. I look at Blondie and Sancho and I know one thing for sure. I may be able to dodge the tough questions today, but it isn't going to work much longer. Someone is going to piece this together and come up with me.

Some force I don't understand is pulling me deeper and deeper into trouble I didn't create. And I have no idea why this is happening. Or how to stop it.

"I helped Jonathon, Mr. Harley, clean up for about ten minutes and then I went home. He was fine when I left. You know, alive and well." I add the last sentence in case they have a definitional problem with "fine."

No one asked but I think it prudent to let the cops know he didn't die while I was there.

Officer Blondie says, "How did you leave the house?"

Is this a trick question? I answer tentatively, "Through the door?"

The cops exchange a look as if I'm trying to be a smart ass. "No, Ms. Crowley, that's not exactly what I meant. How did you get to your car?"

All right, so I'll be more specific. "I went through the door, got on the cable car, pushed the button, went down the hill, left the cable car, exited the cable car building that has its own door, walked down a few steps, and went to my car. Is that what you meant by your question?" Now they definitely think I'm a smart ass.

Officer Blondie gives me a look I can't interpret. "That's

exactly what I meant. Did Mr. Harley go down in the cable car with you?"

"No"

"Did you send the cable car back up to the house when you exited it?"

"No."

"Did you see Mr. Harley send for the cable car?"

"No, but I wouldn't have seen him do anything. I got out of the car and left."

"Would you have noticed if the cable car was ascending the hill as you left?"

I think about that. Would I? And why? What are all these questions about? Is there a time when I get to ask questions?

"Frankly, I don't know. I suppose I might have noticed. I didn't, but it was visible as I walked to my car. I wasn't really looking."

"Did you see anyone walking up to or driving up to the Harley residence as you left?"

"No."

The cops exchange looks again and I continue to understand nothing. I know I'm not helping, but what can I do? I haven't done anything or seen anything.

"Look, I don't know if you're allowed to discuss this with me, but could you tell me what happened?"

Officer Blondie gives Sancho a shrug that I interpret to mean what the heck. "Early this morning Mr. Harley's housekeeper found him stabbed to death in his cable car."

So there it is. Murdered. I wonder if the police have seen the photograph of Jonathon and Peter Perkal. I wonder if they thought it curious that both are now dead from unnatural causes in less than forty-eight hours. Forget the police. I wonder what connection there is between the two men that could have led to their deaths. What connection *other* than being with me.

Blondie continues. "Did you know Mr. Harley before last night?"

"No."

"Did you know that Mr. Harley edited the first two books written by your husband?"

If hearts can sink, mine did at that moment. That's why Jonathon Harley was such a familiar name. I'd forgotten, but surely he would have remembered. Why had he said nothing?

"No. I mean I may have known that once, but I didn't remember it or make that connection."

"What did you discuss with Mr. Harley when the two of you were alone?"

I try to remember but all I can think of is the music playing too loud and his voice going on and on about Bicky and Dicky's desserts. I tell the cops and they look bored.

Blondie and Sancho move. They are walking toward my front door and more or less ignoring me. I take this to mean the interview—inquiry? interrogation?—is over. Interrogation is too harsh. This was pretty painless. So far.

As we get to the front door, Sancho finally speaks. "We may need to talk to you again. If you think of anything, here's our card. Please call one of us. If you think of anything."

Police have serious syntax problems.

I nod my head like one of those dolls with the bobbing head. See Dr. Lana, we both can bob. I take the card and hold onto it like a second grader clutching her report card. I have nowhere to put it. No pockets, no table by the front door. I stand there holding the card, nodding my head, and I feel a foreboding prickle. I know that my next meeting with these guys will not be as mellow.

They walk down my path, get into their car, and drive away. The street is quiet. No doubt every gaze is glued to my house and the departing cop car. I hear a crow cry and think it sounds sad. Maybe that crow is the sole mourner for Jonathon Harley. Poor Jonathon Harley. Until this moment I have been so busy thinking about myself, I haven't considered that he is gone. Gone in an unexpected and horrible way. Did someone hate him so much?

Or is it something else?

I'm not a betting woman but I'm certain something else is the better bet here.

Next door, at Boo's house, I hear a window slam shut and the faint hum of the air conditioning unit turned on. Someone is in the house right now. Are they watching me?

As I go to close my door, Plant Man walks down the street, past my house. It is possible that the tree growing out of his head now has new leaves. Beverly Hills must be one of the nicer places for the homeless to live. If you're not going to have a home, better to not have a home here than in East L.A. or New Jersey.

It isn't until I close my door and go back into the library that I remember something I forgot. As a consequence, I gave the police misinformation. Can they arrest you for having what my Dad calls a senior moment? Is it a lie if you simply forget?

They asked if I had seen anyone walking up to the Harley house and I said no. Well, that is technically correct. I hadn't seen anyone walking. But I had seen someone dancing.

Spandex Man.

I look at Sancho's business card and wonder if I should call him or Blondie.

Maybe tomorrow. Look to literary heroines for solutions. So I take to heart the wise words of the most petulant heroine of all time. Tomorrow's another day.

I, too, am feeling a little petulant.

# CHAPTER NINETEEN

Most days, lately, he felt like the loser of the year. But the phone call that awoke him this morning made him feel a little like Bogart, Mitchum, and Gable. A little like all their best parts. Good. Real good. One smart, super-charged, pistol-packing, macho, desirable hunk. There were worse ways to start a day.

It was 11:30 A.M., too late for even an unemployed ex-cop to be sleeping. But that's how it was when each day blended into the next with no destination and no distinction. The biggest decision of the week was usually whether to try his luck at a late-night card game. When provisions got low, he went to the market. It was too expensive to eat every meal out. Every two weeks or so he bundled up the dirty laundry and went down the hill to the small Chinese laundry where they still charged him 1988 rates for his wash. He thought, *They still think I'm a cop.*

About six months ago he had stopped drinking. He wasn't an alcoholic but becoming one had started to have an appeal. He checked on Grant every day, but the kid clearly resented it. He didn't blame Grant. He didn't blame anyone. The few friends from the past no longer called. They had stopped about a year ago. There's a statute of limitations on how long a guy can be a bad friend.

In the first year, friends felt sorry for him. They clucked, they were understanding, and he could say and do anything. His mom dead. His career gone. His brother all screwed up.

In the second year, friends knew that he needed to start making changes. They were patient and supportive. His withdrawal was understandable. Going through the transition from here to there. Figuring out where "there" was going to be.

In the third year, friends were curious about when he would get things in order. Sure, it had been sad but it was three years. They stayed polite, more distant. They wondered when he would pull it together.

In the fourth year, friends disappeared. It was as if they had never been here or there. They fell into one of two groups. Those who had come to understand that he wasn't going to change and those who had ceased to care and moved on with their lives.

Now the phone never rang. The mail was bills and solicitations. The best company in the world was his television. The TV made him laugh, it made him cry, it entertained and rarely made him think. And he didn't have to give back anything.

Books were good, too. Something he had never before fully appreciated. Jack now had a goal that would have made his high school senior English teacher proud. It was about time he made someone proud. He was going to read the greatest books of all time. As many as he could. He figured it would take at least five lifetimes and so he had set a goal that could remain his forever.

Unattainable and yet time-filling.

He had skipped the card game last night and stayed up until 3:00 A.M. finishing *The Grapes of Wrath*. Last week he had read *Slaughterhouse Five* and the week before *Lolita*. The month before he had read *Henderson the Rain King*, *The Heart of the Matter*, and *Lord of the Flies*.

All these years and he had never known how beautiful words could be. It took a midlife tragedy to show him how he could have improved the soul he once had. Now it was too late. He wished he had listened when his teachers had talked about

Fitzgerald, Greene, Joyce, Dreiser, Hammett, and the dozens and dozens of others.

If he had listened, if he had read, could it have changed anything? Could he have been a contender? Three nights ago, he had stayed up late watching *On the Waterfront*.

Movies made him feel the tragedy of what he had become. Books made him feel the regrets for what he could have been.

And then, late this morning, the phone rang. Almost afternoon and the words of a woman, Samantha, gave him purpose. Her voice came through the plastic box that transmitted and received sound in a manner unfathomable to him, allowing that sound to reach his ear. The voice asked for help.

In the last four years, no one had asked Jack for help.

Help had been offered to him repeatedly and from different sources. He had over and over again helped Grant because he wanted to, and needed to, and it was his job as older brother and protector.

But no one had asked him for help. No one had said, "Listen, could you do me a favor? Take me to the airport, walk my dog, pick up some groceries for me, lend me money, help me paint my living room . . . can I borrow your car?"

The braless woman named Samantha, who was cute and knew about his problems because he had spilled his guts to her, had called him and asked for help.

She didn't want to help him. She had asked, not pleading, but in a way that would be hard for any red-blooded Boy Scout to turn down, that he meet her for a drink, at 4:00 P.M. at Musso and Frank's Grill in Hollywood.

The conversation with her was a bit of a jumble. She had mentioned him being an ex-cop. And that he owned a gun. And that he seemed to be somewhat intelligent. He liked that, and she didn't even know about all the books he was reading. She said that he obviously had insights into the criminal mind, though she made a point of commenting that he didn't seem to be a particularly good judge of character. But she said his judgment of character wasn't that important here, and then said something about him not shaving.

The bottom line was that she needed his help. He didn't have any idea why or what she wanted, but it didn't matter. Because whatever it was, he'd do it. Whatever it was, it was something more than he had done in the last four years. And if she needed him to shave, he'd do that too. No problem.

In fact, he wasn't sure there was anything he wouldn't do for her. Because her phone call had made him feel a little like Bogart, Mitchum, and Gable. All rolled into one guy. And that was the best he had felt in the last four years.

Musso and Frank's. Four o'clock. Hooray for Hollywood.

# CHAPTER TWENTY

Musso and Frank's Grill is the oldest restaurant in Hollywood. This year it celebrated its eightieth birthday, which means "the bar" has seen and heard more stories than those that fill the shelves of most libraries.

And mine will be another to add to the list. Musso and Frank's has a New York rhythm and feel. I've also heard it makes the best martinis this side of the Rockies but I'm not a martini drinker. To be a great bar, you have to earn your place in history. Not every bar can host the Algonquin round table, but Musso's has had its share of creative geniuses warming the barstools.

I get to the bar early and order a Bloody Mary. I figure how looped can a person get on one Bloody Mary. I find out. A warm glow, unlike anything I have felt in a while, is starting to stroll through my limbs after only three sips.

The room is dim with a pinkish, orange glow. A rich-looking cherry wood bar shares a cavernous room with red leather booths that make the dining experience feel a little like you've moved into someone's living room for an evening séance. Because of a large mirror at the bar, the diners, from their booths, can watch the people at the bar. The people at the bar view the reflection of the diners.

There are no secrets.

Interspersed through the room are antique-looking metal coat racks with brass rods that curl up to greet your coat, like a hand hanging in limbo for the handshake. All of the coat racks' spindly fingers are empty. In a city where no one wears a coat, the empty coat racks look like ancient alien skeletons.

Even with it being spring in Los Angeles, Musso and Frank's makes me think of Christmas. The waiters wear red jackets and the busboys slip among the tables in their green jackets. I suspect the uniform has not changed over the many years. The people wearing them have not changed much either.

Some of the waiters look old enough to be my great-grandfather.

But it is the bartender who really catches my eye. He looks like a cross between Mickey Rooney and Clarence, the angel trying so desperately to earn his wings in *It's A Wonderful Life*.

He is tall enough for the height of the bar to be no challenge, but he would have a tough time in a lineup with seventh graders. His cheery, potato-like face looks like it could be remolded and shaped with just a slight push of the hand across his plump cheeks. A crown of soft white hair sits on a bald throne.

I ask him his name and he tells me Lou. Of course, what other name would a bartender have? I tell him I am waiting for someone and he nods. Maybe he believes me, maybe he doesn't. Bartender rule: never challenge the customer.

When I look at my drink, I see it is gone. No harm in ordering another. I go to look at my watch and remember that I decided not to wear it. Instead, I have put on a pretty gold and silver bracelet I purchased at an art fair in Beverly Hills. The bracelet has matching earrings and I am wearing those as well. And both pieces of jewelry look good with my tan safari-type pants that would be nice for any safari in which you don't have to run, climb, or walk more than an eighth of a mile. They fit comfortably but snug and show off my slender waistline into which is tucked a tight-fitting, black ribbed crew-neck spandex sweater.

I dressed with the self-conscious realization that I phoned Jack and told him I had a proposition for him. I want to look good but an obviously suggestive outfit may make him jump to the wrong conclusion. As tempting as a night out with Jack had seemed twenty-four hours ago, I need him for something more important.

Jack is the only person I can think of who may be able to help me sort out what is happening and protect me. There is a strange irony in the thought that the only person I can think to call is someone who pulled a gun on me two days ago. Someone who might have killed me. Ain't life a kick in the pants!

It is even stranger that the only man for whom I have felt that rush, that indefinable hormonal pull—in a very long time—is a guy who threatened my life. What is wrong with me? Maybe I am turning into one of those women who is only turned on by danger. Nah. I would love to talk to Ren, but how can I? Something is stopping me from trusting my most trusted friend. Imagination can play bizarre tricks on you and this is worse than imagination.

The second Bloody Mary has a little more pepper and a lot more Tabasco sauce. I like it. Has Lou decided that my life needs some spicing up? Maybe he thinks I am only pretending to be expecting someone. Or maybe he thinks I am being stood up. Maybe I *am* being stood up.

As I am about to ask Lou the time, I see Jack Sharrow enter the room from the back, which probably means he used the rear entrance of Musso and Frank's, the more common way patrons enter. Through that entrance you walk down a short staircase, with the kitchen to the left and the employee time-cards adorning a wall to the right. You walk past the timecards and through the back door of the restaurant.

Jack doesn't look a lot different from the two occasions we met, although his clothes look neater and some effort has been made to comb his hair back. He is still unshaven, but a few days' growth looks good.

The one difference I sense is more subtle. His eyes. The suspicion, anger, and confusion I had previously detected is gone. Now he looks—well, I'm not exactly sure. The best way to sum it up would be in a double negative, not unhappy.

When he sees me, he gives a wave. His face is impassive as he heads for the empty seat next to me. This is going to be awkward. I need to muddle through the beginning and wait to come out on the other end.

When I say, "Hi, Jack, thank you for coming," I am surprised at how soft my voice sounds. A woman of so many surprises, I've taken to surprising even myself.

Jack sits on the barstool, looks at the room and then at me. His poker face almost undetectably moves in the direction of a half smile.

"Hello to you too, Samantha. Or do you like to be called Sam or Mandy or something else?"

All my friends call me Sam and no one ever called me Mandy, but I like the way Samantha sounds when he says my name so I tell him that I like Samantha. This time I am positive he is attempting a smile. It is still at half mast but inching toward the real thing.

Jack is stroking his unshaven face and I wonder if he considered shaving for our meeting. I don't care that he hasn't. I just wonder if he thought about it. From the way he is examining his face with his fingertips, I wonder if he has any regrets about not scraping it off.

I don't want him to worry. "I like it." I blurt this out in about the least sexy way a girl can pay a compliment. I could take flirting lessons from a twelve-year-old.

And of course he has no clue what I am talking about, which compounds my embarrassment and my idiocy.

"You like what?"

"Your beard. I think it's nice." And then like a complete fool I point to his face as if he may not be sure where a beard is located. Naturally, having made him feel completely self-conscious, his hands drop abruptly from his face.

So this is the flirting singles life? I need a ten-step program, quick.

Jack very graciously ignores my idiocy and says, "On the phone you mentioned that you need my help. You failed to mention what you need it for. But I kind of assumed you have some legal problem since you brought up my former work." I pick up on the slightly bitter edge he gives those last two words. "And you made reference to guns and criminal minds and using good judgment," he continues.

It is a string of sentences that are not questions but stated with the question inflection. I also note that Jack's face is closer to a smile. I get it. When it's at a female's expense, guys have no problem breaking into a grin. Until then, why waste the effort. Girls are so cute the way they overreact. Who now is sounding bitter and defensive? But I don't want him to find this amusing; it isn't a joke.

I need to do what little girls do. Stamp my foot. Figuratively, not literally.

"Three people have been murdered," I tell him. "I guess that qualifies as a serious problem. Particularly for them."

It works. Any sign of an amused look disappears.

Jack puts his hands on my shoulders in a way that, unfortunately, feels more like a big brother than like our karmic paths have crossed, and says, "Yeah, that's serious. Now why don't you start from the beginning, leave out nothing, and take no short cuts?"

Okay, now he sounds like a cop.

And that tone scares. Scares me into being what I should

have been all along. Very scared.

Someone is killing people who cross my path within twenty-four hours of their encounters with me.

Ben's supercilious agent, Carol, is dead. Poisoned, I would guess. Pompous publicist, Peter, is dead. Hit and run—accident or murder? I bet murder. And now poor Jonathon. Stabbed to death in his caboose.

I look at Jack and feel scared but less alone. It is a good feeling, but not good enough. I gulp down the rest of my drink and ask, "Do you mind if I order another before I start the story?"

Jack beckons to Lou who has been hovering, but not too close. My "date" has shown up so I have a little more credibility in Lou's eyes. There are only three other people at the bar. Three men, sitting at the end of bar, are having a lively and heated discussion about a boxing match that was televised recently.

The proximity of Lou and the other three men makes me nervous. I don't want to be overheard. We need a change of venue.

"Jack, maybe it would be a good idea if we went to a booth. I know they're not for drinks so I'll order something to eat. A small price to pay for privacy."

Jack agrees and we slip into a booth, not too far from where we were seated at the bar. It is cozy, too cozy. I shift my rear end a couple of feet away from Jack. I don't want him to get the wrong idea. This really is about business. The waiter comes by our table, leaves two menus, and silently fades away. We must project a desire for privacy.

I look quickly at the menu. "I'm just going to order some sliced tomatoes with bleu cheese dressing," I tell Jack.

He waves to the waiter, who scurries over as if attending to royalty and takes our orders. I am still nursing the Bloody Mary and Jack orders coffee. Time for business.

"Okay, Samantha, we have privacy and you have my undivided attention. Tell me what's on your mind."

It occurs to me I haven't made a decision about what I want to reveal and what I want to hold back. Should I tell Jack about my book? Will he think I'm nuts writing a book for the sole purpose of killing my husband's protagonist? But if I don't tell him about the book, what reason would I have for lunching with Peter, meeting with Carol, joining Jonathon's writers' group?

My book is the glue that holds this story together.

What about my increasing suspicions about everyone, even my best friend, Ren? What about the strange house next door to Ren and me? Should I mention that, too? What about the street people everywhere I go? What about forgetting to tell the police about Spandex Man in front of Jonathon's house?

The more I think about the recent days of my life, the more it makes the rest of my sorry life look not nearly as bad. Was being with Benjamin worse than leaving dead bodies in my wake?

Something to think about.

What will Jack think of me? Screw it. What's the difference what he thinks at this point? I'm scared and need someone to help me sort this out. He was a cop. He knows about criminal minds and a murderer qualifies, in my book, as a criminal mind. He is unselfishly helping his brother, so he has a do-good soul. I hope.

Just as I am about to launch into my explanation, a thought occurs to me. What if the person who killed Peter is not the same person who killed Carol and Jonathon? What if one person killed the two and another person killed the one? What if there are three different killers?

I'm starting to get a headache. I'm not used to drinking. Maybe it's the stress. Or maybe I need another drink.

"Could I have another Bloody Mary?"

Jack looks at my glass with a surprised expression. It was filled halfway only a minute ago.

Great. Now he thinks I'm a lush.

The waiter magically appears again, Jack gives him the order and he vanishes.

I am trying Jack's patience. I can see that without him saying one word. I need to begin.

"This is kind of a long, unusual story. I hope you'll bear with me. I'll try to tell it as best I can without straying too far off the mark."

Jack waits.

"My husband is Benjamin Crowley, the well-known author."

Jack nods and I nod back, as if mutually agreeing I can skip the part where I explain how wealthy and famous he is. That's fine with me. The fewer positive traits attributed to Benjamin the happier I am. Though I'm not completely certain that wealth and fame are traits as much as temporary conditions.

"So, Benjamin told me not too long ago that he wants a divorce. I admit the news upset me, although upon reflection I'm not sure why. I've given this some thought and I think it's just the matter of him doing it. It's unbelievable that it wasn't I who initiated it. If my unhappiness in the marriage didn't surpass his, it had to have equaled it. I haven't loved Benjamin for more years than I can remember."

Jack yawns. It isn't a rude yawn but it is a red flag. He doesn't need to hear and does not appear very interested in hearing the more soap opera aspects of my failed marriage. He is right. I am wrong.

This is precisely what I had set out not to do. I don't want to put him to sleep before I get to the good part.

"I'm sorry. I'll cut to the chase."

Jack doesn't look confident.

"I will. Really, I'll try." I fumble with the fork. "I decided I didn't like the way California law protects me with respect to his literary properties. You see, I think Benjamin's main character, Hunter McCall, belongs to me or at the very least should be divided equally. The idea that Benjamin exits our marriage and completely owns Hunter McCall is unacceptable. So I've written a book, that is, I'm writing a book—it's not quite finished yet—in which one of my characters kills Hunter. Ben will look like a fool resurrecting him, though he can try if he chooses. I guess."

I fail to finish the thought as enthusiastically as I started. I am steadily getting drunker, which is one reason. The other reason is I know my "pitch" doesn't sound nearly as good verbalized as it did bumping around in my head.

Jack's eyebrow arches up and he leans into me, which I take to mean positive body language. I think I detect a spark of interest. He hasn't laughed at me. Maybe he doesn't think I am a lunatic after all.

"You're thinking that because I look interested and because it's a clever idea I won't think you're a nut," Jack says. "What does this have to do with three murders?"

He is tough. Perceptive, incisive, and tough.

"Look, I know this is taking a bit of time to tell but it's important to me that you don't think I'm—"

"Like a Claire Bloom or Joyce Maynard." He finishes my sentence, offering clear proof that he is smart enough to keep up with me.

"Exactly. Though I would hardly compare Benjamin Crowley to Philip Roth and J.D. Salinger."

How does he know about former lovers who tried to literally, through literature, bury their literary men? This Jack is full of surprises.

"Sammi, tell me the tale. And slow down on the Bloody Marys. I want to hear the story today. Coherently and concisely."

I don't know what's happened. It's what Elizabeth and Darcy were all about. You see it in Garbo's face in an old movie when her costar gives her a look that would make any woman's heart shudder to a standstill. Jack called me Sammi and all I want to do is passionately kiss this man until one of us faints dead away.

I like this guy. So maybe I should work a little harder to make him think I am a bright, articulate woman and not a complete moron.

When I describe how I heard about Jonathon's death, the tears start flowing. Jack lets me order another Bloody Mary. I tell him everything. I leave out nothing. I even describe the Belinskys' pastries and muumuus.

When I finish Jack looks at me, but it isn't the way men looked at Greta Garbo. It is probably too much to hope that he feels the same insanely strong tug. Between the drinks and the talking nonstop for almost an hour, I am too tired to do anything other than wait for his reaction.

I have barely touched the food I ordered, which was quietly placed in front of me some time during my reenactment of lunch with Peter Perkal.

"I want to make a few calls," Jack says. "I need to give this some thought. And you need to go to bed."

I smile in the way women who have had too many drinks smile. I heard him say the word "bed."

"Whatever you say, partner." I put on my best western twang, which is not very good at all. I am acting like a dolt again, instead of the enigmatic sexpot I want to be.

"Can you drive?" Jack is being practical and solicitous.

"I can, but I'll stay here a little longer and get a soft drink."

It has been about an hour since my last drink and I can feel the beginning of that horrible, slow descent into sobriety.

"Do you want to meet tomorrow afternoon? By then I should

have some information and we can talk about what I think you should do."

My heart flutters. He is suggesting we meet again. I need to put a business spin on this. I don't want him to think I'm not in need of his help.

"So you are taking what I said seriously. You do see that there's something wrong. Everyone who crosses my path dies. Like I'm some kind of black widow."

Jack's brow is furrowed and he looks unhappy. Real unhappy. "I think there's more to this than you're seeing. I think this is tied into the phone call I got sending me to the cemetery when you were there. I know this sounds peculiar but it's possible that someone wants *you* dead. I'd really like you to be careful. Really careful."

That was my thought two days ago. I had been avoiding it, tiptoeing around the idea for two days. Now he has verbalized my nightmare and I can't tiptoe anymore. I'm scared. Big-time scared.

Sobriety hits me like a brick.

"What do you think is going on? Who's behind this? It makes no sense. How can this be about me?"

"Sammi, don't talk to anyone. Don't answer your door. Lock yourself in tonight and only leave when you come to meet me . . ." He pauses. "How about two P.M. at the Beverly Hills Library. Can you do that?"

Can a cow produce milk? Is a pig good for bacon?

"Yes, I'll be there. I'm really getting scared."

"Good. Scared means you'll think twice. Scared means you'll be alert. It's time to go into condition red."

He is using cop talk but I understand fully.

"Thank you, Jack. I don't know why you're going to help me, but thank you so much."

He gets up to leave. He looks taller, darker, and even better.

"Don't thank me yet. I'll see you tomorrow. Be careful."

We don't shake hands. He doesn't kiss me. But he gives me a wink that sends major goosebumps down my spine. The same kind of goosebumps I bet leading men gave Greta Garbo.

## CHAPTER TWENTY-ONE

I almost have a heart attack when I exit the front door of Musso and Frank's, which takes you right out onto famous Hollywood Boulevard. I think: *I killed Jack.* Well, not that I killed him, exactly, but that this black widow, death mojo, mumbo-jumbo thing that is happening in my life has killed him.

A large crowd is gathered in front of the restaurant. They are looking into the middle of the street where I fully expect to see Jack's corpse. See Samantha and die.

I push my way through the crowd and it parts. People in L.A. don't fight back. That's a New York thing. There in the middle of the street is Button Lady, doing a dance that seems to consist of waving hand movements, casting what I can only assume by the expression on her face, very nasty spells on those cars that are able to pass as she blocks the boulevard. Every now and then she hisses at the throng, which then—as if the hissing has some poisonous venom attached to it—backs up about two feet.

The relief of knowing that a visit with me has not resulted in Jack's death sobers me to the point of a headache. All I want to do now is go home, raid my refrigerator, turn on some soft music, and stretch out on the couch. A little goat cheese and crackers and I'll be as good as new.

When I get home it is almost 8:30 P.M. As I pull up to my house, a black Bentley exits the garage of the house next door. Someone at Boo's house is driving a Bentley. But I can't see the driver. The windows are tinted and dusk has set in.

I can't wait to call Ren. If she saw the car too, my phone should be ringing right now. But as I walk into the front entryway of my house, I hear no phone ringing and there are no messages on my machine. I pick up the receiver to call Ren, then stop and replace it on the cradle. What am I going to say to her? Hello Ren, did you see the car? What do you think is going on? By the way I've been a complete stranger for the last couple of days because I've decided I trust no one in the world, including my best friend. So, how 'bout those Lakers?

Food. Always a good temporary solution to any problem. I take a plate and fill it with crackers and a large helping of garlic herbed goat cheese. I pour a glass of Diet Pepsi and carefully carry my plate and glass out of the kitchen. In the den that has become my writing room, I drop into my oversized, beat-up chair and sink into its warm embrace. I put that first much anticipated cracker, covered with cheese, into my mouth and the doorbell rings. Not once but many times, without stopping.

That's how Ren rings a doorbell. I'd know her ring anywhere. To everything she does, she brings her manic pace. It's what makes her enchanting. And tiring.

There is no need to inquire who's there. Ren stands on my doorstep, smoking a cigarette and holding her cell phone in the hand from which she has let one finger stray to bond with my doorbell. She looks gorgeous and smells like a fresh fruit salad. She is wearing taupe silk pants with a taupe silk blouse and what looks like taupe silk high heels. Giving off sparkling rays like sunshine are a necklace, bracelet, and hairpin. All look like twenty-four-carat gold.

"You can take your finger off the bell now. I've answered the door and am letting you in."

As if her finger has a separate brain stem under whose orders it is acting, she looks at it. Is she wondering whether or not her finger heard me and will obey? She takes a deep drag on her cigarette, her finger lifts off the bell, and we hear silence. Hearing silence, such an interesting concept.

"You look absolutely a mess," she says, a most typical Ren-type comment. "But you're happy. Maybe in love? Am I right?"

Ren has the nerve to say anything to anyone. Not two days ago I suspected she might be having an affair. Did I say one word to her? No. But she has the chutzpah to look at me for less than thirty seconds and speak with the authority of having been my recent confidante. Am I so transparent she can see I am smitten? Let this be a lesson to me never to play poker.

"I'm fine. Come in. I was just going to call you. Did you see the Bentley?"

I want to turn the conversation away from me. It will inevitably return there but I can try.

Ren's reaction to my question is astounding. First she hesitates. Then she blushes. Blushes? Ren?

Once, at Spago, the straps to Ren's halter top literally shredded before the entire dining room and Ren's significant breasts became the *plat du jour*. Not only did she not blush, she stood up and took a solid three minutes to adjust her top just right. The entire three minutes was a joy to every man in the restaurant and perhaps even to a few of the ladies.

Ren doesn't blush.

"Ren, you're blushing."

"Don't be absurd."

By now, of course, her complexion is perfect as always without any evidence that a blush once passed through quickly.

Did I imagine it?

She says, "What Bentley are you referring to, Samantha?"

"The one I just saw exiting from the garage at Boo's house. You didn't see or hear it? That's so not like you. You must have passed it."

"Maybe I was in the bathroom. Maybe I was on the phone.

Maybe it was when I was down in the wine cellar getting a bottle for later."

And that's all she wrote. No questions like: Who was driving? How many people in the car? In what direction was it headed? I know my friend Ren. She has a secret and somehow it's tied into that house. First no reaction to a noise that sounded like a gunshot, and now this.

"Ren, have you met the owner of the house?" I try to make the question sound more casual than I feel.

"Of course not. Wouldn't I have told you if I had? Why would you ask me something so ridiculous?" She doesn't even try to take the snap out of her voice.

We are best girlfriends sniping at each other like an old married couple. She notices too, and her demeanor changes.

"Why don't you tell me what you've been up to, Sam? We haven't spoken and you do look a bit disheveled, but I saw something in your face. Like maybe someone had made you purr."

"Made you purr" is Ren's favorite expression to describe finding a slice of bliss in our less than "purr-fect world," as she puts it. And of course she is right, but I feel like a two-year-old digging in my heels for no good reason. I just don't want to tell her. That's not exactly right. I feel it is a mistake to tell her. But I have to answer, so I try to invent something plausible.

"I've been doing some research about my rights in this divorce," I say. "You know, checking on the computer, reading stuff from the library, talking to people."

"Excellent. Finally. At last. I'm so glad you're doing something. That's the real reason I came over. Just knowing you're still the beneficiary on Benjamin's life insurance isn't enough. I wanted to hear about your meeting with the divorced ladies' group. I hope they've convinced you to talk to an attorney. You've got to be protected. After all these years you've put in, you want to get what's yours."

Ren is being a good friend. She is more concerned about my financial future than I am.

I avoid her comments and say, "I want to apologize. I haven't been a very good friend lately and you're the best. I feel like there's some kind of plot against me and I don't know who to trust and in whom to confide. I know I can trust you but I've been scared."

Ren looks genuinely distressed. "Scared of what? What kind of plot? How could you not trust me?"

All good questions, except the truth of the matter is that even though she is being a good friend, a great friend, I don't trust her. And didn't Jack tell me not to open the door to anyone and not to talk to anyone until I saw him tomorrow? And here I am, doing exactly the opposite of what he cautioned me not to do.

Whatever befalls me, I deserve. I'm an idiot who can't follow simple instructions.

"I'm just being a little paranoid," I tell Ren. "I think I was more upset than I realized about Carol and Peter dying. What I really need is a good night's sleep. I've been tossing and turning and it's starting to fray my nerves." This is a lie with huge grains of truth.

I am convincing and believable and Ren looks like she has bought it all the way.

"You poor darling," she says. "Why don't you hire a lawyer, leave all of this in his hands, and let's go away. We could go to the desert or a spa or bring some of my sculpture to Santa Fe. It's so nice there. What do you say?"

What I want to say and what I say are completely unrelated.

"That sounds nice, Ren. Let me think about it. I need to get organized."

Ren isn't blushing now but she does look uncomfortable.

"I don't want to upset you," she says.

I say, "I'm not capable of being upset anymore."

"People are talking about Ben and her."

"By her I assume you mean his girlfriend."

Ren nods.

"Why would you think that would upset me?"

"I guess I don't want you to feel worse than you already feel."

"Ren, I gotta tell you. I don't feel that bad. I want out of this marriage, too. I'm just angry, you know, about this Hunter Mc-Call thing."

"You're still on that kick?"

I nod. Yup, still on that kick. I wonder why my best friend in the world doesn't understand. Am I being another one of those psycho bitches with obsessive fixations?

I feel bold and say, "So who are you sleeping with?"

If Ren can say whatever she's thinking, so can I. I'll give Ren credit. She doesn't blush, blink, or blanche. She continues to look impassive and beautiful.

"This is certainly your day for absurdities. I have no idea what's gotten into you, Samantha. Are you perimenopausal?"

She hasn't answered my question and she is right. A lot has gotten into me. I am working on becoming the new me and my good friend is finding it a little startling to get fed what she dishes.

I say, "I'm tired. Maybe we should visit tomorrow. It's been a long day. In fact, it's been a long three years."

Ren gives me an odd look. Either she is feeling sorry for me or she is annoyed. It's a little unnerving to realize I can't tell the difference.

We part with overly polite farewells that reinforce my uneasiness about the two of us. I should have listened to Jack.

After Ren leaves, I go to work on the book. I write until two A.M. and then, almost collapsing with fatigue, drag myself up my cool marble stairs to a warm bed. Tomorrow I'll see Jack and he'll help me. I believe that with all my heart. Then my mind starts racing again. Why is Ren so preoccupied with my money and Ben's life insurance and my being financially protected?

Whose life insurance did Ren really want to see that day she went snooping? Anyway, life insurance is only good if someone's dead. That's what *life* insurance is all about.

# CHAPTER TWENTY-TWO

I'm a lousy instruction follower. It doesn't matter if it's assembling a patio table or following the directions of the man I have selected to save me.

It is 6 A.M. and I don't think anyone will be staking out my house or Hollywood Forever Cemetery at this hour. I need the exercise and I want to talk to Bugsy and Bill. Jack said to go nowhere and talk to no one. The drive to the cemetery constitutes my second transgression. It's not that I don't respect Jack's warning. It's just that living like a prisoner makes me feel as if Benjamin has won.

Backing out of my garage, I look in the rearview mirror and there is Plant Man. He's an early riser. He looks calm and no different in the cool morning than in the heat of the day. For the first time I hear him speak. I think he's talking to me. There's no one else around, but then maybe he's just testing his voice in the moist early morning breeze.

"We're all running away. But don't run too fast. You'll lose something." He sagely gestures to the tree growing out of his head and continues his walk down the street.

Prophetic or insane? Only in Los Angeles would one have such a quandary.

In 1908, William Desmond Taylor vanished from New York City where he had been known as William Deane Tanner. He left behind a wife and daughter. He had been vice president of the English Antique Shop on Fifth Avenue. Five years later he showed up in Los Angeles and became a successful silent film director. In February 1922, he was shot in the back with a .38 caliber revolver while in his Los Angeles bungalow. He is buried in Hollywood Forever Cemetery. By the end of 1923, the district attorney's office had over three hundred suspects and confessions in the case. It was never solved. Another quandary.

Santa Monica Boulevard is deserted. When Los Angeles streets are quiet, you can pretend to be almost anywhere. The cemetery is empty, though early morning is the best and coolest time to do gardening maintenance. The city, the little pocket of it I occupy, is quiet and desolate. I walk to the Cathedral Mausoleum where Bill rests in crypt #594. Turn right at the second arcade and walk down a bit and turn to the right. There he is, lying at my chest level.

I speak slowly, with hesitation. "What do you think about all of this, Bill? Am I trusting the right person? I met him here in the cemetery. He pulled a gun on me but didn't shoot. How did it feel to be shot in the back? Someone is killing the people I meet."

My voice doesn't echo. It sounds quiet, calm. It's like being in a church and having a private conversation with God. Only I don't go to church and I'm Jewish and I can't say that I really believe in God or that we have ever had a conversation. At this moment I believe in Bill.

"This is what I think about Jack." I work on the assumption that Bill is keeping up with the players here. "It's like something Esther Williams said in an interview about her affair with Victor Mature. You don't know who Esther and Victor are because they did talking pictures. They came along after you. A little later in time and you could have directed one of them. Maybe. So Esther Williams was a swimmer and became an actress who swam in a lot of her movies. And she was good-looking. And you know, it was no different in your time, actors and actresses having affairs."

I take a breath and stop. This is the most I have ever talked to Bill at one time. I don't want to overwhelm him.

"So Esther said about Victor that it was 'like being with a force of nature.' That's powerful, don't you think? Very powerful. And that's what it's like being around Jack. He's like a force of nature."

I turn my back on Bill and feel a rush of embarrassment. In life we deceive not only others, but ourselves. Who was I kidding? This talk about needing to go for a walk, it isn't about people mysteriously dying and it isn't about my being scared. It's about the fact that I am falling in love, or lust, with a complete stranger. I have come to Bill to babble about Jack, like a schoolgirl's crush.

I'm about as liberated as a caged bird. Open my doors and do I fly? No. But who cares? I meant what I said. Jack is a force of nature. That's how I see him. And I'm going to see him in a few hours.

What am I doing in the cemetery when I should be home trying to straighten my hair?

On the way home there's a lot of traffic. Welcome back, Los Angeles. I listen to the radio and hear an advertisement for Benjamin's most recent book, now in paperback, *Dark Entry.* Another one of my ideas—using the word "dark" as the first word in each title. *Dark Journey. Dark Room. Dark Messenger. Dark Dream. Dark Destiny. Dark Secret.* It was a stroke of genius. I never got the credit, but everyone thought it genius. If a genius comes up with a great theory in the middle of the forest and no one is around to hear it, is it still genius?

It takes me two hours to make myself look as good as I get. Buried in the back of my closet are beautiful, black wool Evan Picone slacks. They may be a little warm, but they look great. I tuck into the slacks my favorite v-neck, gray, ribbed cotton/

spandex-blend sweater from Ann Taylor. The look is smart and sexy. I put on black leather pumps and the little bit of height makes me look even better.

No jewelry except some silver hoop earrings. I am going for the skin look. Let him look at my skin, not my gold.

Rushing to the emergency room with a case of barbecued scalp is always a possibility when I use the process I have adopted to take the kink out of my hair. It looks smooth and wavy, like one of those shampoo commercials. My makeup is subdued.

I look hot. Well, maybe not hot—but very good.

It's only noon. There's no reason why I can't get to the library early. What's the harm? It's a public library in the middle of one of the most affluent cities in the world. Beverly Hills is the sister city to Cannes. Not everyone knows that.

I park my car not far from the library. Canon Drive is one long block away. Am I craving company, excitement, danger? I could just as easily, more easily, have parked in the library lot, but chose a congested street one block away, so that I would be surrounded by people and activity. Just what Jack warned me against. It's a sunny noon on Canon Drive in Beverly Hills. Not exactly a dark, stormy night in Transylvania. We all need a little perspective.

On the other side of the street, I see Bicky walking rapidly. Her skinny frame is moving so quickly at first, I'm not sure it is she. Clutched in her right hand is a copy of Benjamin's fourth book, *Dark Secret*. The distinct cover of the book is more recognizable than tiny Bicky, who seems to have shrunk even further than when I last saw her at poor Jonathon Harley's home. The incredibly shrinking pastry chef.

The street corner lamp post effectively hides her entire body. I call out but she doesn't hear me.

Her head is bowed, her arms are swinging, as if she is trying to maximize her speed by using the air space most effectively. Two cars almost collide at the intersection of Santa Monica and Canon. When I look back for Bicky, she is gone from sight.

Not so for Ren, with whom I almost collide moments later. She is coming out of a camera shop and holding one of those distinctive bags into which they put developed pictures.

Although we come within inches of bumping, Ren is so pre-occupied she hasn't seen me. She looks hassled and beautiful in a white jogging suit with turquoise stripes trimming the jacket and pant legs.

"Hello. Hey, hey, Ren, it's me."

She is hurrying away from me even after my hello. Is it possible she saw me and is ignoring me?

"Oh my goodness, Sam, I didn't know that was you."

"Where's the fire?"

"Huh?"

"Ren, you were rushing like a mad woman. Are you all right? What are the pictures?"

I point to the little bag she is clutching tightly. She looks at her hand and smashes the photo package into her handbag. "These are nothing. They're pictures of my sculptures. I want to send them to various galleries in Santa Fe."

I have shown so little interest in my friend lately. I have some time to kill. I say, "I'd love to see them. Do you want to grab a cold drink and you can show them to me?"

"No, not now. I can't. I have some appointments."

As if cued, her cell phone rings and she is listening and muttering monosyllabic responses. I don't want to watch Ren talk on the phone. Been there. Done that. I give her a wave and she waves to me.

Does she look relieved? Was she trying to keep the photos from me? Am I reading too much into this?

Into everything?

I turn the corner on Santa Monica and have another near collision. This one is entirely my fault. The street person with the tattered jeans and sneakers, open at the toes, is standing as still as a statue on the other side of the corner I was rounding. Only his lips move, and then barely, as he whispers, "Could you loan me $1.83?"

I started the day feeling good. Now everything is unnerving me. It's warm, but I'm getting goosebumps. No money today, my man. The Beverly Hills Library looms ahead like a sanctuary and I walk briskly in a direct line, no detours.

When I enter the library, I do what I always do upon seeing what is there—marvel at the whole wonderful idea of it. We take it for granted that our libraries will just be there to feed our hungry minds.

Thousands of books, information on computers, and microfiche everywhere one turns. We don't know how fortunate we are.

I have almost an hour and a half to kill. Maybe it would be fun to browse through books I don't ordinarily read. I start strolling through the stacks, running my fingertips over the spines of the books, feeling the different textures of cracked and new leather. At one point I just stop and smell. Books smell great. Is it the combination of paper, glue, and leather, or does each book carry with it some trace of the aromas of the different people who have touched it? A nice thought unless you're Howard Hughes.

Across from one set of stacks is a small area with tables and chairs. During school hours the library is usually less crowded and today is no exception. I see what looks like a teenager with a small stack of books in front of him. I look closer and see it's Blake. I am about to approach him when I notice the books in front of him. They are all Benjamin's books. I recognize the spines of *Dark Entry, Dark Passage, Dark Room,* and *Dark*

*Destiny.* What in the world is he doing with Benjamin's books? He is reading one intently. It looks like *Dark Secret.*

Someone has a dark secret all right. I'm not exactly sure who it is, but I'm becoming increasingly certain that my paranoia is justified. How do they say it? Just because you're paranoid doesn't mean you're not being followed.

Benjamin appears from behind a different set of stacks and walks over to Blake. Of course they know one another. Benjamin and I were a couple. He, too, has known Blake from the day he was born, but this isn't an "oops, imagine running into you here" encounter.

I suspect this has been prearranged and that Blake has been waiting for Benjamin.

They talk quietly. Ben doesn't look anxious. Blake looks unhappy and nervous. I feel unhappy and nervous, too. What is going on? Is Ren part of this? Is Bicky? Is the street person? Am I losing my mind? Could Jack be part of this? How did he happen to coincidentally select the one place to meet where Benjamin would be? I haven't "by accident" or otherwise run into Benjamin since our separation.

My clothes feel warm and I am starting to get an uncomfortable sticky feeling. Seeing Benjamin has made me break into a sweat. So much for looking sexy and cool for my meeting with Jack. What do I care anyway? Is he part of this? Part of what? Have I been a fool to think I can trust anyone?

Panic is setting in.

Benjamin is patting Blake on the back in what appears to be a parting gesture. He walks away. That is Benjamin's version of affectionate. I look at him, as objectively as I can, and realize I feel nothing. I'm not angry at this man I lived with for years. I'm sad. I don't lust for him. I can hardly remember what it was like to be intimate with him. I feel nothing other than resentment for all that being with him has stopped me from doing and how little I will be recompensed for what I contributed to his career.

Seeing him does only one thing. It reinforces how determined I feel about killing Hunter McCall.

I guess that makes me as crazy as the rest of the people haunting the Los Angeles landscape. We all seem to want something different or more than what we've got. In Black River Falls, Wisconsin, people wake up and are happy to be alive and healthy, looking forward to a new day. Don't ever try to sell that script in this town.

Benjamin leaves and Blake stops reading the book and looks off at nothing. What did they talk about? Why did they meet? I have about a hundred and fifty questions and I'm too terrified to approach my best friend's son and ask him. I wiped his baby bottom more times than I can remember. I went to his birthday parties and took him on pony rides. I always kept lemon coconut cookies in my house, for him. But I can't ask him what he was discussing with my husband and I don't know why.

I am now functioning on nothing other than instinct and gut, with some hormonal twinges thrown in. This is either going to work out fine or I am making the biggest mess imaginable out of my life.

Everything can't be a coincidence. Three people I speak to die sudden and violent deaths almost immediately after seeing me. Ren is poking though Stephen's papers for "no reason" and finds Benjamin's insurance forms. Blake shows up everywhere I turn and then he's here in the library with Benjamin. I walk in the cemetery and see Jack and the next day he pulls a gun on me and then he suggests meeting in the library where I see Benjamin. And every time I leave the house or go anywhere there are street people. Then there's Boo's house—what about that? Strange gunshot-like noises, Bentleys suddenly leaving, Ren pretending nothing is happening.

I decide to leave. It is the best thing to do. This meeting with Jack is a bad idea. Whatever is happening, he has to be part of it. I dressed like a sixteen-year-old primping for her first date and now I feel stupid. Stupid, ridiculous, and deceived. What was I thinking?

Turning around in the stacks, my heart bumps into my throat. There he is, more than half an hour early. And he looks adorable. I wonder if he has taken the extra time to try and look nice for me, and instantly vanish that thought. I need to get out of here without Jack seeing me.

I turn down into another stack and then another and another. I have lost sight of him and my bearings. I see the dim red EXIT light and head in that direction. In the check-out area of the library I will be in plain view but only if he is looking in that direction. I scurry across the reception area and rush through the exit turnstiles. In less than forty-five seconds I have gone from the stacks to the street. I take a deep breath and walk briskly to my car.

It isn't until I get into the car and start it moving that I see the one fallacy in my analysis. It was I who telephoned Jack and brought him into my problem. He didn't phone me. He didn't offer his help. I asked for it.

Maybe he isn't one of the bad guys.

# CHAPTER TWENTY-THREE

Sanctuary. That's how I think of my home. Only it doesn't feel like sanctuary anymore. As I drive down my street, I am looking for any sign of street people, for Ren's face poking through her designer Venetian blinds, for any activity at Boo's house, for anything at all that looks suspicious. For anyone who looks like a murderer. There, I have said it. At least in my head. Murderer. What does a murderer look like anyway?

The Los Angeles sun, perched in a cloudless azure sky, beats down on all of our perfectly manicured front lawns and everything *looks* tranquil, beautiful, very un-deadly. There's a lot of noir talk about mean streets, but the truth is that murder seems far away when you're on the hot, sunny, royal streets of Beverly Hills. Unless you're Mr. and Mrs. Menendez, of course.

I see no sign of Ren, street people, Boo, or his guests. No one other than the hard-working gardeners who keep my block ready for a film crew's arrival at any given moment.

I park my car in front of the house, not in the driveway, as if I am contemplating the possibility that I may need to make a quick getaway. What I sniff upon walking through my front door does nothing to dispel that notion. Someone has been in my home and unless that person was my husband's clone, the intruder was Benjamin. The blend of his aftershave and cigar is unmistakable. It's not something I'd forget. So, is he still here? And why did he come?

I don't hear any sound other than the one-hundred-year-old

grandfather clock we purchased in a London antique flea market and the soothing flow of water from the marble fountain that perpetually replenishes itself. Benjamin saw the fountain in a store in Tunisia and thought the piece would be a wonderful counterpoint to the outdoor deck off the second den at the far end of the house. My life can be chronicled by purchases— quite the testimonial.

It's time to forget about Jack and this whole mess and get back to something constructive. I need to work on my book. But first, I need to check my house. I also need to stop thinking about Jack's reaction when he realizes I am not going to show for our meeting. Pick a reason, any reason. I can't put it out of my head. Will he be hurt, angry, indifferent, belligerent?

Everything in the room is exactly as I left it, with one exception. I walk to my desk and my book is conspicuously absent. I see neither the pages I printed out nor the backup disk. I look at my computer and see it is already turned on. It takes less than thirty seconds for me to determine that my book has been deleted completely, erased, exorcised from my computer as if it never existed. And without the pages or the disk, it is exactly that. For all intents and purposes, my book has ceased to exist.

Benjamin's smell in the house and the sound of the fountain that I shouldn't have been able to hear from the front door are enough clues for the worst detective in history. I run into the back den and find the sliding door leading to the outdoor deck pried open. I changed the house locks, but not the security code.

Benjamin has broken into our house and stolen my book. Is that what he was discussing with Blake in the library? He must have left the library and come directly here. How would he have known I wasn't home? Maybe he didn't care.

I want to cry. I want to scream. There is no way I can rewrite from memory what has taken so many hours. Any author would know how I feel. The idea of starting over is exhausting to contemplate. Heartbreaking to contemplate. And totally unacceptable.

Two can play at this game. I know exactly where I will find my book. Benjamin is too ego involved to discard the book without reading it. He will take it back to his writing studio, his sanctuary.

So I will invade his sanctuary just as he invaded mine.

After book number three, Benjamin convinced me he needed an office and writing studio away from our home. He suggested we purchase a small bungalow in West Hollywood. At that time, of course, it never occurred to me that Benjamin also wanted a love nest. The bungalow is an older house with two bedrooms, one bathroom, a nice-sized living room with a fireplace, a kitchen, and an adjacent dining area. The larger bedroom became Benjamin's office and writing room. The smaller bedroom is storage for his drafts and research material. He has a bed in case he needs to rest.

A gardener comes once a week. A housekeeper comes once a week. A grocery has a standing order to deliver each Monday morning at 10:00 A.M. The kitchen is always well stocked with the food and drink Benjamin enjoys, so he never needs to leave. I wasn't involved in any of these arrangements.

Benjamin handled everything. Benjamin made it clear that my presence at the little house was neither needed nor wanted. I have not been there in more than four years.

In all this time, I pushed to some recess of my mind that asks no questions the very obvious question. Why couldn't Benjamin have accomplished the same thing in our five-thousand-square-foot home? He had, in fact, done just that with books one, two, and three.

The same Santa Monica Boulevard I travel to the cemetery takes me to Benjamin's bungalow. I will be there in ten minutes.

I still have a key to the house. After all these years I wonder if Benjamin ever changed the locks. I doubt it.

I try not to think about whether or not I care if he is there when I arrive. It is only when I see his car in the driveway that I know the answer. I wish he was somewhere, anywhere else. It would have been easy to stoop to his level and simply turn the key, slip through the front door, and re-steal my book. But that is not meant to be. He gets to steal from an unoccupied house. I am going to have to contend with the occupant. So be it.

The key works. The living room smells like Benjamin. The same smell he left lingering in my living room. There is another odor I can't place. It triggers no memory. This must be how a dog feels, basing so much of perception on smell. Samantha Holmes, Sherlock's younger sister, sniffing her way to solving the problem.

The house is too small for Benjamin not to hear my arrival. He won't hide from me. That's not his style. He Tarzan, me lowly inconsequential woman. In six strides I am in his office. He isn't. In three strides I am in the spare room where he is sleeping like a baby. Next to the bed, on the little colorful hand-painted table we bought from a Taos, New Mexico, artist is an almost finished glass of iced tea. I hate iced tea. Benjamin loves it with lemon and precisely three teaspoons of sugar and mint leaves, which he loves to chomp and swallow halfway through the drink. A high-maintenance man.

I call out his name thinking that will stir him. It doesn't. I shake Benjamin's shoulder to wake him. No reaction. I turn him over, with no resistance, and look at a face that has felt pain at the end of life.

And I feel nothing. Imagine, all those years we spent together, Benjamin is dead and I feel nothing. For me, my husband, Benjamin Crowley, died a long time ago. It is Benjamin Crowley, the author, who now lays dead. In the little bed he bought to rest, may he rest in peace. Or not.

With a certainty that comes only from the gut, I know someone has poisoned him. The mint leaf is gone, eaten by the recently deceased, though some smaller pieces are still scattered in the drink. I leave the room. It is too creepy hovering over his dead body. I sit down in the living room to collect my thoughts. I'm not even tempted to call the police or an ambulance or anyone. This is not a natural death. And I am not an idiot. Even without the other murders, I will be suspect numero uno for this.

I am positive hemlock has been used. I'm not sure why, but with what I've seen, it makes sense. The mint leaf is actually a hemlock leaf. Benjamin would never have known the difference between mint and hemlock. He never did his own research.

Hemlock contains coniine, which paralyzes the muscles. This is not a happy death. One feels pain and a gradual weakening of muscle power as the muscles deteriorate and die. It all starts within half an hour and then shortly thereafter, mere hours, death comes. Sight is often lost, but here is the chilling part. While sight is gone and muscles no longer work, the mind is perfectly clear. The mind stays clear until death arrives. Mercifully arrives? I didn't want to know.

Benjamin and Socrates. Benjamin is finally in good company. I need to find my pages and my disk and get out.

I walk into Benjamin's office and start my search with his desk. The piles of papers are intriguing, and as a snooping wife, I might have been interested. However, under the circumstances, speed is my priority. The desktop and drawer search is unproductive. I move to the shelves and then the file cabinets. I hope I'm not going to have to search the room where Benjamin took his final nap.

In three minutes I cover every conceivable spot he could have stashed my pages and disk. With grave displeasure, I look in the direction of the spare room. Then I have an inspired thought. Think like Benjamin. He didn't associate me with writing. I was the little woman, the former little woman. Would he have "stored" my precious pages and disk in a cabinet in the kitchen? It is the way Benjamin's little mind would have worked.

It isn't until I open every cabinet in the kitchen that it occurs to me I am leaving fingerprints on every surface in the house. But then, why shouldn't my prints be here? This is my house, too.

My frustration level at not finding the pages and disk is only intensified by the prospect of now having to search the spare room housing the body of my late husband. I am starting to feel shaky. I've read about this, the way shock slowly creeps up on you. That I still have the presence of mind to do as much as I am doing is an accomplishment. How much more I can handle is questionable.

Sounds outside the house tell me that I am about to have more serious problems. I hear sirens getting closer and that little cautionary thing we have, way in the back of our brains, is telling me those cops are coming my way and not to some other Los Angeles tragedy.

I yank open the silverware drawer, the last unopened orifice in the kitchen, and can see that the silverware is perched too high. The treasure hunt is over, and just in time. I can see the flashing police lights through the thin drapes and a police cruiser has my car blocked. My car is sandwiched between a cop car and Benjamin's car in the driveway.

There is a back door that goes out to the backyard, but by now the police may be in the yard. In Benjamin's office, there's a window that overlooks a narrow alley between our house and the house next door. The alley is hidden because of the high hedges that run its perimeter on three sides. For some reason, our neighbor planted hedges on the side of the alley abutting his house. We did not. If I climb out the window, jump down into the alley, and push through my neighbor's hedges, I can exit to the street through his backyard rather than my own.

I am thinking like a criminal. Still clutching my pages and disk, I walk into the bedroom, open the window, push hard on the screen, and watch it drop down to the little alley. I am not only thinking but acting like a criminal.

I grab a manila envelope from Ben's supply shelf, shove in the pages and disk, and drop it out the window. Getting my body hunched into the window frame is awkward but not impossible. I want to jump down without spraining or breaking my ankle. I hear the front doorbell ringing. No more time to worry about sprains. After all, Butch and Sundance took a lot bigger leap than the ten feet I am looking at. I jump. I am contorted and twisted, make hand motions to break the fall I anticipate, and scrunch up my face expecting the worst.

Only I land just fine. I pick up my manila envelope, get a little scratched pushing through a hedge that has grown considerably in four years, and find myself in our neighbor's backyard. Everything according to plan.

Now I am a criminal.

# CHAPTER TWENTY-FOUR

As he rounded the last bend toward home, Jack sensed before he saw the kinetic energy near his house. Uniformed police had Jack's street blocked off to all but those who actually resided or worked there. He saw a well-rounded Hispanic woman, whom he recognized as his neighbor's housekeeper, talking to one of the uniforms and no doubt explaining that she was trying to get to the house she was supposed to clean that afternoon.

An officer recognized Jack and waved him on. Jack was accustomed to the occasional inconvenience. No violence in the hills today. Just another movie being filmed on his street at one of the many houses that frequently served as the location for film shoots. It was difficult to navigate the steep hills and narrow streets near his home when the large movie vans took up residence. Usually there were no fewer than four and often more than six vans parked on streets that could barely accommodate two-way traffic.

But the show must go on. It was an easy day for the officers, two of whom were perched atop their motorcycles, drinking coffee and talking to three grips who were waiting for further orders from the person in charge.

Jack remembered when he pulled that detail. It was one of those necessary but useless jobs. A police presence was required by law, but their function was benign and fewer cops were on the streets catching bad guys.

It made him unhappy to think about it. It was no longer his

problem or concern, neither the wasted cop hours nor the bad guys.

Just when he thought he could be useful again, the girl didn't show up. He was back to thinking of her as the girl. He liked her name, Samantha. He liked her look and maybe he even liked her just a little. She had come to him for help and he would have been there for her. Jack had called in favors for the first time in years to find out about the deaths of the three people she mentioned. He had discovered she was one hundred percent correct.

They had all been murdered. The police were baffled by each murder. They had no suspects or motives different than the motives to kill almost anyone in the city. Jack had determined there was no police suspicion that the three murders were linked. Hopefully, his inquiry wouldn't spark such a theory.

Peter had been killed by a hit-and-run. Carol had been poisoned. Jonathon had been stabbed. The entertainment business was their common bond, but there was no other obvious nexus.

Most important, it seemed, the police, in their infinite ineptitude, had not yet cross-referenced Samantha as the person who had lunched with Peter Perkal before his hit-and-run, had drinks with Carol Haber the night of her death, and had been the last to see Jonathon Harley before he took his fateful cable car trip. The reason for this was quite simple. Three separate investigations were being conducted by three different teams. It could be weeks, months—or never—before a connection was made.

So why hadn't she shown up? He could wonder about that for the next century. He had begun to think of her as Monkey Face, though he would never have said that to her. She wouldn't have understood. She had a liveliness, an energy, an ability to make him smile. Not something he did often. The best part of the trips to the zoo with his mother had been the monkeys—the swinging, playful, chattering monkeys. He had loved the monkeys and Samantha made him feel the same way. But she hadn't shown up. Not thinking about it sounded more appealing.

Yesterday Grant had given him a warning to keep away. Grant was tired of brotherly attention and love. If the dogging of his footsteps by Jack continued, Jack might find himself stalked by Grant.

No one wanted his help, so why was he beating himself up about it? He should do the world a big favor and just keep to himself.

Jack picked up the book he had started two days ago, which perfectly fit his mood today. He supposed that most people would call it a girl's book but he thought *Jane Eyre* was a great selection when a guy was feeling particularly tormented. That guy Rochester sure knew about torment.

The phone rang and he ignored it. There was no one he needed to speak to and no one who needed to speak to him. Whomever it was hung up without leaving a message on his answering machine.

Maybe he should disconnect the machine. Why did he need a device to catch phone messages? He should get rid of it. Maybe get rid of the doorbell, too. Isolate himself, like Rochester. The idea appealed to him.

He could give away his TV and radio. He was carrying his disillusionment to ridiculous heights. He had gone mad, but not that mad.

It was only the knowledge that he had gone slightly mad that was keeping him sane.

Contradictions were the fuel that made the world a challenging and interesting place.

And now that he was philosophizing, maybe he should be

wondering more about what happened today. Maybe the ringing phone had been Samantha and not some solicitation. Maybe there was something wrong and that was why she had not shown up. Maybe she was injured, or in danger, or had been followed.

Maybe not answering the phone was the same as being ten minutes late again. Trust Jack and die. Maybe that would be his legacy.

He didn't want to read. He wanted and needed to act. His inaction was an impotence that could only be understood by a man who knew what it was like to be knee deep in the fray. For her not to have shown up meant something was wrong.

If the phone rang again, he would answer. And for now he would put aside the Rochester philosophy and watch some TV. He flipped channels for five minutes, barely seeing what was on the screen. He finally settled on a local news broadcast.

The lead story was about the birth of a kangaroo at the city zoo. That story segued into a piece about people not using the proper car seats for their young children. He waited and hoped it would not turn out that a celebrity talk show was more informative than the afternoon news update.

A commercial came on, blaring so loud that Jack almost spilled the apple juice he poured. It was a clever device these advertisers had, pumping up the volume for commercials. Well, he had a clever device too. It was called the mute button, which he activated. The picture, quiet, was far less offensive.

On the muted screen, he saw Samantha's face above the caption LATE BREAKING NEWS, and in his haste to get some sound with the picture, he again almost spilled the apple juice.

Samantha's famous husband had been found dead in his writing hideaway in West Hollywood. They showed the bungalow and Samantha's car in the driveway. The only sign of Samantha was the picture that kept flashing on the screen. The newscaster didn't say Samantha was a murderer, but the implication was clear.

Jack didn't know whether to laugh or cry. When this gal said she needed help, she wasn't kidding. With the instincts of a former cop, and the even more confident instincts of a man who was a good judge of character, Jack knew she wasn't guilty of killing her husband. Or anyone else.

And much to his delight he also knew something else. She may have thought she didn't really need him before, but she sure as heck needed him now.

He switched off the television and walked into the other room to sort through the mess in his closet. It was time to get his white knight duds out of mothballs.

## CHAPTER TWENTY-FIVE

Considering I stood the guy up and was wanted for murder, I could probably have started the phone call in a slightly more diplomatic fashion.

"So, you finally decided to answer your phone," I say.

Can you hear a person grin? I had not thus far seen Jack smile, but I know he is doing something close to it now. Sometimes a voice smiles.

"That was you calling before? I didn't get to the phone in time."

Now I can tell he is grinning and lying. That's the oldest lie in the book. He hadn't gotten to the phone because he hadn't wanted to, or the thought that made me sicker than I cared to admit, someone had been there with him . . . distracting him.

I'm standing at a payphone on the corner of Melrose and La Brea, very close to the famous Pink's hot dog stand where people line up for blocks to get hot dogs. It seems awfully odd to wait on a long line for hot dogs, but the place has been in business for sixty years, so what do I know?

I know I need help. I need the cavalry to come to my rescue as I stand in this graffiti-ridden phone booth.

"Look, Jack, I'm in trouble."

"Uh huh."

"Big trouble."

"Uh huh."

"What do you want? Do you want me to apologize for not

waiting for you at the library?"

Jack says, "You mean you were there?"

Verbalizing my stupidity makes me feel worse.

"Yes. I was there but I left."

This conversation is going backward not forward, which is where I need it to head. The library feels like a million years ago, but Jack has no way of knowing that.

"Jack, listen, I'll say I'm sorry, I'll say whatever you want, but something has happened which I think you'll agree really needs to take priority over why I left the library. Are you alone? Can I talk to you right now because it's kind of a major emergency."

"Yeah. I think killing your husband qualifies as a major emergency, but really it's more like his emergency."

I gasp and almost choke. How could he know? I look through the smudged glass of the booth and see Button Lady sitting very quietly on a bench in front of Pink's and staring directly at me. I am being given the evil eye. Or is it a sympathetic eye? For a fleeting second I wonder how she has gotten from Musso and Frank's on Hollywood Boulevard to Pink's on La Brea. If these street people have some underground railroad that transports them to different points in the city, I sure could use a rail pass.

"How do you know about Benjamin? I didn't kill him. You don't really think I did, do you?" I'm trying not to sound desperate, but if Jack doesn't believe me I have nowhere left to turn.

"No, I don't think you killed him." Jack's tone changes, sensing the time for joking, as if there really had been a time, is over. "And if you had met me at the library, I would have given you the information I'd gotten. You were right about the other deaths and it's pretty clear now what's going on. I'm not sure someone is out to kill you, but someone is certainly trying to frame you."

"How did you know about Benjamin?"

"I've got some bad news. It's all over the TV. With your picture. You left your car in his driveway. Why didn't you just leave a calling card and a confession?"

"Very funny. The cops showed up and blocked my car and I had to jump out a back window. I can't go into all of it now. I need to get to your house, if that's okay with you. I need to hide so I can come up with a plan. Can I come to your place?"

My voice has deteriorated from desperate to hopeless. I wonder if life will ever be normal again.

Talk about relying on the kindness of strangers.

"I'll pick you up as quickly as I can get there, but you might want to think about changing your look. Your picture has been all over the afternoon news."

"Oh my God!" Hopelessness has reverted back to desperation. "I could go into one of the stores near here and buy something." My brain has shut down. I can't think. "What should I buy?"

"Maybe sunglasses, a hat, a scarf."

Jack is functioning even if I'm not. My survival instincts, dormant for years, are completely out of shape.

"Okay, I'll do that. I can do that."

"Only don't use your credit cards. Pay in cash."

"What?" I'm acting and feeling like someone has taken an ice cream scooper and excised my brain in one clean swoop.

"Sammi, your name is on the card and your name is all over the news. Someone could recognize you or your name. And if the cops worked fast, they could track you through the credit card."

I scour my handbag as Jack speaks and take stock of my cash situation. Everything from my groceries to my haircuts are charged on my credit card. The only time I use cash is to tip valet parking. Today I hit an all-time low. I have a total of four dollars. There is no place within a ten-mile radius of my location where I can buy a scarf, hat, glasses, or even a hot dog for that price. This is Los Angeles. Four dollars is barely enough to tip the valet parking man.

It isn't Jack's problem. I can't make everything in my life his problem.

"You're right, of course. I'll come up with a disguise. How long will you be?"

"Hopefully, no more than ten, fifteen minutes."

I try to sound light. "I'll see ya when I see ya."

Then, an important afterthought. I say, "Wait one second, Jack."

"Yeah?"

"I think I forgot to say thank you."

"Hey, that's what white knights are for. Damsels in distress."

This guy sure can put a smile on my face during the worst of times. I can't resist a taunt.

"Hey, yourself. Who says you're a white knight?"

"You will."

The phone clicks as he, I hope, hurries off in his Ford Explorer "steed" to come to the aid of, I hope, his Guinevere.

I'm acting as though the only person in the world upon whom I can depend is this man. A charming but complete stranger. Is that really possible? Am I that alone? I pull out the precious change I should be using to purchase plastic sunglasses and dial Ren's number.

She answers the phone after three rings, sounding more throaty than usual and decidedly distant.

She hears my voice and says, "What's up?"

She isn't exactly abrupt but she sure isn't warm. Was it today I bumped into her coming out of the photo store, or a million years ago?

"I need to talk to you."

"Okay."

This is not like Ren. Something has to be going on.

"Are you alone?" I ask.

"No, I'm not, and I'm not really interested."

Huh? This answer makes no sense.

"Is someone there?"

"Hold on a minute," I hear her say. Then, "It's just one of the women calling me about my helping her host a luncheon."

Her lie helps the obvious register. If I want to remain a fugitive, I need to get swifter.

"It's the police? The police are at your house?"

"That's right. So I don't think we have anything further to discuss, don't you agree?"

"Thanks, Ren. You're a good friend."

"Goodbye. It was nice of you to call."

The police haven't wasted any time. Only three or four minutes have passed since I phoned Jack.

I can't stand in the payphone indefinitely. I can pretend to be talking on the phone, but hiding in a phone booth seems too obvious. The police may be cruising the area, looking for me. This is unbelievable. I have stepped into *The Fugitive.* I've done nothing wrong. Four people are dead, but one is my husband, and I am the logical suspect. Except there is nothing logical about it.

Button Lady is still staring. She hardly moved a muscle in all the time I was in the phone booth. With two or three of her scarves, I could change my look dramatically. She has no less than ten or twelve colorful scarves wrapped around her body, neck, and head. Will she sell me a few for three dollars and sixty-seven cents?

I walk out of the booth and sit down on the bench next to her. The truth makes things less complicated. That has always been my philosophy, so I don't deviate here.

"Hello. We don't know each other but I've seen you on

Hollywood Boulevard and other places. I really need to change the way I look a little and I was wondering . . . I only have three dollars and some change, but I would be happy to give all of it to you if I could just purchase a few of your scarves, which would be most helpful in allowing me to alter my appearance."

My words sound weird and stilted to me. I am talking to her as if she is a child and as if English is not my native language. I am losing my mind. Button Lady, covered in hundreds of buttons, who puts her mojo on cars passing down the street and who may not have bathed in the last four months, looks at me like I'm crazy.

Does she speak? Does she understand English? Maybe she's deaf. I live in a house that costs two million dollars and spend seventy-five dollars for T-shirts. Now here I am, asking Button Lady if I can buy some of her scarves. I understand what is happening. God, or someone or something, is humbling me. The growing up that was stunted by my marriage is over. I'm spurting like kids do during that summer vacation between their thirteenth and fourteenth birthdays. Only it isn't that I'm getting taller, just smarter. I hope. I am getting some long overdue life lessons.

"My name is Betty." Button Lady speaks in a surprisingly pleasant and cultured-sounding voice. "What's your name?"

Betty the Button Lady is now teaching me about manners and class. I failed to introduce myself when I plunged into my entreaty. I still have a lot to learn. Police sirens are audible in the distance and for all I know coming my way. But I'm not going to ask this woman for her scarves again until I tell her my name and apologize.

"I'm terribly sorry. That was very rude of me. I'm Samantha and it's very nice to make your acquaintance, Betty."

Amazingly, she peels some layers of scarves off her colorfully layered body and wraps them around my face and head in such a way that I look right out of the Arabian Nights, a not unfamiliar sight on the multi-ethnic streets of the City of Angels. And here I am, face to face, with one of its angels.

Betty smiles and starts chattering about her daughter who is an accountant in another city and an ex-husband who broke up with her and left her penniless.

Betty the Button Lady is neither crazy nor ignorant. I could be Betty the Button Lady.

When she is done with her pinning and tucking, she stands back to admire her handiwork.

"Now no one will recognize you."

She has overheard only my half of the conversation with Jack, but she is a fast study. Betty completely understands what I need to accomplish. She asks no questions and gives me something I've never gotten from any other human being. Unconditional friendship.

I know it would not make most normal adults feel special that a street person bestowed upon them unconditional friendship, but that's just how I feel. The old Samantha would not have done what I decided to do next. Germs and dirt be damned, I give Betty a hug that literally lifts her feather-like body up from the sidewalk.

I tell her, "You are the kindest person I've ever met. Thank you."

I go into my purse and pull out the meager three dollars and change and hand it to her. But she waves away my hand and looks embarrassed.

"We're friends now. I don't need it. You might. You can have my bench."

She gets up but I don't want her to go. Not just yet.

"May I buy you a cup of coffee?"

She nods.

So I stand on the long Pink's line and buy my friend Betty a cup of coffee.

When I hand it to her, she says thank you. Then she delicately dances away with the coffee cup in one hand while the other hand opens a parasol I hadn't seen. She twirls down La Brea Boulevard like a monarch butterfly set free from its cocoon.

I sit on the now empty bench and wait for Jack. My scarf wrapping makes me feel empowered again. Maybe the scarves carry the power to cast mojos. But on whom do I want to cast evil spells? Who is doing this to me?

The cast of characters is small and shrinking. The number of characters immediately surrounding me, however, is expanding by the minute. The Pink's line is now almost a block long. A man wearing a bright yellow jumpsuit is talking in an excited tone and explaining to the woman he is with that it will be impossible to expect us to inhabit Mars until they find a way to make space travel food as good as fast food. The woman is applying black mascara to already heavily mascara-laden eyes and doesn't appear to be listening to one word he says. I, on the other hand, am fascinated at how she is able to juggle her handbag, the mirror, the mascara, and still inch forward with the line.

Two women whose combined weight is no less than 550 pounds debate the merits of sharing an order of French fries or each getting her own. At no point in the conversation does either woman seem to consider the possibility of passing on the fries altogether.

Wouldn't it be nice if my greatest concern at the moment was the pros and cons of more calories?

I am surrounded by people without a care in the world. At least that's how it seems. Is it possible that someone standing in the Pink's line has more worries than I? More worries than being homeless and wanted by the police? Because at the moment

I am homeless, virtually penniless, and jumping at every siren that passes.

Empowerment is fading fast. I feel silly and conspicuous sitting, wrapped like a mummy, on the bench. If I could just walk a bit or talk to someone, I'd feel better. I stare intently at the traffic, as if I can will Jack's sport utility vehicle to appear.

When he finally pulls up to the curb, my attention is distracted by a homeless man yelling that we must praise the lord. It isn't until I hear a loud whisper calling my name that I snap out of the almost hypnotic reverie into which I have been transported by the homeless prophet. I quickly climb into Jack's passenger seat.

Jack chuckles at my attire but I don't care. At least he can see I am a girl who, at long last, has followed instructions.

"Laugh all you want. I'm disguised, aren't I?"

"That you are. I'm not sure who or what you are, but you do look different."

"Where are we going?"

"To my house, of course. You'll be safe there and we can talk about what we need to do."

I don't know if I feel more relief from the fact that Jack is taking me to his house or his use of the word "we" instead of "you." In any case, the relief that washes over me is both welcome and exhausting.

I am safe. My body finally has permission to feel tired. I close my eyes and let someone else be in charge.

Jack will take care of everything. I close my eyes. I am in that twilight state where the body is like a sponge, soaking in sounds that are incorporated into a waking dream.

The bumping and twisting of Jack's Explorer on the steep road to his home finally forces my eyes open. What I see makes me start choking. I can't speak.

There are police all over Jack's street. Waiting for me. Staking out the place as if the Hillside Strangler and Charles Manson have planned a rendezvous in the Hollywood Hills.

"Oh my God! It's all over. And now you're going to get in trouble. Jack, I'm so sorry."

Jack gives me a bored look and as scared as I am, I also feel majorly irritated.

"What is the matter with you, Jack?" Considering he has just come to my rescue, I could have phrased my question a little better.

His left hand stays on the steering wheel as he expertly executes the twists in the road. His right hand touches my face. Okay, now I know what those romance novelists mean when the heroine says that his touch was scorching. A flush of heat rushes through my body. This man either turns me on or estrogen is evaporating from my body and causing me to undergo an instant and early change of life.

"I would never take you into harm's way, Sammi. Trust me. The only reason you see cops here is because they're filming a movie on my street. As usual." He adds the last two words with what sounds like more genuine irritation than mine.

I am fully awake. I see the movie vans and the camera crew and the cops sipping coffee and chatting with grips and the normal buzz of a Hollywood movie in progress.

After all the time I've spent with Bill—William Desmond Taylor—you'd think I would have recognized that we have just driven into a genuine Hollywood movie-making moment, security police and all.

For sure my guardian angels are looking down on me. I'm riding into safety and freedom with my very own Captain Alvarez. Before he became a director, William Desmond Taylor had a starring role as Captain Alvarez, the pistol-packing hero of a rebel brigade.

I look at Jack. White knight. Captain Alvarez. What's in a name? This is Hollywood, the land of magic and make-believe.

# CHAPTER TWENTY-SIX

Jack is explaining. "Love, revenge, money . . . those usually sum up the motives for murder. Benjamin didn't love you anymore, he found another woman, motivating you to revenge, and then, of course, you get all the money, honey. You were at the scene of the crime and you ran away. What more do you think the cops and D.A. need to issue a warrant for your arrest?"

Not necessarily in the order of importance, I need a manicure, liposuction, and a new face like Humphrey Bogart got in *Dark Passage*. I wondered if Jack likes old movies. Me and Bogie. Who would have thought we'd ever have anything in common?

I love that movie. Bogie plays a man convicted of murdering his wife. He escapes from prison with the goal of proving his innocence. Definitely some similarities. The problem is that a convicted felon's face is too well known. Hello. Bogie didn't have to contend with breaking news every ten minutes on CNN and the Internet.

Bogie picks a clever, somewhat drastic, way out. He gets a new face. The portion of the movie that is pre-surgery is filmed from Bogart's eye view. We see him for the first time only after the surgery, when his face has been transformed into the one we all know.

As solution solving as it might be, I'm not having anyone reconstruct my face, even if I am on the Los Angeles County's ten most wanted list. I'll prove my innocence using the face my parents gave me.

I say, "I didn't love him and I didn't care if he had a girlfriend, boyfriend, or a harem."

Jack shakes his head to show he understands and says, "I'm convinced. Now all we have to do is persuade the other ten million inhabitants of our fair city. Or at the very least, the police and prosecutors."

"Your home is wonderful. It's comfortable."

Jack gives me a quizzical look. I am starting to be able to read this interesting man. I like his face. I like him. Don't ever let your face go under a knife, Jack.

Sure it sounds like I'm a dizzy dame replete with nonsequiturs and with my priorities out of synch. But I mean what I say, and at that moment it is more important to me that Jack start to know Samantha Crowley than dwell on the manhunt for Samantha Crowley.

I can see it now. One day I'll go to one of my high school reunions in Queens, New York, and we'll be sitting around telling tales. One of my old friends will relate a wild and wooly adventure she had in some exotic foreign country, and another will tell about the amazing life-saving surgery performed on her or her spouse or her kid, and another will tell about how she broke a fingernail and had this idea for a new product and three years later it was a ten-million-dollar company going public.

And I will tell them about the time I was the target of a city-wide manhunt on the mean streets of Los Angeles.

I don't know if I'll tell them the really good part of the story. How I met an irresistibly sexy man who kept me hidden in his home. Because I know those girls from high school will not understand one bit. And never believe me.

"You have such comfortable furniture and everything just looks good together. It's as if you've lived here a hundred years and the home belongs to everything in it as much as it does to you. I know this sounds dumb, but you have a great home, not house. You don't really appreciate the difference until you've lived in a house."

Every piece of furniture in the den is worn. I can envision one of Jack's body parts rubbing the sofa and armchair and desk edges to bring it to its current shiny patina. We were once like new furniture. Now we're frayed, faded, older, and broken in. Everything ages and changes.

Jack's five o'clock shadow has become more growth than shadow. His dark hair is rumpled. His eyes are tired. His shirt has pulled out of his pants, but I see no thickening in his waist. The practical side of my brain kicks in and sends a message: *Get your mind out of the bedroom and back to the business at hand— saving your neck.*

We are sitting on a faded green love seat and Jack is close to me. Close enough so I can smell his body in a way that makes me feel self-conscious. The smell is too personal. This is the odor his lovers know. It's the combination of his skin and his sweat and his chemistry with the house and the room and me. Well, his lover, if he has one, doesn't know the smell that includes me. We become part of the smell of the people whom we touch.

Jack smells like leatherbound books when you open them, and almonds, and dusk at the pool hall. He smells the way a man is supposed to smell. At least the men about whom I fantasize. He is John Garfield and Errol Flynn and Robert Mitchum and Kirk Douglas when they fought, swashbuckled, punched, and wisecracked their way to the girls and the fortunes.

I feel something touch my shoulder. It is Jack. He isn't shaking me, just holding my shoulder and trying to look into my mind. He is trying to get me back to our space. He is without a clue as to where I have drifted. His eyes are searching mine and I have the sinking feeling that he is seeing nothing.

Romanticizing like a schoolgirl is unbelievably absurd given my current situation. I am glad he can't read my mind.

"Sammi, you're talking about my house and furniture and stuff when we need a plan. Your problems aren't going to magically go away. It's only the two of us who will make it go away. Sam Spade and Philip Marlow aren't here to help you. I know it would be nice if Charlie Chan could gather everyone in a room and solve this puzzle, but at the moment he and Number One Son are on an extended vacation on the other side of the world. Do you get my drift?"

Here is what I get. Apparently he does like movies, though our tastes are not necessarily in synch.

But more importantly, Jack referred to "us" making this go away. Not just me, Samantha, one person. It may be the wrong kind of progress, but I can still remember my dating days and this is progress.

"You're right, of course. I'm sorry. It's a lot easier to drift in and out of wishful thinking than to deal with this. Death wasn't real before. Then one person dies and it's real. Then a lot of people die and it again stops being real. Do you know what I mean?"

Jack looks even more tired than when we started talking. I have that effect on people.

"Yeah, I do know what you mean. I guess I haven't been particularly sensitive to how shocking this must be for you."

He doesn't know that he is pushing my guilt button. What I said was true but I didn't say it because I'm shocked. In fact, I'm shocked at how strangely calm I feel.

"Don't worry about me. I'm fine. The whole situation has taken on a surreal quality. It's as if I'm outside of my body observing some woman's life that has taken all sorts of unexpected twists and turns and is going down an unknown path."

We both hear loud noises outside and look toward the front door.

Jack says, "It's the film crew wrapping up for the day. They're off to happy hour and dinner. Six o'clock on the nose each day. No one wants to pay overtime."

We look at one another and say nothing. The den has only one large window facing north and looking out on hillsides and the house next door. It is the only source of natural light in the den and as the day moves on, the room has gotten dimmer.

If nothing else, the lighting serves to flatter my features. It flatters Jack, too, but he doesn't need the advantage.

I break the silence. "You know, we should think about dinner. I haven't done much cooking lately, but usually I can whip together a meal that goes down without difficulty."

When did I start talking like one of the ranch hands at the Ponderosa? My many personalities have far exceeded Eve's three and I am now working toward Sybil.

Jack, blessedly, doesn't seem to notice. "That's not a bad idea, but I'm not sure I have much in the kitchen for you to work with."

"Don't worry. I'm sure I can mix and match enough of what you've got to get us through dinner." Now I sound like I'm putting an outfit together.

This is our cue, at least my cue, to move off the comfortable loveseat and go to the kitchen, but I don't want to budge. I could have sat there for the rest of my life. All right, big exaggeration, but at least for another hour. I'm hoping Jack will touch me again. Say something personal. Tell me about his childhood. Probably that wouldn't be such an upbeat idea, considering what happened to his Mom and the way things are with his brother. Tell me about summer camp? I don't know or care. I just want to hear him talk.

If there was a spell, it is broken by the ringing telephone. I feel Jack's body shudder. Maybe he is startled. Maybe a ringing phone is never good news. I hiccup. Without question, I am one dazzling dame.

He mutters words about having to grab the phone. I mutter words about heading to the kitchen to start dinner. Our assignments are in place and we rise from the loveseat to put them in motion.

Jack's kitchen is old with real wood cabinets that were once probably painted some awful harvest or avocado. Someone has stripped and stained the wood with a cedar-type finish. Whatever wood it is, the cabinets now look nice, like something you'd see in a fancy log cabin. The kitchen floor is hardwood like the entire house. It looks like pine but I'm not a wood maven. The counters have to be new. They are a smoky black granite and I'm positive no one originally put granite countertops in these old houses. The refrigerator is black, as is the stove and microwave. The sink is the only splash of white in the room, looking like a virgin in a whorehouse.

I open the cabinets and find what you find in most houses. I don't know what I expected. There are dishes, enough of them but incomplete sets, some obviously missing, lost, or broken. In the lower cabinets I find bowls and pots and pans. There are heavy crystal glasses. The cutlery is stainless steel. One drawer has lots of serving pieces thrown in randomly.

Below the sink are cleaners and paper towels and sponges and disinfectants and ant-killing products. What did I expect? He's a person with normal stuff. Cut him and he bleeds.

The upper cabinets, near the refrigerator, contain cans and jars of food. Beer, soda, mustard, spices, cereal, pasta, and a very large bag of chocolate chip cookies. There isn't much in the refrigerator.

The freezer contains frozen chopped meat. I can defrost that in the microwave. I go back to the cabinet to retrieve spices and olive oil and spaghetti.

We're in business. I have enough to throw together one of those dinners from the days when Benjamin courted me and we lived on a tight budget but still wanted everything to taste good. My special cheeseburgers won Benjamin over, way back then. Can they do the trick again?

My recipe for the spaghetti is simple. Boil al dente and then sauté in olive oil with spices and ingredients of choice.

I putter in the kitchen, feeling great and humming a Joni Mitchell tune from her *Blue* album. I haven't cooked and hummed in a long time. I shouldn't be happy and I'm not. I'm ecstatic.

Until I see Jack's face. When he walks into the kitchen, I can see the news is bad and my reality comes back as swiftly as a boomerang.

"What's happened? They know I'm here, don't they?"

Jack's face is ashen. His dark good looks have an almost ghostly aura.

"Relax. It's not about you."

"Talk to me. Tell me. What is it?"

"It's not your problem."

"And I'm not your problem. Let's not be that way. Just tell me what's wrong."

"That was an old friend of mine at the police department. He thought I might want to know that they've got Grant under investigation. They know he has no means of support and he's down at one of the missions in downtown Los Angeles handing out twenty-dollar bills to indigents. They know he's been doing cons and they figure he's spreading around the money he stole."

"But . . ." I hesitate because I don't know where I'm going with this. "But if he took money, he wouldn't be giving it away."

"Yeah, well, that's not exactly how Grant does things. You can be Robin Hood without the green outfit. Not everyone plays him like Douglas Fairbanks."

So now I have two more pieces of information. Stay away from questions about the family, and Jack does know a little about old movies.

# CHAPTER TWENTY-SEVEN

Sanctuary. Forget what I ever thought or believed before today. That's how I feel about Jack's house. Every sight, smell, and sound is different and better than anything I ever experienced in the past.

Jack still isn't ready to talk but he isn't leaving me alone, either. He sits down on one of the corduroy, burgundy-colored bar stools at the kitchen counter and is silently watching me sauté onions and blend ingredients into the raw chopped meat.

The kitchen light gives the room a yellowish hue. Outside it is too dark for the kids to continue with their ball game in the street, but light enough that some cars haven't turned on their headlights. I can hear neighborhood children shouting to one another, making tentative plans for when they will meet up the following day. Three dogs bark intermittently, as if passing along the evening status report to one another. The birds are chattering in anticipation of nightfall.

Life is lived differently with open windows. Latin music and a hammer beating as if keeping time echoes through the canyon and spirals into the kitchen. Jack and I have not spoken a word since he told me about Grant.

Next door, someone is cooking bacon and its aroma wafts through our kitchen, melding with the sautéing onions and the hamburgers I've placed in the broiler. From somewhere I catch the whiff of cut grass and then a sour smell as if a garbage pail has overturned.

I try to imagine who I would now be if every day of my life had smelled and sounded, looked and tasted like this twilight in Jack's kitchen.

And then I start to cry. The simplicity and complexity of my thoughts have put me on sensory overload and the result is tears. Not a torrent, just the soft, weepy, quiet tears that men sometimes don't even notice. But Jack does notice and, unlike most men, he elects to comment.

"Why are you crying?" he asks in a gentle but matter-of-fact way.

I wonder if I will sound like a complete idiot if I tell him I'm crying because I've been cheated by living my life without the sights and smells and sounds of Jack's kitchen. I am spared finding out the answer as he speaks again before I have a chance to respond.

"I'm sorry. That's not a fair question. I don't know you. Maybe you cry all the time. Maybe it's because you peeled that onion. Or maybe you'd rather not say."

I answer right away. "After everything you've done for me, there are no unfair questions. Anyway, I'm not crying anymore. It was a pang of self-pity. Do you want to talk about your brother?"

"I've been sitting here, watching you cook and thinking. I have an idea that's a little far-fetched but could be a solution to your problem. It's a gamble and we're going to need some money."

"Money isn't a problem." I hate the way I sound after the words are spoken.

Jack raises an eyebrow and says nothing for a few seconds. Then he looks pointedly at me and says, "You can't get money from your bank accounts or credit cards unless you want to risk being found."

"I know. I understand that. I have quite a bit of cash squirreled away in my house. If we can get in my house, I'm sure I have enough there. I think it's probably ten or twelve thousand."

Jack whistles. "So is that what you rich folks do? Hide your money in the mattress?"

That's a little annoying. I don't want to apologize for being wealthy and ten thousand dollars isn't exactly a king's ransom.

The steam from the boiling water has given my face a sheen I can feel. I don't want Jack to mistake the moisture for discomfort, so I turn, give him my best full-force glare, and speak in what I've come to think of as my nasty voice.

"Aren't we getting off track here? Is that enough money for your idea? That's the question we should be addressing."

"That and how we intend to get into your house to retrieve the money."

Touché. I hit, he hits back. He has a good point.

"And while we're contemplating that, how about my getting some clothes and personal stuff."

For a moment I forget I'm annoyed and revert back to infatuated girl. It would be nice to have my clothes.

Jack waves his hand impatiently and in agreement. "Let me think a bit more here."

I go back to cooking. As I check to make sure my pasta isn't overcooked, I watch Jack. Watch Jack think. He's still on the barstool with his hands intertwined behind his head. I can see the dark hair on his forearms and the pull of the muscles in his upper arms. His face looks as if he is resting, but his eyebrows are knotted in concentration that doesn't appear restful at all.

Jack says, "My idea is a little over the top."

"Speak. Tell me."

I feel a little flutter in my stomach and a tingling in the fleshy part of my palm. The idea of taking action, any action, is both appealing and repulsive. One part of me wants to end this nightmare. Another part of me wants to continue being a fugitive in this idyllic setting. I have definitely watched too many 1940s melodramas.

"We need to get the killer's attention, Sammi, but we don't have much to work with. When will dinner be ready? I'm going to take a shower."

There was a leap of thought.

Jack gets up and starts walking toward the bedroom. Men can do that. Men are contained. They don't need to blurt stuff out when an idea hits. When I get a brainstorm, I can't wait to find the nearest rooftop.

I call after him. "You have about eight minutes before it's on the table."

He yells back from the bathroom, "See you in ten."

I scramble around the kitchen to find what I need and something I want—candles. Somewhere he must have candles. After all, this is Los Angeles, the place destined, according to prognosticators, to suffer the big quake one of these days, and candles are one of the necessities of earthquake preparedness.

Logically, they should be in the kitchen. And they are. They're not the elegant candles I have in mind, but they'll do. Short waxen ivory stumps will throw off the same moody glow as the most beautiful candles.

When Jack emerges from his bedroom, he has a scrubbed look, like an eight-year-old coming to the dinner table after his bath. Only he isn't eight and I would be arrested, had he been eight, for what I am thinking as I look at him. His dark hair is slicked back and he's shaven.

"Dinner smells good."

"I hope you like it," I say in a pseudo Martha Stewart voice.

"It looks great."

Sitting down to dinner with Jack feels natural, as if I have been doing it my entire life. Go figure.

Admittedly it is hardly a gourmet meal, but Jack and I dig

into the hamburgers and pasta as if it is our first meal in a long time. Life crises can give you a hearty appetite.

We start out eating in silence. Jack breaks it with a sweet platitude. Or maybe he's sincere and I'm too tough on myself.

"These may be the best hamburgers I've ever eaten. I find it hard to believe you found, in my kitchen, the magic ingredients you need to make these taste this good."

I blush. "Not magic. Just something most people don't think to put in the raw meat and normally use after the meat is cooked."

"And what is that?"

"Mustard. Just plain ordinary mustard."

"Really?"

"Uh huh."

"When you stop being a fugitive from justice, you can open up Sam's Burger Stand next door to Pinks Hot Dogs."

Jack is kidding me and it feels awfully nice.

"I'm going to be too busy being a best-selling author to run a hamburger stand, you know."

"Good segue."

"What do you mean by that?"

Jack finishes his burgers, pasta, and two bottles of beer that appeared at the table without me noticing. How does he do that? How did the beer do that? How do men and beer do that?

"I mean that my plan ties in with your book. Here is how I see it. We have a killer out there. This killer is clever. He probably killed all these folks and then killed your husband."

Jack's right hand counts off on the fingers of his left hand. "Peter, Carol, Jonathon. I think his goal was for you to be implicated in those deaths. But it didn't work. The murders were like a back-up plan for your friend when he didn't succeed in setting me up to kill you."

"Mistake number one." I say it as a compliment and he takes

it that way. I see facial movement on both sides of his face. One day he may even smile.

"Your killer did his or her homework and knew how to push my buttons. There's no question in my mind that the objective was for me to kill you. When you weren't killed, getting you arrested for Peter, Carol and Jonathon's murders was the next best choice. Only that hasn't happened."

"Okay, that takes us up to the present. That person killed Benjamin and knew I'd be implicated. Made sure I'd be implicated. And of course I made it much easier by getting to the house within hours of the murder. He correctly calculated that I would go searching for my disk. But how would he know Ben took it?"

So many questions. My head is spinning.

"And how does this have anything to do with my book?" I ask.

"It doesn't, but it will when we're done."

"I don't get it. Should I?"

"We need to advertise for the killer."

"Huh?" That is as brilliant a response as I can muster.

"Sammi, here's what I'm thinking. We have an almost impossible goal—to find this killer—but first we have to figure who it is or at least who it could be. You haven't been able to do that, the police don't seem highly motivated, and I don't know enough about the victims to even hazard a guess. So, how do we find the killer?"

Everything he says is true. I've been thinking the same thing while wondering how long it's been since Jack had a girlfriend. And I've been a widow one day. I can't imagine this is how my mother's canasta group envisioned widowhood. If my life were an episode of *Perry Mason,* they'd call it "The Case of the Lusting Widow."

I look at Jack's clean-shaven cheeks and want to run my

fingers down his face and along his neck. I don't want to talk about catching a killer. I want to know if my face also looks interesting in the flickering light.

Jack senses my mood shift. "You do want to find the killer, don't you?"

"Of course I do." I try to sound indignant but who am I kidding? Jack is trying to save my life and I'm indulging in one-sided fantasies.

"Jack, are you saying that my book and advertising for the murderer and finding the murderer come together in some way?"

Jack bangs the dining room table. "Exactly."

I jump so high I could start a new Olympic event. Leaping from your dinner table chair. Judged for height, symmetry, and realism of astonished expression.

"Jack, tell me what you're talking about. I'm not good at puzzles. You can't mean that we take out an ad and request that the killer of Benjamin Crowley and the others simply turn himself in. What do you mean?"

"Not just yet, Sammi. I'm still thinking it through. But whatever we do, it has to make the killer believe that you know his or her identity."

"That's your idea, Jack? Your idea is that you're going to find a way to let the killer think I know who he is?" I'm trying not to sound as hysterical as I feel.

"Yup. Pretty good, don't you think?"

"I don't know if I'd call it good. I have no idea who killed Benjamin. And how does my book tie into this?"

"I'm not sure yet. The pieces are just coming together. And if you don't know Benjamin's killer, so what? Our killer doesn't know that you don't know. If he or she thinks you know, that's good enough. I need to think of a way to make the killer fear you. Be terrified of you."

"Me. Me. This is the idea you love!" Now I am hysterical.

"Yeah. Don't you see the possibilities?"

"Of course I do. The killer will go after me directly, try to kill me."

"Exactly. That's our objective. He will have to rise to the bait, which is you. Once I figure out precisely how to let the killer know that you know who he is. He can't take a chance. Then we'll expose our murderer."

Clearly, if Jack had a romantic agenda for us, a long-term relationship wasn't part of it.

"So, in other words, I set myself up as a target."

"Right, and then we catch the killer in the act of trying to kill you." Jack sounds positively gleeful. I feel like someone just told Bin Laden I'm the reason for all of his problems.

"Jack, has it occurred to you that the killer could succeed? That the killer has a perfect track record? That I could end up dead? You know, d-e-a-d? Dead is when one is no longer breathing."

"Don't think that way. We'll be very careful. You'll be fine. Do you have a better idea?"

Jack's idea wasn't much of an idea. Not yet. But what did I have? A week ago I had anguished over the dedication in my book. Now, maybe it was time I started thinking about my epitaph.

Did I have a better idea? Not to catch a killer. But I had one for my headstone: *For lack of a better idea, she went bravely and stupidly into that good night.*

# CHAPTER TWENTY-EIGHT

Sometimes you forget that Los Angeles is at the edge of a desert. The heat of certain days in winter, the coldest season in most other places, can toast your skin, leaving that browned, healthy look that doctors warn isn't healthy. Spring arrives overnight, and if rain hasn't come during winter, the brush of the hills waits patiently for a stray ember to start one of the many conflagrations that plague our dry city.

Buds and sprouts venture out cautiously from the oddest places. A lush cactus springs forth between the tarred freeway and cement retaining wall. Small purple flowers grow in the cracks of concrete stairways. Palm trees, with their freakishly long trunks, sprout new green fronds and sway, but never fall, during the tremors and quakes that ripple under this strange city.

While late winter and early spring storms ravage the Great Lakes and kill those who dare to trifle with the wind chill, surfers here don wet suits and ride the Malibu waves. The air is filled with salt and sound. Birds circle and caw. The Pacific Ocean drums the shore, and traffic on the Pacific Coast Highway sounds hypnotically like a waterfall.

Jack and I are sitting on his deck. I had begun the dishes and cleaning up chores when Jack suggested we sit out back, talk and sort out what we want to do. But instead of talking, Jack chain smokes and I reflect on the topography and climate of L.A.

It's getting late and we should be strategizing, but I've noticed Jack isn't much of a talker, even when he has something to say. After all my years with Benjamin, it's refreshing to be with a man not enamored of his own voice.

"Jack, are you ready to share your plan with me?"

"I think I am. I've come up with an idea for our first problem. How to get your money out of your house."

"And after that, we're going to use the money to make our killer fear me." My shoulders shudder when I say the last two words.

Jack takes a drag on his cigarette and in the faint glow I see an approving look. I didn't know there was anyone left in this city who smoked, besides Ren. It's not for me, but I don't share the same revulsion as most folks. No one cringed when Paul Henreid lit cigarettes for himself and Bette Davis. No one ever told Sam Spade, "I think I'll find a nonsmoking private eye."

"I have an idea about getting into your house that may also help me with Grant. He doesn't want my help, but this is different. He befriends the homeless and gives them money he takes. He steals," Jack corrects himself unhappily. "How about if we pay them for some legitimate work?"

"I'll bite. We're going to hire the homeless? To do what?"

"Be movie extras. We rent a truck, put on lettering to make it look like a movie van, pull up in front of the house next door to yours, and make it look like we're filming a movie there. Grant will handle our 'crew.' I'll be the director and you'll be a cop. No one will challenge a cop poking around your house. You'll scoot over to your backyard, break into your own house, get the money, and hightail it back to our movie truck."

It simultaneously sounds like the best and stupidest idea I've ever heard. The best because there is logic to it. The stupidest because how in the world can we ever pull it off?

"I don't want to be the voice of doom and gloom, but may I?"

Jack shrugs and gives me a half smile. "Go ahead, start poking holes in the dam, 'cause if I can't plug them, we need a new plan."

"Who's going to know what we're really up to?"

"Just you and me."

"Isn't Grant going to wonder? What about the people he recruits?"

"I don't think so. Everyone is being paid to do something, not think. Grant won't care. Advancing his agenda is his only concern. For us, it's about getting the money so we can do what it takes to get the killer's attention. For Grant, it's about his people getting paid hard dollars. If you figure ten people at one hundred dollars each, that's one thousand dollars right there."

"How will I pass for a cop?"

Jack chuckles. "Be serious, Sammi. What does a cop look like other than the uniform? Once you put it on, you're one of the clan."

"How do we deal with the people who live in the house next door if they object or ask questions or call the real police?"

As I ask the question, I know the question that has been unanswered now for months may finally get answered. Who lives in the "Boo" house? I remind Jack about the mystery occupants in the house.

"That's a potential problem. Maybe the smarter move is to get your friend Ren's cooperation, park our truck in front of her house, and then we're only two backyards away from your place instead of right next door. Either way should work. What do you think?"

Finally, I am asked to participate and I have absolutely nothing intelligent to contribute. Isn't that always the way?

I say, "Part of me thinks how can we take the chance? Another part of me says that whoever lives in the Boo house is not going to come out of the house or protest or ask questions no matter what we do. I can't believe they, he, she, whoever has remained this secretive and would risk being exposed because a movie truck is parked in front of their house. On the other hand, you never know. I hate to ask Ren because I haven't been confiding in her like I used to, but that's my fault, I think, not hers."

"We're not going to be there very long. There's a good chance that we'll be in and out before the person or the ghoul of your mystery house even realizes something is going on." Jack raises his arms and pretends he's a poltergeist. He looks as scary as Casper the Friendly Ghost.

I'm glad one of us can be playful about this.

I think out loud. "I don't know about the Boo house. Maybe they're dangerous. Maybe they have a drug lab in the basement, or it's a clearing house for stolen goods, or they're printing money, or who knows what."

On Jack's clean shaven face, his half smile looks particularly good. His mouth may not take the full route, but his eyes are sure laughing when he says, "You've been watching too many Edward G. Robinson movies. There's nothing illegal going on in that house. At least not that kind of illegal. Everything you've described smacks of a different kind of hiding. Whatever they did that they shouldn't have done has already happened."

I hate and love Jack's know-it-all attitude.

"How can you be so sure, Mr. Smarty-Pants? Who died and passed the crystal ball on to you?"

It's starting to get cool outside. A stray bird screams in the night, as if frantically trying to find a missing friend. The wail of a trumpet spreads through the hills like a mist blanketing the landscape. It's hard to tell if someone is playing a real trumpet or a recording. Throughout the canyon there is the occasional dull glow of lamp light straining through shuttered and curtained windows. The tip of Jack's cigarette is the brightest spot in the panorama.

"I don't have a crystal ball, Sammi. If I did, lots of things would be different." Jack looks the same but sounds wistful. "A lot of cop years give you an instinct. I don't think your neighbor is a professional bad guy. But that doesn't mean he's not someone with a secret. Many people have secrets. More than you might imagine."

I listen to Jack inhale. I hope it isn't blackening his lungs. It would be nice to know him as I grow old. I think about what he said and realize he is right—very right. Everyone has secrets and that's why it's so hard to know where to begin, who to suspect, who has a motive.

"Jack?"

He doesn't answer and I am surprised to see I have startled him out of his own private reverie. He still says nothing, but from the glow of his cigarette I can see that he is looking at me intently. I now have his full attention. I'm getting cold but I don't want to lose my thought.

"You're right. About the secrets. That's why no one can figure this out. Think about it. It started with me distrusting my best friend Ren and thinking she has secrets from me and a hidden agenda. She changed her look, her food, her scent, even her attitude. She started poking into her husband's files. I know she never did that before. She pretended to see and hear nothing from the house next door when a month ago she was consumed with curiosity. She came out of a photo shop with pictures she didn't want to show me."

"All of that could be innocent."

"I know, but it's not just her and it can't all be innocent. Benjamin had secrets up the wazoo. I'll probably never know a fraction of them. Then, of course, there was the girlfriend, Laura, his biggest secret. Now here it gets really odd. Bicky, who I hardly know, invited me to a writers' group. It turns out that Paul, the quiet beer-guzzling computer geek, knows Laura and has offices down the hall from Peter Perkal, victim number one. Bicky and her sister are as odd as can be and they met with Carol Haber, victim number two. Bicky is darting around Beverly Hills like a squirrel hiding nuts, with a copy of Benjamin's book under her arm. Why?"

I give Jack one of those intelligent piercing looks Angela Lansbury perfected when she played Jessica Fletcher investigating the deaths of two hundred of her closest friends in Cabot Cove.

"Sammi, really, it could all be coincidence. It's amazing how many investigations end up with precisely that as the answer."

"Let me finish, Jack. Maurice shows up at our meeting with a Tanya Brown book in his hand. Tanya Brown is . . . I mean was . . . Jonathon Harley."

"Aren't you getting a little off the beaten path? Secrets, remember? Maurice was holding a book. Not exactly qualifying conduct for having a deep secret."

"I'm making a bigger point, don't you see? It's all interconnected and doesn't seem to make sense, but it must. Then there's Blake, Ren's son. He's everywhere I turn and he's either crying or rushing or having clandestine meetings with Benjamin. Very suspicious."

"You said he met Benjamin in the Beverly Hills public library. I'd hardly call that clandestine."

"Everyone knows that the most private place is often public. Plain sight can hide a secret better than many cubbyholes."

"Did you read that in your last fortune cookie?"

I mentally stamp my foot. "No, but I did read it in Edgar Allen Poe."

He isn't laughing because Jack doesn't laugh. But he is laughing at me.

"And Stephen Martel, Ren's husband, what's the story with

him? Is he crooked, is he straight? Where there's life insurance, there's money, and even you said money is one of the primary reasons for murder."

Jack says, "Poor guy. He's hasn't even figured into this equation and he ends up getting the short end of the stick."

I shove Jack lightly in the arm. "Stop it. You don't know him. In a way, I hardly do after all these years. Why did you say that?"

"To show you how foolish you sound. Somewhere there is a connection but all you're doing is taking every conceivable oddity and throwing it against the wall to see what sticks. And nothing's sticking. And nothing will stick until we fill in the missing pieces."

"So how do we do that? And there's still the Boo house. Which has the biggest secret of all. I think we should park our movie truck there. Boo probably won't ask questions and Ren will ask too many." Without intending it, I am plotting and planning with Jack.

"I agree with you," he says. "As far as finding the missing pieces, I think we need to be patient."

"All things come to those who wait." I put my hands together and do an Oriental bow.

"Ah, more fortune cookie wisdom. I'm not sure about the wait part, but all things usually have a way of revealing themselves."

"So when do we make our debut in Beverly Hills?"

"I think we should be able to get everything we need in the next two days. Tomorrow is Tuesday, so I think we should plan on Thursday. I'll call Grant in the morning."

Jack's mind is going a mile a minute. I can tell.

"I'm going inside, Jack. It's getting cold out here."

"You're right. We should pack it in. We have a long day tomorrow."

Both of us stand up and start walking toward the sliding deck door to enter the house. Jack and I are so close we are almost touching. When he leans slightly to slide the door open, I can feel his body heat and I get a faint, fleeting whiff of his scent. Slightly musky, very masculine. Momentarily, I feel lightheaded. It's intoxicating.

"I just need to clean up. Wash some dishes before we . . ." What was I going to say? Go to bed?

Have I lost my mind? "I need to wash the dishes before we talk about tomorrow. Or we can talk about it while I clean up." Good save, I think.

"Yeah, that's fine. I'll get some clean towels for you and make up the sofa for me in the living room."

I was going to protest, say I'd take the couch, but then we'd end up sounding like one of those conversations from a 1960s movie and I don't want that. I don't want to spoil everything by having him think of me as Doris Day.

Jack joins me in the kitchen when I'm almost done. I have a lot of questions, but I'm tired. I want to thank him for his help, but it seems like the wrong time. Instead, I say, "Do you think I can go for my morning walk in the cemetery tomorrow? It's so close to here and I could be there and back before you want to get the day started."

Jack says, "Do you like movies with happy endings or do you prefer the ones with sad endings?"

It's such a peculiar, plucked-out-of-the-air question that I don't know how to respond. My automatic reaction is that I like happy endings. Doesn't everyone?

What are some of my favorite movies? *Bonnie and Clyde.* Driving their car unsuspecting and then ambushed on a warm summer day and dramatically shot dead. *Butch Cassidy and the Sundance Kid.* Butch and Sundance holed up in a mud-built hacienda in Bolivia, joking that they can outgun the few guys out there as the cavalry bombards them with artillery. And when Ingrid Bergman left *Casablanca* without Humphrey Bogart, that may have been a happy ending for freedom fighters everywhere, but it certainly didn't leave a dry eye in the audience.

Happy endings do not always a great movie make. Is that the answer Jack expects?

"I guess I like movies with sad endings. I mean that's not to say I don't like happy endings too, but just now, when you asked, I thought about some of my favorites and none of them have happy endings. What does this have to do with my taking a walk tomorrow morning?"

"Nothing at all. I could think of a thousand reasons why you shouldn't, but the more you try to outguess life, the more it tends to outguess you. So why not? If you want to take a walk and visit your pals, go ahead."

I am still confused. Very confused. How does this man's mind work? Will I ever figure it out?

"What does any of this have to do with movie endings?"

"Not a thing, directly."

"Why did you bring it up?"

"Because I'm thinking about the rest of our plan. The finale. That's the most important part. Just like in the movies. And we need a good finish and we want a happy ending. And I knew if I asked you that question, your answer would very likely be what it was. Sad endings are often a lot more interesting. We need to set our goal to be very uninteresting."

"And this relates to my taking a walk in what way?"

Jack shakes his head as if he feels sorry for me. It's such a sad look, it makes me feel sorry for me.

"Sammi, Sammi, long-suffering wife. Death dogging your footsteps. Wanted for murder. Daily visits to the graves of two men gunned down in their prime. Did you ever ponder the common denominators in your life?"

Perhaps not before, but now I am. So what exactly is Jack saying? That I am interesting but surrounded by sad endings? How am I supposed to respond?

"Jack, this isn't going to end up sad. We're going to pull this off. We'll trap the killer and the good guys will prevail. There'll be no sad or interesting endings."

I am saying this to a man who has a life littered with sad and interesting endings. I don't need to remind him of that because I can see it consumes him. He looks worried, skeptical, and alone. He is supposed to be my rock, but even a rock needs protection from some elements.

My father taught me the way to deal with this kind of adversity. So I give it a try.

"Look, Jack, I've thought long and hard and no matter what happens, I promise you I'm not going to suggest we go to Bolivia . . . like Butch and Sundance."

My dad, as always, was right. When in doubt, turn to humor. It works.

Jack laughs. I have pulled off the close to impossible. Jack laughed. It isn't long and it isn't hard, but the doubt has left his eyes and the spark is back. We are going to plan for a happy ending. It is the kind of ending that is long overdue for both of us.

Let the games begin.

# Chapter Twenty-Nine

I borrow Jack's car, a T-shirt, and ten dollars. The kind of borrowing married couples take for granted. The kind of borrowing girlfriends in new relationships read to mean there may be a future. I am trying not to jump to any conclusions.

From Jack's house, the drive to the cemetery takes five minutes instead of the usual thirty. How very convenient. Another point in Jack's favor. Not that he is in need of more points.

I leave a note saying I'll be back by 8:30 with juice, eggs, bagels, Diet Pepsi, and cream cheese.

The previous night I trundled into Jack's bed at eleven, curled into a cocoon, and lapsed into the best dreamless sleep I've had in ages. The sheets were tangled from Jack's sleep the night before. When I straightened them out, I imagined what it would be like to have Jack lying beside me. Nice.

The cemetery looks especially grim and unwelcoming today. It is starting out as one of those rare gray L.A. days. A sunless day in a city that has constant sun carries an ominous feeling of foreboding. The air is raw and damp. If you're a fan of horror films, it's one of those days you'd expect to find Freddie or Jason or any fictional nightmare character pop out from behind a tombstone.

I don't need a bleak day and unusual noises to make me jump. My imagination is already working overtime and doing an excellent job. It was a dumb idea to go walking alone in the cemetery.

The killer knows this is where I walk. What's to stop this demented being from showing up and finishing me off? I hear a whirring sound and let out a yell that could have awakened some of the less restful inhabitants of Hollywood Forever.

Visions of chainsaws and what I've seen them do to quivering innocents in horror films race through my head. Other kids watched sugar plums dance, but not me. The grotesque recollections of cut-up bodies makes me hyperventilate. I shut my eyes tightly and then quickly open them to locate the source of the noise.

Month after month I walk in this cemetery and never have I seen a gardener, yet today, there he is. Like a busy industrious bee, buzzing away at dead branches on one of the few oak trees in this palm tree–studded cemetery.

The presence of a friendly or at the very least non-deadly person allows my breathing to return to normal. My step gets back a little spring. I'm not off to see the wizard but I think I'll hike over to Bugsy and then Bill for a nice walk and a little one-sided conversation.

Someone else has visited Bugsy recently. There is a small but pretty bouquet of purple and pink flowers in the little brass-colored vase that hangs from a small suspended fixture next to his crypt. On gray days like today, the Beth Olam Mausoleum has a hollow feel to it, like one of those huge, old, tiled train stations long since abandoned. I start to tell Bugsy the whole story of what has happened, but then I stop. If he can hear me, it's fair to assume he can read my mind.

Even when we're adults, we make up the rules as we go. After months of talking out loud, I now decide he can read my mind.

The best lesson I can learn from Bugsy is to watch my back. For no good reason I get that prickly feeling like someone is creeping up on me. I turn but no one is behind me. Above me, I hear a sparrow vigorously pumping its wings, looking for an escape, after finding itself trapped in the mausoleum. The bird's flight is the sole sound in this huge cavernous building, and that only makes it seem louder and lonelier.

I leave the building and glance up at the Hollywood sign, which looks different than it does in the picture postcards they hawk on Hollywood Boulevard. Those pictures are taken on perfect, sparkling, sunshiny days. Today, in the gray somber of the morning, the sign looks singularly out of place.

Walking briskly, I reach the Cathedral Mausoleum within minutes, but hesitate to enter. If someone knows my routine, he can be hiding in the second arcade not far from Bill's crypt and waiting for me. I can still hear the gardener's whining machine chopping away. But why will that scare off a killer? I could be dead for minutes, hours, days before the gardener discovers me.

I don't go in. I turn around and start on the winding path back to the car. A few aerobic moments and a one-sided conversation with a dead director isn't worth the risk. In better days I'll return here and do all the explaining I want to Bill. He'll understand. He wasn't exactly a conventional by-the-book guy.

On the way back to Jack's house, I stop at one of those overpriced mini-marts to pick up soda and the breakfast staples I promised. Standing in front of the store, as if he moves around the city by some secret wand, is Plant Man, panhandling and drinking coffee from a paper cup. It looks like the tree growing out of his head has some new buds.

It's 8:15 when I knock on Jack's door. He answers, fully dressed, a cigarette hanging from his mouth, a cup of coffee in one hand and a gun in the other.

I look at the gun. "Is there something I should know, or is this your usual way of answering the door?"

He turns away from the door and I hear him say, "It's never boring."

A little panic and paranoia have returned.

"Has something happened?" Disregarding the tingles of alarm, I am unpacking the bagels and cream cheese and pulling dishes and silverware off shelves to set the table. In so many ways I've become my mother.

"Nothing's happened. Just being cautious."

Jack pulls a bagel from the bag and walks around the room, talking, eating, and making crumbs. Every woman notices the crumb-makers, even if it's not her house.

"Why don't you wait the extra thirty seconds it'll take for me to set the table?"

Jack flashes me one of those looks that lets me know he thinks I am acting like a clucking ninny.

Men hate that. I like him. I need to stop.

As if we experienced simultaneous regrets, Jack sits down at the table, stops chomping on the bagel, and waits and watches as I set out the dishes and food. Forget necessity. Compromise is the mother of invention. I like thinking we are on the path of inventing Sam and Jack.

"I spoke to Grant and he's in. In fact, he loves the idea. He's on the way to the mission now to recruit some 'players,' as he refers to them, for our Beverly Hills adventure tomorrow."

"Tomorrow?" It comes out sounding like a croak, which isn't what I feel. What I feel is panic. "Why so soon? Aren't we rushing this? Don't we have a lot to do?"

Jack gives me an appraising look. "That's what we decided. Have you changed your mind?"

Reluctantly, I shake my head.

"In that case, we need to get moving. You know what they say, strike while the iron is hot."

"Whatever that expression really means."

"Sammi, we need to get your life back to normal and we can't do that without finding the killer and we can't find the killer without our plan and that plan requires money which is in your sealed and cordoned-off house. Right?"

He is right about everything except getting my life back to normal.

"So," I say, "where do we start? What do we do first?"

I'm going to put myself in Jack's hands. He looks comfortable and confident. I am feeling neither. I guess that's how we pick leaders, kings, captains of teams.

"We need to rent a truck and get some lettering. If we put Studio Rentals on the truck, that should be fine. We can buy the letters at a hardware store or sign store. We need to get you a cop uniform and we probably need to pick up some clothing for the crew. They'll be in clean clothes when we pick them up, so if we buy ten matching jackets, maybe inexpensive windbreakers or something like that, I think they'll look like they're part of a team. If we could put the name of the movie we're making on the backs of the jackets, it would be even better. Maybe when we're out and about, we'll find something we can glue onto the jackets."

This man really does have a plan, really does have organizational skills. I feel pride in the fact that I picked him. Even though I really didn't. The killer picked him. Something about that still doesn't sit right. My mistrust of Jack is gone, but I'm not a big believer in coincidences.

"Why did the killer pick you to confront me in the cemetery?"

"Because your friend found my Achilles' heel, my brother. She or he thought I was vulnerable and desperate and might pull the trigger."

I'm still not satisfied. "Right, but that doesn't answer the question, Jack. Why you? Why would this person know your story? It would take ages to investigate different people to find the right person. She couldn't have selected random individuals and investigated all of them until she found one with a vulnerable spot, so to speak. How did she get to you?"

"What are you suggesting? That we look for a person who knows about my past and hates me?"

"Yes and no. I'm suggesting that somehow you and I have a person in common who hates me and knows about your past."

There's an expression: *The silence was deafening.* That's how it sounds in Jack's dining room all of a sudden. He gets quiet, puts down his half-eaten second bagel, and looks pensive, distracted.

He is thinking hard.

"We should deputize you, Sammi. You're right. I didn't think this through carefully. Sloppy thought process has led more than one cowboy down the wrong trail."

I'm not certain if Jack is pleased at how clever I am, or angry at how remiss he thinks he's been. At the moment, it doesn't make a difference. Figuring out the common link is what's important.

"So, how do we do this? I mention names and you mention names and we see who we know in common?"

Jack shakes his head. "If it were only that simple. Who knows how many people I've met? Perps, unhappy victims, other cops. The list could go on forever. We can give it a shot, but I have a suspicion it's not going to work that way. If it did, we'd have a killer who was significantly more nervous than he appears to be."

I make the obvious point. "Or she. After all, it's a woman who phoned you. It could be a woman."

"Could be. If it is, she's a very dangerous woman."

I think about the women recently in my world. Ren. Bicky. Dicky. Not the sort I would characterize as dangerous. Dr. Lana Green wanting to take revenge because of my Tom Cruise/Little

Rascals crack? Not likely. Bea, the realtor, gone wildly insane because she didn't get a listing? I don't know dangerous women. At the moment, I am the most dangerous woman I know.

I say, "Or dangerous man?"

Jack sighs. "Always leave your options open until you catch your man . . . or woman."

Recent men in my life: Could that idiot Denny Brillstein have gone berserk because he not only didn't get my divorce case but couldn't take Ben's case, either? Too ridiculous to consider. How does a dangerous man act? Did Jupiter feel his artistic integrity had been slammed when I didn't take Diane's hair appointment? Dr. Dan didn't think I was going to call the next day to have my body parts rearranged, right? Bob Kirby sells cars. He lives with rejection.

Maurice. Now there's an interesting character. He could have plotted this. But why? Because his real victim was Carol Haber and he was killing the others to draw attention away from him? He was reading Jonathon's Tanya Brown book that day—

What about Paul? The quiet, unassuming type is always a logical suspect. He was part of Jonathon Harley's writers' group. He has an office in the same building as Peter Perkal. He knows Benjamin's girlfriend, Laura. In fact, quite well it seems. Maybe they were in it together. But a gold-digging pinup girl hitching her star to Paul rather than Benjamin? Hard to imagine and to what end?

How about little and big Martel. What connection could Stephen Martel have to any of this? He is always busy wheeling and dealing. On the other hand, Blake popped up everywhere I was in the last week, and was with Benjamin in the library. Am I reduced to suspecting a fifteen-year-old as the prime suspect in a diabolically deadly murder plot? A major ingredient is missing: motive.

How do any of these people have even the remotest connection to Jack?

The cloistered and unhappy life I've led in the last couple of years has left me with few friends and few viable suspects.

"I can't think anymore, Jack. My brain is going to explode. The more I think about this, the less it makes any sense at all."

"Not uncommon with most puzzles. You're over-thinking it, which doesn't work. Let's go get these errands done and give your mind a rest. Let's accomplish something positive."

Jack has a patience that comes from understanding process rather than fighting it. I always fight it. When I couldn't be Barbra Streisand after four voice lessons, and knew I'd never be Charlie Byrd after three guitar lessons, I abandoned those pursuits. Result oriented without the patience for the process to get me there. And that partially explains why I married the wrong man.

"I never made you eggs. I bought them but . . ." I falter. The sentence has nowhere to go.

"There'll be other breakfasts."

A simple, slightly ambiguous statement that could mean nothing or everything, but my heart is bursting with optimism and happiness. The nice thing about ambiguity is that it's so ambiguous.

# CHAPTER THIRTY

If you live in Hollywood, you already know. Glamour, glitz, and galas left Hollywood years ago.

Forget what you've heard and read—it ain't pretty.

The face of Hollywood changes weekly. Hollywood Boulevard has turned into a T-shirt emporium with stores that go in and out of business as quickly as the traffic signals change. One day it's tired, with boarded-up stores and faded hookers. Other days there's a sparkle and there's talk about Hollywood seceding from Los Angeles and being a city in its own right. But one thing for which it is famous never disappears.

Hollywood Boulevard sidewalks are bronze star–studded with the names of famous film, radio, music, theater, and television personalities. Often, you can find a homeless person nesting for the night on one of those bronze stars embedded in pink terrazzo, curled up for the evening on the Hollywood Walk of Fame, resting his head on Jimmy Stewart's star. Maybe in the poor soul's dreams he's won the Oscar or Tony or Grammy and it truly *is* a wonderful life.

Near Highland, the handprints and footprints of the stars remain undisturbed by the earthquakes and graffiti-crazed gangs of Los Angeles. The only disturbance to those cement treasures is the name change of the theater that surrounds them. Grauman's Chinese Theater became Mann's Chinese Theater. I think it's Grauman's again. Ownership always takes precedence over history in this city.

Few visitors know that the prints originated as an accident. Silent screen star Norma Talmadge, while visiting the newly constructed theater, tripped and stepped into a sidewalk of wet cement.

And thus footprints, forevermore. Little Norma Talmadge and her sister Constance both buried at Hollywood Forever in the Abbey of the Psalms. Thirty years after she stumbled and became part of Hollywood history, she was interred in a cemetery a short distance away, a cemetery picturesque enough to be the background location for many Hollywood movies.

The famous HOLLYWOOD sign, reigning over Hollywood-land and now Hollywood, is the majestic, all-seeing presence. The most famous sign in the world. No one looks at it and ever thinks of the actress Lillian Millicent Entwistle, who committed suicide by jumping from the "H" in 1932.

Now Jack and Samantha will be "doing" Hollywood. Our first stop is a truck rental agency to obtain a credibly sized truck for our movie crew. After that, we plan to go to a store on Hollywood Boulevard to find suitable cop attire. It may sound like a strange place to look for a police uniform, but among the many stores on the street of bronzed stars are those that specialize in providing outfits for any sexual fantasy. It isn't a stretch to understand how cops play a role in the fantasy world.

Renting the truck is going smoothly, but the rental fee plus the steep security deposit is taking us close to maxing out Jack's credit card.

"I can charge another three hundred dollars and then we can hit my savings account, but that's probably at best a couple of thousand."

"Jack, I feel terrible, and I'll pay you back. We shouldn't need to touch your savings. Tomorrow we'll get the money from my house and then, when this is straightened out, well, you do realize I'm rich, don't you?"

Jack finishes the paperwork and the man helping us leaves to process the charge and get the keys to the truck. I'm driving Jack's car back to his house. He's going to drive the truck there and put it in the garage. Then we'll leave again in his car to go down to Hollywood Boulevard and get the windbreakers for our homeless crew. And my cop outfit.

I hate the way my words come out. This apologizing for having money has to stop. There are worse things a person can be than rich.

But rich I am, if I can vindicate myself. I hope I can use my own money to hire a lawyer because a casual turn of the head makes me realize how badly I'm going to need one. The *Los Angeles Times* is lying on one of the chairs in the truck rental office. The lower right-hand corner of the first page has an article about Benjamin's death that leads off by stating the prime suspect for his murder is missing . . . and is me.

Jack says, "Sammi, are you okay?"

I suspect that one paragraph has bleached ten years of California sun out of my face. I make a shushing noise. Jack looks startled and says, "What?"

"Don't say my name."

"Of course. You're right. But what's wrong?"

We're whispering in an empty office. We're like kids who started out playing a kid's game that has turned out to be an adult game . . . very adult.

I hand Jack the newspaper, but he waves it away, a dismissive gesture.

"I don't need to read what it says. They're looking for you. We know that already. That's what this is all about, and if you're going to fall apart because now you've seen it in black and white, then fall apart now and get it over with."

Of course he's right and he isn't being mean or even insensitive. Jack is sticking his neck out for me and I need to focus on our plan without crumbling over the obvious. There'll be plenty of opportunity for me to fall apart up the road.

I need to toughen up. As I come to this conclusion, Jack comes to one of his own, and in what is a definite softening of his hard line he says, "I'm sorry. I know this must feel like you landed on an alien planet. There must be a soda machine somewhere in this office. Do you want a cold drink?"

I'm flattered by his caring and further flattered by his starting to remember my likes and dislikes. I am a non-coffee drinker and it's nice not to hear the typical "Can I get you a cup of coffee?"

"That would be nice. Thank you."

As he is almost out the office door, I say, "And Jack, I'm really okay. You're right."

It's lousy timing because the words bounce off Jack's retreating back and land right in the face of our friendly truck rental salesperson, who is looking at me quizzically. *Very good, Sam.*

The man, whose name I've been too impolite to remember, is more polite than I and doesn't inquire about what I mean. He merely asks if everything is all right and I assure him that everything is peachy and we are ready to leave with the truck, if he is ready to give it to us. He gives me a strange look.

Maybe I acted too cheerful. Maybe I look too pale. Whatever it is, he now seems suspicious. I desperately try to think of a mundane, conversational comment. I need to do some normal boring talk like people do all the time. So how come I can't think of one thing to say?

"I guess we never really think about trucks until we need one, right? I suppose people must discover they need trucks all the time."

My statement is completely stupid. Worse than stupid. It sounds like an invitation to ask why we need the truck. And if he asks that and I don't have a prompt, reasonable-sounding answer, I'll look even more suspicious. Stress is causing my IQ to drop at an alarming rate.

In my head I am so busy planning the story about how I'm moving my home office to another location that I fail to register that Jack has returned, put my soda down on a table, exchanged the paperwork with the nameless salesman, and gotten the keys to the truck.

We are out of there.

"Don't forget your soda." Jack points at the cold drink he was kind enough to get me and which I have walked right past in what has begun to feel like my slavish devotion to following Jack. Whither thou goest, so do I, babe.

I follow Jack back to his house. No film crew today. It was a short shoot, just like the one we will appear to do tomorrow in Beverly Hills. Jack puts the rental truck in his garage. I keep the engine running, scoot over to the passenger seat as he climbs into the pilot's seat of the Explorer. Fly me to the moon.

We wend our way down the hill. Neither of us speaks. The silence would have been peaceful, almost comforting, if my stomach hadn't started growling in a less than ladylike manner. It sounds like a mourning dove's cooing call.

"We'll get something to eat when we get down to Hollywood Boulevard," Jack says.

I want to protest and say I'm not hungry, but I am. More importantly, we can't afford to squander the little money we have on food. I have to watch every dollar I spend. A week ago this would have been inconceivable.

"That's just my stomach wanting attention. I'm fine. We can grab a slice of pizza later. Let's get the things we need first. That's much more important." Than feeding my fat face. That's what I want to add but don't. After all, maybe one day this man will look at this very same face with lust and I prefer if he doesn't think of it in terms of smothering my fat face with kisses. Angelic face. Wounded face. Dare I hope beautiful face? But not fat face.

We find a meter in front of the Hollywood Roosevelt Hotel. Another part of Hollywood history. They've redone the hotel in an art deco fashion that plays up its long-standing role in the drama of Hollywood. In 1929 the first Academy Awards presentation was held at the Hollywood Roosevelt Hotel, where 250 attended and paid $10 per ticket. The first actress to win an award was Janet Gaynor for her performances in *Seventh Heaven, Street Angel,* and *Sunrise.* Just across the street from the hotel, one can find her footprints in the cement. And further up the road she is buried in Hollywood Forever. Janet Gaynor Gregory, born 1906, died 1984.

We feed the meter and start our walk up the boulevard. I can hear Jack's breathing. He smokes too much. Within seconds of my thinking that, he stops, pulls a cigarette from the pack, and with his thumb, lights a match single-handed. Just like a PI in a 1940s film noir.

In front of the Hollywood Wax Museum, a costumed employee dressed like Frankenstein is trying his best to induce customers to pay the price of admission and view tinsel town's celebrities in wax. On the south side of the street, where we are walking, I can see the giant toothy dinosaur that appears to have broken through the roof of Ripley's Believe It or Not "Odditorium." A huge clock is lodged in his mouth, much like a pacifier. Tick tock. I think of the clock always ticking in the alligator's stomach in *Peter Pan.* Tick tock. What am I forgetting?

The day has turned sunny. Gray in Los Angeles often disappears in a paintbrush stroke. People walk and talk and hip-hop down the boulevard, oblivious to Frankenstein and the dinosaur. Oblivious to the monsters. If only my monster was as easy to ignore. But it isn't. My monster kills people and my monster is after me. My monster is far more deadly.

While I ponder the philosophical unfairness of what is happening to my life, Jack attends to business.

"Look, I think these would be perfect." Jack is holding up navy blue windbreakers made from some material that literally crackles in the almost nonexistent breeze. It is the kind of jacket that will never survive the first dry cleaning.

I am trying to look at the price tag while Jack is showing me the bold yellow lettering on the back of the jacket. It says OUR GANG and then, in smaller letters: "in Hollywood."

"How much are they?"

"For a hundred bucks, plus change, we can get ten."

Ever the female in our gang, I say, "What sizes should we get?"

"Who knows? Let's get larges and a couple of extra larges and we should be fine."

I agree and start wandering the store to see what other jewels we can mine. In the row beyond, harboring ashtrays, erasers, paperweights, and snow globes, all bearing the likenesses of such Hollywood notables as Mickey Mouse and Marilyn Monroe, I find plastic handcuffs for $7.95.

I hold the cuffs up in the air, shake them slightly, and call out to Jack, "Do you think we could use these too?"

At least three tourists in the store snicker. Even Jack looks amused. Not to be the spoilsport, he answers more than audibly, "Sure. I think you'll look like a truly tough enforcer if we attach them to your uniform."

Now one woman looks angry and the two men have changed their positions to check me out. I feel their gazes warm my body. If we weren't in such a hurry and this wasn't as serious as it is and I wasn't wanted for murder, I might have been inclined to give them a little bump and grind.

Jack signals that he has paid for the jackets. We hurry out to the street and continue our march down the boulevard. When

Susan Goldstein

we get to Frederick's of Hollywood, Jack stops. "I think we should try here."

There is something, though I'm not sure what, that one should say about a lingerie store that has survived since 1946. It isn't just about musical panties that play "Happy Birthday." Frederick Mellinger had a vision. Maybe it originated with some girl he liked in her bra and panties, but Frederick's is one of the survival stories on the boulevard.

One can ascend a short flight of stairs to enter "The Celebrity Lingerie Hall of Fame," an exhibition of movie stars' underwear. I'm still trying to understand the attraction of Ethel Merman's girdle worn in *There's No Business Like Show Business* or Lana Turner's slip from *The Merry Widow* or Judy Garland's nightgown from *Presenting Lili Mars.*

Maybe it's just a question of there's no accounting for entertainment or taste.

In 1992, Frederick's got a more unusual footnote in Los Angeles history. After the Rodney King verdict, rioting spread to Hollywood Boulevard and Frederick's was looted.

Approximately $200,000 worth of lingerie was stolen. That's a lot of bras and panties. In another city, rioters would have zeroed in on the stores selling expensive appliances, but our rioters went for undergarments. They don't call it tinsel town for nothing.

"This isn't the type of stuff we need." Jack holds up a diaphanous slip. "Let's get out of here and find another store."

Jack is getting impatient. I don't blame him. Tomorrow is in place, all arranged, and we need to get our task done.

He grabs my arm, we hurry back onto the street . . . and we find the store. The mannequin in the window wears her cop outfit tight enough to make the prospect of her chasing any perpetrators an impossibility. But she doesn't need to worry as she already has her suspect under control. In fact, he is cowering under the whip that is clenched in her odd-colored man-nequin hand, while her face has a painted look of twisted determination.

I buy the cop outfit two sizes larger than the one in the window. Jack and I agree I should be able to both breathe and flex. It costs a lot more than I expected. These stores take advantage of people with unconventional tastes and weaknesses.

We leave the store and a man is walking with a board on his chest advertising the newest museum to arrive on the boulevard: The Museum of Death. A museum designed to educate the public about the many aspects of death.

I can skip that museum. I'm getting my education in the field.

# CHAPTER THIRTY-ONE

"Now let's get you something to eat. What would you like?"

Jack hasn't forgotten my grumbling stomach. We are walking past a pizza parlor and I point. We have little money left and I don't want to be a bother. Two slices of pizza can be a late lunch or an early dinner. Jack eats nothing.

Men are bigger. Food is the fuel. So why is it that we women always seem to eat more? Is there absolutely no justice?

We get to the car and head back to Jack's house. Neither of us has said much for a number of minutes.

"Jack, is anything wrong?"

We're driving up the hill to his home and I'm nervous. If Jack is starting to lose interest in this, I am doomed. I can't do it by myself and I can't be seen in public. I didn't worry when we were on Hollywood Boulevard, but that was Hollywood Boulevard. It's like an unspoken rule. No one there wants to be seen. Or to see.

Jack doesn't answer. If he's trying to worry me, he's succeeding. "Jack, hello, are you there? Have I done something wrong?"

He gives me that movement with his mouth that I am beginning to understand is sort of a smile. Not like in happy smile; more like bittersweet.

"Don't be silly. You haven't done anything wrong. I'm just thinking. We need tomorrow to go smoothly, very smoothly. One slip-up and someone could start thinking that something's not kosher and check with the Beverly Hills police. That's the last thing we need."

Jack sounds sincere but something is missing. Two days with this man and I can read the nuances in his tone. Years and years with Benjamin and I never had a glimmer.

"Jack, is there something else? Something you're not telling me?" I ask quietly, bordering on intimate. "I need to know everything. I don't want to be shielded like a child."

Jack looks at me. We are pulling in front of his house and the look is so startling, I gasp. It is as if he is looking right though me. Clark Kent has shed his suit. Hello, Superman.

"I don't want you to go to jail. Not even for one minute. I don't want you to ever know what that feels like. We have to find the killer. We have to make no mistakes. This time I'm going to get it right."

This is about me, but not completely and not only. This is about Jack's mom. This is about Grant. This is about Jack getting to his mom's house too late four years ago. Too late to stop the murder.

So now I know. Am I glad I know? Yes, no, maybe, I'm not sure. Yes, I'm glad I know. Not everything has to be about me. For the scars he carries, I am going to be the beneficiary of Jack's best. He is giving me his best.

He parks and we walk up to his house. It still looks warm and cozy. Jack would hate that description. He's not the warm, fuzzy type. I stop him as he puts the key into the door lock. I take his hand in mine and without expecting it to happen, I start to cry. I'm becoming a regular water works.

"I don't know how to begin to thank you. You are the luckiest thing that has happened into my life. You are a good man, Jack, and I hope one day you'll start to believe that."

Jack doesn't answer. No surprise. He turns the key, opens the door, enters the house, and avoids looking at me. The thought crosses my mind that maybe he is overwhelmingly touched.

Susan Goldstein

"I don't want you to thank me and I don't want for us to ever discuss me again. I'm not blaming you because I personalized this, but that was my mistake. From now on we have a project, we have an objective, and there is nothing other than that. We need to approach it with a single-mindedness that neither of us has ever given to anything."

Forget about overwhelmingly touched. Jack's words aren't intended to wound, but they cut through me as effectively as a sharp knife through watermelon.

Maybe my romantic delusions are my defense mechanism against what's happening. Truth be told, I haven't given more than a passing thought to what could happen to me if we don't find the murderer. I've avoided all thoughts of what a criminal trial entails. Mounting a defense or not being able to mount a defense, and going to prison for the rest of my life.

Thinking this way isn't constructive.

My grateful tears turn into self-pitying tears.

"I'm going to jail forever," I tell Jack. "I'm going to be one of those stories you see on *20/20* or *CNN* fifteen years from now, where they do one of those retrospectives about whatever happened to convicted murdering wives of famous dead authors. I'll be disgusting and old and babbling after fifteen years of prison life."

I stop for a minute and think about what I've just said. "No, it'll be worse. No one will talk to me in prison, so when a snoopy reporter wants to talk to me, I won't care what he says or does just so that I can have human contact with a non-convict. I'll be willing to confess to anything for some conversation and a good pastrami sandwich."

Now Jack is definitely smiling. The oddest things amuse this man.

"I'm glad you find this funny, Jack. First you say take this seriously and when I do, it's a big joke."

We are in his kitchen. I am sitting on one of the barstools and watching him do something. I have no idea what he's doing though I am watching intently. The result is what looks like red water.

"We should take this seriously, Sammi, and it *is* serious, but Joan Crawford melodrama isn't going to help. Are you nervous about tomorrow?"

Interesting question. Just as I hadn't thought about going to prison, I haven't given much thought to tomorrow. At least not the kind of thought that would make me nervous.

"No, I don't think I am. I guess it's because the idea of breaking into my own house doesn't feel criminal, even if it is. Hey, what are you doing?"

Jack holds up a long cylindrical glass with a fluted platform at the bottom. It's a hummingbird feeder. He has just filled it with a strawberry mix for the plump hummingbirds who have adopted his deck as their meeting place.

It is twilight and Jack's kitchen and living room have taken on that same soft glow as the night before. It's not a room that makes it easy to remember our circumstances are about life and death. "I guess we should turn on the news," I say.

I am trying to focus and be adult. All day I have religiously avoided the news, avoided radio, press, and television. But it's time for a reality check.

"Why don't you turn it on while I go outside and hang this for the hummingbirds?"

When Jack leaves I don't turn on the television. I sit and look at the room, his room, his space.

We each have our space and we each fill it differently. On the kitchen counter is *Heart of Darkness* by Joseph Conrad. From the placement of the bookmark, Jack has started the book recently.

Maybe last night.

He comes back into the room and looks surprised.

"I thought you wanted to watch the news."

"I did. I do. I was just looking at this book." I hold it up. "I read it a long time ago."

"I never read it. I told you that I'm on this mission to read great literature. Find out what I've missed and learn a thing or three."

"Yes, I know. I remember. It's just an interesting selection. I mean, did you see *Apocalypse Now*?"

"I watched it the other night on TV, and it gave me the idea to read the book. It's not the same."

"I agree. If I had never read the book and had just seen the movie, I would have done the same thing you did . . . get the book and read it." I hadn't intended for this innocent comment to come out sounding like I was a hyped-up, overzealous teenager, but it did.

Jack gives me a look. Sometimes I should just shut my mouth.

Am I a competitive show-off or the biggest kiss-ass in the world? Is he debating which?

Ignoring my comments, he says, "Are you hungry? Can you handle one of those frozen dinners? The cupboard is bare. Or I could run down the hill and go to the market?"

"No, don't bother. A frozen dinner is fine."

Jack heats up the oven, pours himself a beer, pours me a Diet Pepsi, and turns on the six o'clock news, which has already started. I'd hate to think I'm the lead story.

I'm not. After the first commercial break, they mention Benjamin's murder. They remind the viewers of his better-known books and two major films adapted from his books. Both received a lot of attention, though little respect. Then the too-cute newscaster says, "The police are now conducting an investigation to determine if there are any links between the murder of Benjamin Crowley and three deaths that occurred shortly before his. A publicist, Peter Perkal, who had worked with Crowley in the past, was killed in a mysterious hit-and-run accident. Crowley's agent, Carol Haber, appears to have been intentionally poisoned during a trip to Los Angeles. And Crowley's former editor, Jonathon Harley, was stabbed to death just outside his Studio City home only days ago. Until very recently, none of these deaths were linked, but now it appears, notwithstanding the different causes of death, that there is a connection. The police have declined to divulge what they've found as the investigation continues. Meanwhile, the wife of Benjamin Crowley, Samantha Crowley, remains missing and wanted by the police for questioning in connection with her husband's death. No one will say if she is linked to the other three deaths, but our inside sources tell us that she was definitely with one of the victims before that victim's untimely death."

By referring to "that victim," the broadcaster has made it impossible for me to know if it was male or female. Only Ren knows I saw Peter Perkal. Only Bicky and Dicky and Paul know about my meeting Jonathon. And only Maurice knows about my meeting with Carol. So one of them talked. One of them leaked the connection and it will be easy for the police to start making the other connections.

Someone is sabotaging me. My tie to Maurice is the most tenuous, so he is the most likely candidate, I think.

"Someone is trying very hard to get me in as much trouble as possible."

"So it would seem." Jack shuts off the TV. He has taken the frozen dinners out of the oven and scooped the contents onto plates for each of us. "You can eat as many as you want, Sammi. I've got a freezer filled with them."

I taste mine . . . cheese cannelloni. It isn't bad. "I think one will be enough for me, Jack."

We sit quietly and eat. It doesn't feel awkward. It has the

natural feeling of the ritual of a long marriage. I wish I could shake this comfortable feeling. It has been so easy coming to me and is going to be so hard to forget when I'm gone. Gone to prison or back to Beverly Hills—both now seem like jail.

"We should get to work soon," Jack says. "We need a good night's rest and it'll take about an hour to get the truck ready."

His words mean nothing to me. I'm not tracking the conversation. It's as if I picked up in the middle of a monologue.

"I'm sorry, Jack. I don't understand. Get to work? What are we doing?"

"The truck. We have to buy the lettering and glue it on, remember?"

Where are we going to find lettering at eight o'clock at night?

Before I can ask, Jack says, "There's a Home Depot near me, open twenty-four hours. We can go over there now. It shouldn't be too crowded."

Twenty-four hours? Who shops at Home Depot at two or three in the morning? Do people sit up in bed at 3:00 A.M. and think *I've got to go buy a wrench or nail?*

I promise myself that when this is behind me, I will set my clock for two-thirty in the morning and drive to Home Depot to see who is actually shopping at that hour.

At the much more respectable hour of 8:00 P.M., Jack and I are on our way. Although I insisted on coming along and he didn't fight my somewhat incoherent doggedness, he decides we shouldn't press our luck, so I wait in the car while he runs into the store. What's that expression about idle hands? With nothing to do other than sit, I open Jack's glove compartment. It's snooping but I mean no harm.

The glove box is jammed. I run the risk that if I remove one thing, I may not be able to cram it all back. If the past few days have taught me nothing else, it's to be daring. I remove the flashlight first, which gives me access to the good stuff . . . papers.

Registration papers, insurance card, maintenance records, two maps, a business card of a woman named Rita, her home number written on the back, a parking ticket, and a newspaper clipping about Peter Perkal and his public relations firm, an article from eons before Jack and I first met in the cemetery.

I will myself to postpone falling apart until after I've squeezed everything back into the glove box. By more neatly stacking the papers, I am able to make it all fit. I feel zero concern about whether or not Jack will notice. In fact, I hope he does.

Why is this man, a total stranger, being so nice to me? I am flooded with the old suspicions and new ones. I stopped thinking for myself and literally thrust my entire safety into Jack's hands. Why does he have an article about Peter Perkal if he doesn't know Peter and he hadn't yet met me? I can't think of one good explanation.

I hear the car door opening before it registers what I'm hearing. I let out a scream that would have gotten me, in a heartbeat, the lead in yet another remake of *King Kong*.

"What's the matter? Are you all right?"

Jack looks concerned and I feel sick. I decide to stick with the truth.

"I feel sick."

Now Jack looks genuinely dismayed. "I'm sorry. I should have insisted you stay home. Look I can do the lettering myself while you hit the sack. You need a good night's sleep."

I don't agree. I don't disagree. One minute I'm ecstatic, one minute I'm sick. I wonder if Jack has gotten to Charles Dickens yet. If he has, he may better understand that—for me—life is flip-flopping between the best of times and the worst of times.

For the second time today, we pass the Museum of Death. Maybe I should take it as an omen.

## CHAPTER THIRTY-TWO

I tiptoe very quietly to the refrigerator to look for a soda. It is only 6:00 A.M. and I don't want to wake Jack. From the position of the bookmark, he made no further progress reading *Heart of Darkness*.

When I open the refrigerator door, I am startled at how brightly the refrigerator light illuminates the kitchen and I peek at the couch to see if I have awakened him.

He isn't there. The bad feeling that started last night when I found the article in his glove compartment comes flooding back full force. I drink the soda straight from the bottle and slam it down on the counter, loud, as if to say, *I don't give a damn if I wake you.* Strong body language for an empty room. I choose my audiences carefully.

We aren't expected to pick up Grant and his group until 9:00 A.M. Jack isn't the jogging sort, so I have no clue where he is. After my pronouncement the previous night that I felt sick, we had a silent ride home and I went straight to bed. When I fell asleep, I heard Jack in the garage working on lettering the truck . . . without me. I feel guilty, but mostly I feel confused.

I pad through the living room, into the hallway, and open the door that leads to the garage. Jack has done a good job. In prominent yet understated brown letters, the truck now bears the moniker Studio Rentals. It looks authentic and yet surreal. I like this Dickensian thing. You can affirm and contradict simultaneously. It pretty much sizes up how I'm feeling about life these days.

I hear the front door opening as I reenter the house. I am still in my sleep outfit, Jack's oversized T-shirt, which my nipples now prominently pierce in response to the very cool garage air. Jack looks at me. I look at Jack. He pretends not to notice and I pretend not to notice him pretending not to notice.

I go for casual, nonstop sentences. "Hi, where have you been this early? I thought I was up before you and was tiptoeing around not to wake you. I figured you would sleep in a little after being up so late. I saw the lettering and it looks great. You did a really good job. I'm sorry I wasn't much help."

I would have continued babbling if Jack hadn't held up a bag and his hand to give me the cease-and-desist signal.

"Whoa, slow down, Sammi. Are you feeling better?"

I nod yes and squeeze my eyes tight to stop myself from crying. He's considerate, he's smart, he's good-looking, he's capable. Why am I constantly looking for excuses to distrust him?

"Good, I'm glad, because we've got a long day. I left to get more coffee, eggs, and bacon, you know, protein. We don't want to lose steam. Anyway, I wasn't up all that late. The letters went on pretty easily and I think it looks good."

He isn't beaming and he isn't bragging. Jack just tells you what he thinks. I don't respond.

Staring at him, I experience too many conflicting emotions. I am starting to better understand the expression the kids on my street frequently use: "This is getting weird." I'm standing in a T-shirt in a strange man's house, a man who has just done breakfast shopping for us, as if this is my normal routine. And I am wanted for questioning about multiple murders. This is getting weird!

"Sammi, why don't you shower and get your gear together and I'll make breakfast."

So that's what I do, and emerge from the bedroom to the smell of sizzling bacon.

My stomach starts a low growl, my new mantra. I refuse to look in the mirror to see what I look like. I already know. Ridiculous. The cop outfit feels stiff and awkward. I should have thought of that yesterday and run it through the wash to soften it up.

Under different circumstances, it would have been fun to walk into the kitchen and bark a cop line like, "Put your hands where I can see them," but I'm not feeling frolicsome this morning. Instead I say, "That bacon smells good."

"Officer, we'll soon have you fed and ready to hit those mean streets." Jack gives me a half grin.

Maybe he doesn't think I look as ridiculous as I feel. Or maybe he's just being nice.

"I look stupid, don't I?"

"No. Actually, you look like my old partner except for the rounded hips, smaller, nicer butt, shapely legs, protruding frontal extremities, and good-looking face. Otherwise, I wouldn't know the difference."

I think it's a compliment. Does good-looking face mean pretty, or that I had a smoother shave than his old partner? I'm back in the flip stage of flip-flop. Liking him and wanting him to like me.

Jack says, "Once you put on the shades, you'll look like the real thing. The uniform looks good. A cop would know the difference but not a civilian. Do you have sunglasses in your bag?"

I don't think so. I shake my head no while I attack the scrambled eggs and bacon. Jack is eating standing up while he talks and paces. At last a man who can walk and chew gum at the same time.

Benjamin never liked to talk at meals. Or maybe he didn't like to talk to me.

"No problem, I'll lend you my sunglasses. We're picking up Grant and his gang near the courthouse. We should probably give ourselves half an hour to get there in case we hit traffic."

I nod and let Jack speak. My Svengali. There has to be a good reason the Peter Perkal article is in his car. Why don't I have the nerve to just open my mouth and ask? Since when am I a shrinking violet?

Answer: Since now when there is so much at stake.

"I'm all set, Jack. What time is it now?" I look at the clock and see it is 7:40. "We have a little less than an hour."

He hits the remote and the TV screen fills with the smiling face of a *Today* host, whose normal grin turns somber when she says, "Coming up we'll be doing a retrospective on the life of the much-loved and respected author, Benjamin Crowley. We'll talk to some of his friends and discuss the mysterious circumstances of his tragic and untimely death."

A commercial for fabric softener follows. I wonder if Benjamin is watching from his new abode and finding it undignified to be remembered and then segued into a fabric softener ad.

Jack looks at me with no expression. "Do you want to watch or shall I switch it off?"

"Maybe we'll learn something, who knows? Let's keep it on."

"You have a point. What friends will they interview?"

Good question. As far as I know, Benjamin had no real friends. I shrug.

The retrospective is complimentary and factual but nothing new. Benjamin's accomplishments, including his books, the movies from his books, computer games, and other marketing gizmos that had evolved from the character, Hunter McCall, are summed up in five minutes. We are forced to endure another commercial break before my curiosity is satisfied.

The first person interviewed is Maurice. If you gave me a hundred thousand guesses, he would not have made the cut. He looks perfectly coiffed and even more effete than usual. He explains his relationship with Carol and her relationship with Benjamin and his relationship with both of them. He explains his connection to the two in a way he would never have had the nerve to do if either of them were still alive. Little Maurice is getting a taste of celebrity and power. He ends the interview with the enigmatic comment that he has his own theories about their terrible, terrible deaths.

I wonder who would rate only one terrible. At least Maurice has a connection of sorts to Benjamin. The next interview is more astonishing. I almost spill my glass of soda. Bicky and Dicky, in what look like new yellow and purple matching muumuus, are being asked how they knew Benjamin. Bicky is shyly answering that he encouraged them to write their book.

Apparently, Benjamin frequently bought pastries from Bicky and occasionally from Dicky and they had engaged him in a running dialogue about their desires to write their family history. According to the sisters, Benjamin told them "write, write, write," and that's just what they did. Now they have a seven-hundred-page opus, which they hope some publisher will want to look at since it had Benjamin's seal of encouragement.

I am dumbstruck. Neither of them ever told me they knew my late husband, let alone that they had any relationship with him.

The next interviewee is equally disturbing. Can I still be surprised? Most definitely.

It's Ren.

My best friend, the same person who held my hand and took me to a divorce lawyer, is about to eulogize my dead husband. But all she says is that Benjamin was her neighbor, friend, and her son's godfather, and his death left everyone saddened and shocked. Ren is so good, I wonder if she has a publicist. She looks fantastic. Her magic red hair is shimmering and bouncing gently with the movement of her head. Her body is wrapped in a forest green pantsuit that fits like a second skin and makes her look like some exotic jungle creature.

I point at the TV. "That's my best friend, Ren. She's gorgeous, isn't she?"

Jack looks at me and shrugs. "She's okay. But if she's your best friend, what's she doing on the *Today* show?"

I shrug back. I'm out of answers.

The last person interviewed doesn't know Benjamin at all, but considers herself an expert on almost everything. Dr. Lana Green is being asked if there doesn't seem to be an abnormally higher rate of tragic deaths in tinsel town compared to other cities in the country where lives are more humdrum.

Dr. Lana's numerous bestsellers are all about relationships. I wonder when she became a homicide expert. I suppose one could make the leap. She insipidly drones on. I am mentally wandering off when I hear my name. Not one of the other people interviewed mentioned me. Dr. Lana says, "I made numerous efforts to volunteer my services to Benjamin's wife, Samantha, before this tragedy occurred. I blame myself a little. Perhaps if I could have been more persuasive with her about getting help, this incident could have been averted."

Dr. Lana has just referred to Benjamin's murder as an "incident."

But of far more horror to me, Dr. Lana Green just told the world on national television that I'm a murderer. Jack is looking at me strangely. I'm not sure what he thinks, but I have a pretty good idea of what the rest of the United States is thinking. Right now in Red Cloud, Nebraska, a mother is probably making breakfast for her children and husband before they go off to school and work, and she's saying, "Look at that, honey, the famous lady doctor in Beverly Hills says that this famous writer, Benjamin Crowley, was killed by his wife. You know that guy.

He writes the books about that Hunter feller you like so much."

The show goes to commercial and I look at Jack and ask him to shut it off.

Jack says, "Do you know Lana Green? Have you ever met her?"

I explain to Jack the sum total of my two brief encounters with Dr. Lana, the luncheon a long time ago and her accosting me the other day in Beverly Hills.

Jack looks incredulous. "That's it? She went on national television just now and said what she did based on that?"

I nod.

"Do you think there's more to it?"

"I don't know. I wouldn't think so. She didn't know Benjamin or me. Neither of us has ever seen a therapist. I just don't know."

"Leaving only one other explanation."

"That being?"

"She wanted publicity for herself. You saw how they plugged all her books again and gave her a highfalutin introduction. This is Hollywood. You can never be too thin, too rich, or too famous."

*Is that a fact, Jack? At the moment, I am feeling far too famous.*

# CHAPTER THIRTY-THREE

Six homeless men and a guy who bears a strong resemblance to a young Alan Ladd are standing on the corner when Jack and I pull up in the rental truck. It is really happening.

The men quietly shuffle into the back of the truck as if they are under arrest. It makes me nervous and sad and self-conscious about using people. But we are going to pay them for their time and the back of the truck is loaded with doughnuts and thermoses filled with coffee. A last-minute idea that came to Jack and me at the exact same time. We are in sync in so many ways.

Grant and Jack don't look alike, but do look like brothers. They have similar eyes and the same kind of mouth. The kind that is reluctant to smile.

Grant nods at me and gives Jack a slight touch on the shoulder. I am sandwiched between the two of them and disinclined to be the one to get the conversation rolling.

Jack speaks to his brother without taking his eyes from the road. "Grant, this is Samantha. Samantha, this is Grant."

Grant nods again and I say "hi" a little shyly. I am suddenly aware of the fact that I want very much for Grant to like me and that we couldn't be meeting in a more unusual way. Grant doesn't know who I am and why we're doing what we we're doing. I am sitting next to him, wearing a police uniform and Jack's sunglasses, which are so dark I am certain no one can see my eyes. Usually, a lot of what I say is in my eyes.

It's a good minute before anyone speaks again. It feels like a long, awkward silence, but when I look at the brothers they don't seem to notice.

Jack says, "We have jackets for the guys and you in the back. Like I told you, I don't expect them to do anything other than stand around and drink coffee. I don't want them to go wandering off. You make sure of that."

We discuss what people would expect to see our crew doing. Jack and I agree that most of the time when you pass studio trucks filming in residential areas, the only thing you see is the token uniform cop and a lot of guys standing around doing nothing, except drinking coffee.

"It'll be fine." Grant's voice is not as deep as Jack's. "I'm a few guys short. Is that a problem? I think they drank too much last night and I couldn't wake them."

"It's no problem at all. In fact, it's probably better to have fewer. It makes it less likely for anything to go wrong."

We are back to silence. Until Grant says, "So, Samantha, I understand that we're going to your house so you can get some things. And you needed a diversion. I don't imagine you're really a cop."

I'm flustered and unsure how to respond. If this is how I react with one of my co-conspirators, I don't want to think how I will act if confronted by a stranger. I hope this goes smoothly. Jack and I never had the conversation that starts with "What if?"

"No, I'm not a cop. Grant, I want to thank you for doing this. You don't know me and it's really a great kindness. Even your brother doesn't really—"

I catch a fleeting look from Jack and stop. He hasn't told his brother anything other than what he needs to know and I am babbling unnecessary information. I'm already involving Grant in a crime. The less he knows, the better. It's still hard to believe

I need to break into my own home.

"Anyway, Grant, it is my house and I need to get some stuff and, well, life has been complicated lately. We don't have your money yet but I have it in the house and I'll bring it out for your guys."

Jack is frowning. I should shut my mouth.

We drive the rest of the way without conversation. In the back of the truck, we can hear the guys occasionally talking and laughing. Life can be ironic. It feels like there is more normalcy in the back of the truck than up front. Six homeless men can still find something to laugh about. Jack, Grant, and I look like grim, grimmer, and grimmest.

My heart almost stops when I see my street. It feels as if I've been gone for a long time. The past few days make my life before feel like a different lifetime. I am a stranger looking at someone else's house. Never before have I seen my house this way. It is beautiful, grandiose, monstrous.

Jack glances at me and then, as we agreed, he drives another block and lets me out. It won't look right if the cop gets out of the truck with the film crew.

I watch the truck drive off toward my house as I start walking in that direction. It is 10:00 A.M. Four gardeners are attending to a massive lawn. At one house, painters on a ladder are scraping off old paint at a slow pace. A nanny has a cute little boy out in his stroller for a morning walk. He smiles and waves at me.

This is a place where I've had little joy. I'm sad and disappointed with my life.

Jack is parked in front of the Boo house. I don't see him or Grant and assume they walked to the back of the truck to let out our gang. I walk to the rear of the truck and enjoy the sight. It's kind of cute. The guys have already discovered the jackets and put them on. One of the men who weighs no more than

120 pounds has put on the extra large, which is almost down to his knees, but he looks happy. His left hand is shoved deep into the pocket while his tongue licks his sticky right hand. I glance at the box of donuts and see it is empty.

Grant decided caps would be a good idea and purchased them for the guys. Each guy has a navy blue cap with the imprint #1. Some of the guys have buzz cuts, others have hair that one would kindly call untamed. They look like the cast of patients from *One Flew Over the Cuckoo's Nest*.

Grant is talking quietly to the guys and though one of them is distracted by a candy wrapper that is floating down the street on a gentle wind current, the others are looking at him with rapt attention.

Our plan is that Grant will stay by the truck with the guys and they will periodically look like they're checking something in the back of the truck. I am going to circle my house to the rear and break in through the back patio door. Jack will be coordinating between the front and back to make sure that everything is going smoothly, and he will field any questions from passersby if we are unlucky enough to have someone ask questions.

"Wish me luck." I don't know what else to say.

The stiff black patent leather shoes we purchased with the police costume are already starting to pinch in two places. I can tell I will be contending with blisters tomorrow.

Jack tries to be low key and supportive. "That's just what I was going to say. But you won't need luck. It'll be fine. Don't forget to grab a garbage bag and get some of your clothes."

As if I would have forgotten clothes, makeup, shoes, conditioner.

I walk along the side of my house and look at my roses. I haven't thought about them once. I have a little pang of guilt. I think about George Washington making the time to tend to his flowers, and then consider that clearing myself of a murder charge might be even more work than George had in running a brand new country.

The sound of a basketball bouncing on pavement and clanging against the metal rim from a missed shot resonates from the house next door. Boo's house. What in the world is going on?

The way our backyards are situated, I will be able to clearly see the basketball player and he can see me when I make the turn to my rear patio door. The large trees that decoratively and effectively divide our yards have what I've always referred to as a midlife bald spot. It's a small clearing where we can each see into the other's yards when standing in particular spots.

I make the turn and see two boys playing basketball. I gasp when I realize that one of the boys is my godson, Ren's son, Blake. I don't recognize the other boy. Blake sees me, too. Jack and I should have talked about the "what ifs." I haven't yet broken into my house and already I'm busted.

The other boy runs into the Boo house. Blake, never a shy child, yells loudly, "Mom, Mom, there's a cop here! She's in Samantha's yard!"

Blake doesn't recognize me. How is that possible? A cop uniform doesn't change who I am. But then I consider the fact that my hair is pulled back, I am wearing dark sunglasses and, most significantly, no one expects a cop to be me or for me to be a cop. It is true, after all, that our perceptions can be manipulated. What we expect to see can control what we see. Blake is seeing a cop. Samantha is not a cop. The cop is not Samantha.

What is more astounding is that he has called for his mom through the door of the Boo house and not their house on the other side. I am living a tale stranger than any of the novels Jack is reading. Ren walks out the back door of the Boo house. She holds a dishtowel to wipe her wet hands. Has she been washing dishes in the Boo house? A cigarette hangs from her mouth.

Will my best friend in the world recognize me? I step backward, trying to put as much distance between us as will appear natural. The farther away I stand, the more difficult it will be for her to see my features.

"Blake, get in the house. Now." Blake scoots into the house. "Hello, officer, is there a problem?"

I push Jack's dark sunglasses further up the bridge of my nose. Then, I turn my head as if examining something in the yard. A profile will be harder to identify. How am I going to sound like a police officer? How does a police officer sound? I think about Blondie and Sancho and get no guidance.

She will recognize my voice. Can I change it?

And, what am I doing at the house?

I have to answer her question with a different voice. The fewer words I speak, the safer I'll be.

"No problem. They're filming a movie. I've been assigned to . . ." What have I been assigned to do? This was the part we envisioned Jack playing. He was the voice.

But Ren isn't all that interested and I don't need to finish. She cuts me off. Of course she isn't all that interested. I suspect she has as much to hide as I do.

"Oh, sure, I understand. They're shooting movies all the time in this city."

She laughs with what I know to be her phony laugh. She is nervous and wants me to go away as much as I want to go away. But I want to understand what's going on.

In my new lower and slightly nasal voice, I say, "I'm sorry to have disturbed the boy's game. Are those your boys?" Her face burns pink. If I had been a real male cop, I would have thought she looked adorable. If I had been a female cop, I would have been inappropriately jealous of her. But I'm her best friend and I know the pink means she's deeply upset.

"Yes, those are my boys. You didn't disturb them. They have to come in and clean up and get ready for lunch."

"Is this your house?"

She gives me a suspicious look and I realize I've crossed a line. There would be no earthly reason why a police officer would have ever thought for one minute that this isn't her home and ask such a question.

"Of course," she says with an edge that I detect.

"Sorry to have bothered you, ma'am. Have a nice day."

I start walking toward the patio door and her voice follows me. "I don't understand. If you're supervising a film shoot, how come you're going into the house?"

Ren is always smart. She didn't like the cop asking her questions, so now she's putting the cop on the defensive. I'm smart, too.

"There are some things I've been requested to do here, ma'am, but if you have questions, I don't mind coming into your home and calling headquarters and having you speak to my lieutenant."

"No, I'm sure it's fine," she says, her bravado gone. "Have a nice day, officer."

Getting into the house isn't hard. I pry the patio door open with plenty of time to punch in the alarm code. No one bothered to change the combination. The hard part is walking into a house that used to be mine and now feels like a strange place. I want to cry. No time for self-indulgence. Eight men are in the street sticking their necks out for me.

I twist the oak newel post at the bottom of our stairwell and it resists. I twist harder and it budges and then turns. A long time ago, when I first started feeling unloved, I got it in my head to hide money. It was a silly thing for a wealthy woman to do, but I did it anyway. I hope each dollar doesn't represent each day I felt unloved, because if that's the case, I've been a very unhappy woman for a very long time. I shouldn't take the time to count, but I do. There's eleven-thousand-two-hundred-and-fifty dollars. Jack and I are rich. Temporarily.

I cut through to the kitchen, grab a garbage bag from under the sink, and head upstairs to my bedroom. By the time I'm done with clothes, shoes, cosmetics, and such, I'm dragging the bag. I should have double bagged it. Hopefully, it won't break before we get into the truck. Hopefully, it won't break right in front of Ren. I can see the headlines: LOCAL BEVERLY HILLS COP STEALS ACCUSED MURDERER'S HAIR CONDITIONER.

I am done and ready to leave. I exit the same way I came in. Now I'm hurrying. The heavier items in my garbage bag bang against my marble steps as I drag it down the flight of stairs. At the landing I decide there is one last thing I should do: play the messages on my machine.

Jack and I agreed that it was too dangerous for me to call in for my messages. The cops may have a way of tracing the number I am calling from. But I'm here now and the only downside is time. It would be foolish not to check. There may be a clue.

The machine isn't blinking, which means either there are no messages or someone has listened to them. It's possible they may not be erased. I end the suspense and push the play button.

A voice announces, "Ms. Crowley, this is Maurice. I think it would be a good idea if we got together. I think it's important. I'm staying at the Beverly Hilton Hotel. You can reach me there."

Message Number Two: "Samantha, this is Bicky and I'm calling for Dicky, too. We just think that everything happening is so dreadful. We're so sorry we didn't tell you that we knew your husband but we didn't want to upset you. We would really like to see you and try to make it up to you. The best place to reach us is my bakery. Hope to see you soon. Bye."

The machine moves on, "Ms. Crowley, this is Dr. Lana Green. I want to, once again, offer my assistance in your troubled time. I think we should get together. I strongly suggest it. You can reach me at my office."

Message Number Four: "Sam, I am so worried about you. I love you and I've been stupid and kept secrets from you. I hope you get this wherever you are. I must see you. Please see if you can find a way to contact me." It is Ren. Only five sentences and I hear her inhale twice. I have a feeling she is smoking more than usual.

The machine says, "You have no other messages."

My callers are the same four people I saw on the *Today* show. Jack and I will sort it out later. I rush out of the house and head to the front. Jack sees me and I hear him call out, "Okay, guys that's a wrap for today. We're going to head back and hit the other location tomorrow."

I watch my little motley crew grinning and passing around the thermos. Grant is the head cheerleader while Jack stands away from the group, acting as the lookout. I'm not so sure we are as inconspicuous as we think. A curtain moves in the Boo house and I'm certain someone in there is watching us do nothing. I am equally sure no one in that house is going to call the police. That house has its own mystery.

One of the men has his cap on backward like a good old homeboy. Another has removed his cap and it is sticking out of his jacket pocket. Yet another has folded up the cap and it's protruding from his shirt pocket like a handkerchief. The men are slowly climbing into the truck. Grant looks calm. Jack looks relieved. It's over.

"Did everything go all right?" Jack asks the question rhetorically, the way we do when we assume the answer is "fine."

"Almost all right," I reply, startling him. "Let's say more

245

interesting than either of us expected, but I don't know if it has anything to do with me. We'll talk when we get home."

He nods and we roll out of Beverly Hills, making a clean getaway—me and my #1 gang.

# CHAPTER THIRTY-FOUR

"Sammi, you have to think of this as the first half hour of a poker game that's going to go all night."

Since dropping the "boys" downtown, returning the truck, and getting back to the house, Jack has been repeatedly reminding me that it is too soon to celebrate victory. Liberating my money was only step number one. We are still no closer to finding Benjamin's killer.

I want to talk about finding Ren and Blake in Boo's house. I want to talk about the messages on my answering machine and what they mean.

Jack wants to talk about one thing: How do we go about keeping me hidden but having one person, a killer who we don't know, find me.

"It's impossible." That's what I've been telling Jack for the last hour. "You've created an impossible scenario."

We turn on the TV and I find myself looking at me. It's pretty strange to see your face on the afternoon news. My fingerprints were found all over Benjamin's writing studio. What a stroke of masterful police work. I am the man's wife and there is little doubt I was at the studio right before the police. I guess the real point is that they haven't found anyone else's prints. No surprise there. Our killer doesn't leave any calling cards, other than me. Someone is throwing me to the wolves.

And if someone is throwing me to the wolves that means he needs to find me as much as I need to find him. Or her.

"Jack, think about this. Whoever is doing this needs to find me. It's got to be better for that person to locate me before the police do. Our killer isn't sure what I know."

"I agree. That's been my thinking all along, except for the problem you pointed out before. We don't know who it is."

"But maybe we do."

"What do you mean?" Jack gives me a questioning look.

"Four people called me, if you count Bicky and Dicky as one. All of them said they wanted or needed to see me. Four people are looking for me. No one else left messages. Isn't it probable that one of them is trying to find out what I know and where I am?"

Jack is looking at me intently. The sun is beaming into his living room where we are sitting, and I hope it doesn't illuminate every wrinkle and the little baby crow's feet that have taken up residence in the corners of my eyes.

"Sammi, you're a genius." Jack's look makes me blush.

Is his look a display of a proprietary interest? Is Jack thinking of staking some new territory? Because if he is, I'm ready for him to plant his flag.

I wait for Jack to resume. I don't want to ruin the moment.

He says, "I've figured out how to let the killer know what you know and give our friend a good reason why he or she really wants to see you before you're found by the cops or turn yourself in. We're going to make someone very scared of you."

I grimace at the idea of the killer being scared of me. "How are we going to accomplish that?" I don't wait for Jack's answer. I need to vent my frustration. "Jack, I'm not getting this. How are we telling a killer, who we don't know, anything? And what could we possibly say that will rattle him?"

"I think I've got this worked out. I agree it's probable one of the four people who telephoned you is responsible for the mayhem."

I wonder if only cops and former cops use the word *mayhem*. "You mean that one of them is the killer? That's not possible. I didn't say that. If I said that, it's not what I meant." I'm having a hard time formulating my thoughts "I just said they wanted to know what I know. I can't imagine any of them being the murderer. It makes no sense. Bicky and Dicky didn't know Benjamin well and hardly know me. Maurice was Carol's gofer. Dr. Lana doesn't know us. Ren is my best friend. They'd have no reason." I can tell by the sound of my voice that I'm becoming unglued.

Jack ignores my pending hysterics. "Remember how I said we need to advertise to make the killer fear you? We need a quick attention grabber. I've given this a lot of thought. There are many ways to do something like this. We could take out a full-page ad in the *Los Angeles Times* but that would cost more money than you took from your house. And there would be too many questions and it would be too difficult to do anonymously. There is one thing, however, more visible than a full-page ad."

"What?"

"Billboards. They're all over the city and all over Sunset Boulevard and Wilshire Boulevard. We take two billboards and put up a sign that says 'Hunter McCall and his creator are both dead, killed by the same person. If you want to know who, how, and why, read KILLER ON THE LOOSE by Samantha Crowley, soon in your local bookstore.' That should blow our killer away."

I feel myself turn pale. Maybe white. "That should make our killer want to blow *me* away, Jack. The killer in my book isn't Benjamin's killer. I don't know who Benjamin's killer is."

"Sammi, we've been over this. It doesn't matter what you know. It's what the killer *thinks* you know."

"So he'll think I've written a book about him?"

"Precisely. And that's why he'll be anxious to set up a meeting."

Jack's logic isn't wrong but it has two flaws. A minor one to him, perhaps, but major to me is that I could end up dead. The other is more of a technicality. How can we go about renting and posting our own billboard in the very narrow time frame in which we are operating? I need to have this mystery resolved in days, not months.

I try to calmly express these concerns to Jack without showing my distress at how casually he seems to value my life, my body, the territory in which I hoped he wanted to plant a flag.

Jack looks almost relieved when I tell him what I'm thinking. "That's what you're worried about? Well, don't. I'll be protecting you every minute. You'll be fine. We'll set up the meeting in a public place. As far as the billboard goes, when I got the idea I considered the very problems you raised. I came up with a solution. It'll be a piece of cake."

A piece of cake is what I wish I was eating right now. Preferably one with lots of chocolate, so I could drown my agonies with a massive sugar rush.

I go back to my first argument. "It makes no sense, Jack. There's no reason for any of those people to have killed Benjamin and the others, or to wish me harm."

"There's a reason, Sammi. We just don't know what it is."

"I don't see how renting a billboard and getting the sign constructed then erected on the site can be less expensive and less complicated than taking out a full-page ad in the *Times*."

"That's because you don't know how to liberate a billboard."

I have no idea what Jack is talking about, but I have some suspicions. I'm guessing that to exonerate oneself from a crime one did not commit, it's necessary for one to commit many crimes.

First, I had to liberate my own money. Now, Jack wants us to liberate a billboard. It's at times like this when it's easy to remember when unliberated wasn't so bad.

# CHAPTER THIRTY-FIVE

We used to have how-to books. Now we have how-to websites. Jack tells me his idea for liberating a billboard came from a site dedicated to improving an environment that had been desecrated by big business.

I tell him I like to think our motive has equal merit.

We need a ladder and one-inch-by-four-inch pine boards, as well as canvas, glue, staples, staple gun, fast-drying epoxy, and high-gloss, oil-based lacquer paint. Jack needs to make a trip to the hardware store and an art supply store.

The great philanthropist Samantha says, "Here's ten C-notes from our recent heist." If it is my fate to be a felon, I may as well start speaking with felon-type words. Jack backs away and protests.

"It may be too much," I say, "but take it anyway. This way you'll have enough money for anything you think of. What's the difference? At this point, it's like play money to me. I can't go anywhere to spend it, so let's use whatever we need to get me out of this."

We discuss the pros and cons of our plan being executed in the night or day. The cover of night would be great, but we think there's a good probability one or both of us could fall and break some bones.

In some cities we would look conspicuous in the daytime, but this is Los Angeles and we are probably less likely to call attention to our activities by doing them in broad daylight. On the streets we have in mind, during daytime hours, the problem is the traffic.

Another mystery of this city: *When do people work? How can roads and stores be so crowded during normal working hours?*

We resolve that the best time is around 6 A.M. Proving my innocence is turning out to be very early morning work. I'd be more rested with a full-time job.

"Also, Jack, since we have some money, I'm thinking we could have a nice dinner delivered tonight. We've earned it. What do you say?"

"Sure. Anything you want."

Jack is half listening to me. His primary focus is on the shopping list he's compiling. All of the items we need to purchase in order to work tonight on our billboard scheme.

Jack and I will paint on canvas the words he composed earlier about Hunter McCall and Benjamin being killed by the same person, who is revealed in my book. Jack needs to be sure to get a fairly heavy canvas so that it can withstand the strong winds that occasionally descend on L.A. The type of paint we are purchasing is water resistant. The canvas doesn't have to remain in place for long. We figure my four phone callers will either see it or hear about it within forty-eight hours.

We will then glue and staple the pine boards to the horizontal length of the top and bottom of the canvas. We then hope to simply drop the top of the canvas, weighted by the pine boards, over the top of the billboard and have it held in place by the board on the bottom of the canvas. This sounds a little like wishful thinking on our part, so we are bringing a heavy-duty epoxy to try to attach the pine boards to the top back and lower front of the billboard. The website is our teacher and we are its students.

The good news is that it doesn't have to work for more than a couple of days. But it does have to work. We have two different locations in mind. The billboard we intend to cover on Sunset Boulevard currently has an advertisement for a new movie starring a major box office star. He won't miss any meals by my actions. The billboard on Wilshire Boulevard has a car ad. One less billboard won't put a dent in their profits. All my rationalizations mean nothing if we're caught.

Jack is also getting us white coveralls to wear so we look like the real thing.

After he leaves, I check the phone book to see what restaurants deliver to the Hills. There aren't many, but I find an Italian restaurant and call. I place an order and a delivery time for approximately seven P.M.

I'm restless and nervous. I try not to think about the Peter Perkal article in Jack's glove box. Or getting caught by the cops tomorrow. Or why Ren and Blake were at the Boo house. Or why Ren is so anxious to talk to me. Or why Ren lied to me, disguised as a cop, about who her children are and where she lives. Or why Dr. Lana Green keeps popping into my life. Or for that matter, why a rather odd assortment of people are haunting my steps. And, why Jack is doing this for me.

The more I try not to think, the more I do. I decide to take a nap, and sleep seamlessly until 5:45 when I hear Jack coming through the front door.

I hear him say, "I've parked the car in front of the house and left the garage empty so that we can spread out the canvas to paint later."

When he looks at my face, he says, "I'm sorry. I didn't mean to wake you. I wouldn't have come in like a tornado if I'd known you were sleeping."

"It's okay. Don't apologize. You're out doing all this work for me."

Jack showers and I set the table. In the middle of the greatest crisis of my life, I am stunned to find that this whole situation feels perfectly comfortable. We already have a routine, a rhythm. Some couples never get that, no matter how long they're married. Benjamin and I were one of those couples. So this is how the other half lives. This is what I've missed. And all this with a guy who I can, at best, call a partner in crime. I reel to even think about how much better it can get.

The food arrives early and is good. To make up for the last couple of days, I ordered a lot, figuring we could wrap up leftovers. They deliver minestrone and two different salads, a veal dish, chicken dish, pasta, and lots of bread. We are having a regular eating orgy. One day, if life ever gets a little fairer, I'd like to thank Jack by taking him to dinner at a nice restaurant where we can sit in public. Oh, the little things we take for granted.

We make a pact to talk about anything but me, Benjamin, and the murders. All of a sudden the dam bursts and Jack starts telling me about his concerns for Grant.

In response to his unhappy comments, I say, "But he seems normal and nice and, I don't know. He's quiet, likeable." It's not that I'm trying to make Jack feel better. Grant has been cooperative and pleasant.

"Yeah, I know. He was thrilled that I asked him a favor. I told you he doesn't like me looking out for him, checking up on him, and bailing him out of jams. It's all right that I'm big brother, but it's not. You know what I mean?"

"I think so." But I'm not sure.

"You say he seems normal but you know that's not true. His behavior is not acceptable in the world we live in. I'm the big bad brother of a Robin Hood. He only befriends the underdog and underprivileged. He hates the haves and loves the have-nots. That's not exactly what I would call normal. Nice? Yeah, fine. But what good does it do him?"

"Nice is its own reward."

Jack looks askance.

"What I mean is that Grant is this little pocket of good fighting evil. He keeps the scales of justice balanced. Tragedy touched him and he became sensitized and committed to righting the wrongs of the world. Does that make sense?" I look at Jack and can see it may make sense, but it doesn't make him any happier.

We finish dinner and head into the garage. I put on old jeans, as does Jack. He looks cute and I look a little like Marjorie Main.

It takes hours to do one canvas. It looks amateurish. But you can read it clearly and the black letters are big enough to make out our message from far away. It looks a little like those painted bed sheets you see people drape from the freeway overpasses. Jack bought the wood boards pre-cut and we just need to staple and glue them to the canvas. By the time we finish one canvas, it is after midnight.

Jack looks at me and I look at him and our thoughts meet. I say, "We'll just do the one billboard. I think Sunset. What do you think? Wilshire or Sunset?"

"It's your crowd, Sammi, so I'll defer to you. If you think that's the more likely spot for exposure, let's do it there."

First I hear kitchen noises and then I look at the clock. Jack is making coffee. In my old life I would have said "three more hours please," but in my new world I grant myself three more minutes. Then I will jump into the shower and from there into my new white overalls.

We're on the road by 5:45 A.M. The way we prepared our substitute billboard is practical. The canvas rolls up like a carpet, making for easy transportation. The ladder is more of a problem, but Jack fastens it to the roof of the Explorer. We decide the smart move is to leave the ladder behind, rather than try to bind it to the roof after our mission.

It takes only four minutes to get to Sunset Boulevard. For fame and stardom, Sunset Boulevard can't compete with Hollywood Boulevard, but it has had its moments. Certainly, Sunset Boulevard is forever memorialized in the classic 1950 Billy Wilder film of the same name.

But nearer to Hollywood, Sunset Boulevard is more faded glory. It boasts nightclubs and the Rock Walk/Guitar Center, where those interested can check out the handprints, signatures, and memorabilia from rock's greatest musical performers and innovators.

There is no traffic at this hour. Sunset Boulevard looks like a ghost town. The billboard we select faces west so that it will be viewed driving east. The billboard is not situated too high off the ground, which is good news. It will make our fall shorter and less painful.

We could use a third person to stand guard while I hold the ladder and Jack does the climb. But we considered and ruled out calling Grant. Jack's goal is to keep Grant out of trouble, not find new and unusual ways to get him into it.

A few cars pass us. No one slows or stops or gives any indication that they have any interest in what we are about. The epoxy is clumsier and stickier than Jack or I anticipated. A lot more than the pine boards are covered in glue by the time we're through.

After thirty minutes, our canvas hangs crookedly, glued in place. The lettering is clear, but we have somehow allowed a ripple in the canvas—after spending nearly half an hour pulling it tight before attaching it to the wood boards. As a result, my name looks, at times, like "Samtha" instead of Samantha. I would have fired any publicist who did this kind of sloppy work, but Jack and I are amateurs who got the job done in twenty-four hours. I'm proud of us.

I let my concentration drift for three seconds and the ladder shudders when my grip loosens. I yelp. Jack calls out in the loudest whisper he dares, "What's wrong?"

"Nothing. I thought for a minute that I screwed up. Are you all right?"

"Yeah. I'm coming down. It's done."

Jack climbs down and I notice there is glue in his hair. We each lift one end of the ladder and carry it to an area where there are trees and shrubbery. We plant it gently in the middle of the tangle. By tomorrow it will be part of someone's garage sale.

"We should beat it," Jack says and he's right. We can admire our handiwork as we drive away. Just as we start to get into the Explorer, a police car comes driving down Sunset, going west. Jack keeps moving, unconcerned. At least he appears unconcerned. I freeze and can't get my hand around the door handle. I hear Jack whisper, "Get into the truck."

Jack is afraid I'm going into shock, but I'm not. I feel fearless. You know that sensation you have, almost exclusively when you're high school age, where you think that nothing and no one can ever hurt you?

Then I remember that defacing a billboard is the least of my problems. Once a cop gets hold of me, I am going to have to explain about Peter and Jonathon and Carol and, of course, Benjamin. I jump into the truck and we take off.

Jack is quiet, coming down from his adrenaline rush. After all, he did the hard part of our task. The canvas is heavy and I'm not certain Jack is used to that kind of physical work. He did go through the police academy, but that was a while ago and I'm mixing up the Academy with all those movies I've seen about training for the FBI and Quantico.

"Jack, how do you think it looks?"

"Lousy. But it'll have to do."

"Is it good enough?"

"Sure. In any case, it's done, we did it, and now we wait and see. So how does it feel to announce your book and have your name in big letters?"

"Lousy. But it'll have to do."

# CHAPTER THIRTY-SIX

When I tell Jack "lousy," I'm not kidding. I was seriously writing my book and the billboard makes a mockery of the whole thing. I understand why we had to do it, but that doesn't make me feel any better. Who will I be when this is over? Can I ever write a book and be taken seriously?

I know it isn't the best idea, but I ask Jack anyway. I want to stop at the cemetery to take my walk. Considering the lunacy of the idea, Jack is kind about my request.

"Let me buy a newspaper and coffee first. I'll sit in the truck, read, and keep guard until you're done. Then we'll head home. Anyway, you can't start making the phone calls until later this afternoon."

Jack is referring to the next part of our plan. We decided I would telephone the four who left messages on my machine. One of them should now be especially anxious to meet with me.

We assume all of them will have seen or heard about the billboard by late afternoon. Who knows how long it will be before our billboard liberation is unliberated? We can't afford to wait and our four suspects, as we now refer to them, will be thinking about the puzzle solved in *Killer on the Loose:* Who killed Hunter McCall and Benjamin Crowley?

One of our suspects will not want the book published, or me around to talk about it.

When we get to Hollywood Forever, I leave Jack sipping coffee and reading a front-page article about me. Heading in the direction of the Cathedral Mausoleum, I turn to look at him and give him what I hope is a brave wave.

I glance at the sky. A brilliant sun has broken through. It is going to be a gorgeous day. Above me, about fifteen miles away, is the 450,000-pound Hollywood sign, and ninety-three million miles away is the sun, the largest object in the solar system. The universe keeps these heavy objects peacefully perched in place. I can't keep my one-hundred-twenty-pound body peaceful anywhere. I am suffering from a massive attack of "poor me." That's why I want to see the boys.

It occurs to me that I could have cut some roses to bring to Bill when I was at my house. It's sad to think that though he was an actor turned director in early Hollywood, he is probably best remembered for his brutal and mysterious death.

The mausoleum is empty of all living souls, except for me. It doesn't take long to walk there. I feel compelled to let Bill know that he is appreciated for who he was and not just remembered for what happened to him, so I say, "I think it's great that from 1914 until 1921, you directed more than forty films and that you served as a captain in the Canadian Army during World War I and that you were the president of the Motion Pictures Directors' Association. You weren't just fodder for front-page headlines and tabloid gossip." My voice sounds strange in the empty, cavernous mausoleum. Can Rudolph Valentino and Peter Lorre hear me? They are interred here, too.

Bill did things that mattered, that changed and helped the world. Even Valentino, the silent screen lover, and Lorre, who played creepy parts as a character actor, made contributions to society. What have I ever done? My major contribution to society, thus far, is being the subject of titillating innuendo and speculation on the evening news and the front page of the newspapers.

The walk isn't making me feel better, after all. I go outside and look at the trees and water and flowers and all the effort that goes into trying to make the cemetery a peaceful and harmonious place to visit. But I am still feeling bitter and negative, so I decide to visit Bugsy another time. He has to have cornered the market on bitter and negative when he got shot down and his girlfriend, Virginia, didn't miss a beat. Or a meal.

I walk a little, aimlessly, and then start back to the parking lot where Jack is patiently waiting.

He senses my mood, at least I think he does, as we drive back to his house in silence. At the house, we turn on the news. I'm not sure what we expect to see. Maybe both of us think there is the possibility camera crews are at the billboard to publicize our morning's work. It could happen. I'm wanted for questioning by the police and a billboard suddenly springs up announcing that I'm going to have a book published that reveals Benjamin's murderer. In any city that would qualify as news, not just Los Angeles.

The television commentators are preoccupied with talk of spring being in the air. That's another remarkable thing about L.A. Compared to other places, we have no weather. It's never cold, rarely very hot, never snows, hardly rains, and the sun is out approximately 350 out of 365 days a year. Yet they talk about spring coming as if we are arctic dwellers who have hunkered down for winter and are eagerly anticipating the thaw.

"Sammi, are you all right? Why don't we go out on the deck with a cold drink, relax for a while, and watch the birds make lazy circles in the sky?"

"I'd like that a lot."

Jack notices my mood changes. Maybe this is a good time to ask him about the Peter Perkal article in his glove compartment. Maybe this is exactly the wrong time for me to let him see what a sneaky mistrusting soul I can be.

We go outside. The air is warm and smells good. The wind

carries an aromatic blend of cut grass and jasmine and that sort of nutty smell of rich soil freshly watered. These are comfort smells, like freshly baked bread.

Going outside is a good idea. Jack starts talking to me about *Heart of Darkness* and the way Conrad writes and how different it is from someone like Jane Austen. Jack just read *Pride and Prejudice* for the first time. We talk about Darcy and Elizabeth and Jack tells me his next book, after Conrad, will be *The Sun Also Rises* and then *The Sound and the Fury*.

Fitzgerald and Faulkner. I tell him that's a heavy undertaking. Twice we get up to replenish our drinks. I discover packets of lemonade in the cabinet and make a big pitcher. We are two people sitting and drinking, talking and sharing. I want to hang on to the lemonade, Jack, and these moments forever. I push aside the frustration of knowing I can't.

The light outside is dimming and it's getting cooler. The day has passed swiftly. The day has been delicious. Jack isn't quiet. He just picks and chooses when he wants to talk and what he wants to talk about.

I get up and stretch. Jack looks at me and says, "It's time?" I nod and we both go inside. We have already decided the order of my calls, the suggested times of meetings, and the places. We hope only one of the four will still be interested in seeing me. Then we may have our killer. It's possible, however, that more than one will want to meet me, so to be on the safe side, Jack selects four locations. Jack and I think the murderer will go wherever I propose. I'm the bait. I'm the one our killer wants.

Jack chooses locations where he can remain easily hidden, or inconspicuous in plain sight. He can check out if our suspect is alone, and even more importantly, protect me if our suspect does what we know is a possibility—try to abduct or kill me.

The afternoon on the deck has been calming. I've stopped being afraid. I've stopped the self pity. Jack and I are going to pull this off. We will walk into the Hollywood police station, escorting a multiple killer. It doesn't cost to hope.

My first call is to Maurice at the Beverly Hilton. I ask to be connected to his room. The phone rings three times. I think for sure he isn't there, and then he picks up on the fourth ring and says hello.

I recognize his voice. "Hello, Maurice, this is Samantha. I got your telephone message."

"Samantha, oh my God! Samantha Crowley, oh my! Yes, yes, I left you a message, but do you know about that billboard? Do you know the police are looking for you?"

Maurice is breathless, excited, overwhelmed. Should I believe that this is a man capable of killing four people? It feels as likely as Bugsy Siegel resurrecting himself to help me avenge my persecutor.

"Maurice, do you still want to meet me?"

"Most definitely, my dear. Even more so now that I've seen the billboard."

What in the world does that mean? That he now has good reason to fear me and wants me dead? Is Maurice our murderer?

"Well, I'm sure you can appreciate the need for secrecy, Maurice. Do you understand what I mean?"

"Of course. Naturally."

"I'll meet you at Grauman's Chinese Theater at nine A.M. tomorrow. You must be prompt. I'll try to be on time. Just wait if you don't see me."

"Could we make it a little later? I wanted to—"

"That's the place and time, Maurice."

"Fine, fine. I'll see you there."

I add, "Alone."

"Yes, certainly. Alone."

I hang up without saying goodbye. The guy makes my flesh crawl. I give Jack a thumb's-up and he notes down the time and place of the meeting and the time of my phone call.

The next call is to Bicky's bakery. A man answers and I ask to speak to her. He inquires as to who I am and I ignore him. When I tell Bicky who is calling, she squeals.

"Bicky, I would appreciate it if you didn't attract attention to this call."

"Oh, I'm so sorry. Where are you? Are you all right?" Now she is whispering in a melodramatic, little girl–sounding voice. "Have you heard about the billboard sign? Everyone is talking about it."

Jack was right. The billboard was a stroke of genius and we have not overestimated the speed with which it disseminated our words.

"Yes, I know about it. Listen, Bicky, you left a message that you and Dicky wanted to see me. Do you still feel that way?"

"Absolutely. Is it okay? I mean we don't want to get you in any trouble. We don't believe you hurt anyone. Dicky is devastated by Jonathon's death, though. She says she wants to believe you wouldn't do this to her."

And all this time I thought it was *Bicky* who had the crush on Jonathon.

Listening to her, it's impossible to imagine Bicky and Dicky being cold-blooded killers. Bicky sounds worried about me. She and Dicky could never have killed Jonathon Harley. On the other hand, they do want to be famous writers. But how will these killings make them famous writers? How does implicating me help them?

"I'll be fine. But Bicky, you are to tell no one I called or that you and Dicky are meeting me. Go to the Griffith Park Observatory at eleven A.M. tomorrow morning. Come alone. If I'm a little late, wait."

"Well, that cuts it close to lunch time when we get busy, but I suppose I can get away. Maybe Dicky will call in sick tomorrow.

It gets difficult for her to handle too much in one day. You know what I mean?"

Bicky would have just gone on chattering if I hadn't stopped her. "I have to go now. Do you understand where and when?"

"Oh, sure. By the way, did you see us on the *Today* show? It was my idea to wear matching outfits. What did you think?"

I think that if these two silly women are the reason I have been terrified and hiding out for the last few days, it may be a toss-up whether I kill them or myself.

My next call is to Dr. Lana Green. If I time the call close enough to the top of the hour, I may catch her between her fifty-minute hour appointments. It is 5:45. I decide to wait five minutes more. I fill Jack in on the contents of both calls. He agrees that Maurice and Bicky don't sound like murderers, but then one has to ask how does a murderer sound? They have seen the billboard and are anxious to meet.

I dial Dr. Lana's number and listen to it ring. A machine picks up. I have no intention of leaving a message identifying myself, but if I start speaking, she may figure out it's me and pick up the phone.

It works. All I have to start saying is, "Lana, you left a message that you wanted to see me."

"Hello," she says. "Is this Samantha Crowley?"

I wait until I am sure the machine is finished recording. I'm confident she won't hang up and she doesn't.

"Yes, it is. You phoned and said you wanted to see me."

"Right. I did do that. Now I see you have a book about to come out and that's funny because it's related to why I wanted to see you. Are you agreeable to meeting me?"

No other questions, like how are you, where are you, can I help you?

Is Dr. Lana the murderer?

"Yes," I say. "I'm willing to meet you."

"Splendid. When can you come to my office?"

"I can't. I'll see you tomorrow at one P.M. at the Wilshire Boulevard Temple. In the Edgar Magnin Sanctuary. Do you know it?"

"Yes. That's a little unusual. Oh, I think my six o'clock appointment is here."

"That's fine because we have nothing more to talk about. Come alone and wait if I'm delayed."

I hang up the phone and feel the same surge I experienced the last time I spoke to Dr. Lana. I think it's called hate. I have no good reason to hate the woman other than she is so hateable. I would love for her to be the killer. Wouldn't that be perfect? But finding a reason is even harder than imagining how or why Maurice or Bicky or Dicky did it.

The final call is to Ren. She is the last call. I hope she doesn't want to meet me, and if she does, I hope I never arrive at our designated spot. Because if I do, it means the other three are not murderers and, most probably, my best friend is.

Sure, I talk fondly about my dead friends in Hollywood Forever, but I haven't completely lost my mind. It's good to have an alive friend, even if she does spend too much time on the phone and smokes too much. We forgive our friends their excesses. But I will never forgive Ren if she has set me up. Is it such a stretch that a woman like Ren could be a murderer? Murder is crime of passion. Her art, her sculpture, her life is passionate. My red-headed friend blazes, but it doesn't address the bigger question. *Why?* It doesn't make sense. Why would she hurt me? What was she doing in Boo's house? Why has she been so secretive lately? I hate to admit it, but she is as likely a candidate as everyone else.

I dial her cell phone, where she can always be reached. She answers on the first ring, which means she isn't on another call. I hear her take a deep inhale from a cigarette I can visualize parked between her two red lips. Always sexy and scrumptious.

"Ren, it's me."

"Oh, God. I need to sit down. Sam, I've been so worried about you. Are you all right?"

My eyes are welling up and tears are about to cascade down my cheeks. This is how friends are supposed to sound. I take my own deep breath and compose myself. This is business.

"I'm okay, Ren. I can't go into it now. You said you wanted to meet, so I'm calling you back. Do you still want to meet me?"

"Yes, but everyone is looking for you. We have to meet somewhere private. That billboard is your doing, isn't it?"

So it has worked. All of our suspects know about the billboard and all of them remain anxious to see me. One of them is now more motivated, though our conversations have failed to give me a clue as to whom that may be.

"Ren, I can meet you tomorrow at four P.M."

"Fine. Where?"

"At Hollywood Forever cemetery. As you walk up toward the Beth Olam Mausoleum, there's a section slightly to the left, where Mel Blanc is buried. I'll be there."

"Mel Blanc?"

"You know, the guy who did the voices for nearly all the classic Warmer Brothers cartoon characters."

"That's where you want to meet? How will I find it?" She sounds overwhelmed.

I need to make it simpler. She'll never find a specific grave. "Meet me in front of the Cathedral Mausoleum. It's huge, you can't miss it."

"The Cathedral Mausoleum." She repeats it as if memorizing for a final exam. "Are you sure?"

Her voice has a quiver. I need to be strong. The usually strong Ren doesn't sound that way at the moment.

"Yup. I know what I'm doing. If I'm late, wait for me. And be sure to come alone. And don't tell anyone."

"All right, I guess. Samantha, are you sure you know what you're doing?"

"I'll see you tomorrow."

Am I sure I know what I'm doing? Of course I'm not sure I know what I'm doing. Did Butch and Sundance know what they were doing when they raced off to Bolivia? Did Bonnie and Clyde know what they were doing when they took that last drive into town? Did Bugsy Siegel know what he was doing when he decided to spend a quiet evening at home?

Spin the wheel. Take a chance. I hope I'm guessing better than Bugsy, Bonnie, and Butch. If not, I may be seeing all of them—and Benjamin Crowley—entirely too soon.

# CHAPTER THIRTY-SEVEN

Subterfuge can be exhausting. I feel like Dorian Gray in reverse. Somewhere a picture of me is getting younger while I rapidly age.

"Do I look as bad as I feel?" Oops. I didn't mean to say that, certainly not to a man for whom I feel more than a modicum of lust. The fuzzy growth has returned to Jack's face and he looks similar to the day I first saw him. Why is it men can look tired and strong, worried and resilient?

"You look very nice," Jack says. "Sitting outside put some pink in your cheeks."

"I'm sorry. I wasn't fishing for a compliment. The phone calls wore me out. I'm surprised."

"I'm not. You find that with police work. Being in the field can often be less tiring than the mental work of trying to understand and get into the psychology of a case. So I know exactly what you're talking about."

"I don't want it to be my friend, Ren. It's too discouraging to think that my one good friend could be setting me up."

"So, don't think it."

Jack is trying to be nice, but he can't really be advocating my sticking my head into the sand.

"Let's face the facts," I say. "The phone call you received to meet 'her' in the cemetery, the call that attempted to incite you to kill me, was made by a woman."

"Right. But there are other women in the picture. You're

meeting them tomorrow. Lana Green and Bicky and Dicky."

I consider what he's said, then shake my head. "But they have no meaningful connection to me or Benjamin. Ren has some connection. And she was in the Boo house and pretending it was her house and that both boys playing outside, not just Blake, were her children. And I saw Blake in the library, talking to Benjamin. And Blake saw me going to the Peninsula to meet Peter Perkal."

I watch Jack's face to see if he reacts. He doesn't.

"And then I bumped into Blake at the Regent Beverly Wilshire when I went there to meet Carol."

"What are you saying, Sammi? That it's a diabolical mother–son team against you?"

Hearing the idea out loud makes it sound as ridiculous as it probably is.

"I know it's early, but maybe I'll go to bed and try to get a good night's sleep. I'm not very hungry."

A little part of me hopes Jack will say we need to stay up and plan and plot for tomorrow. But a bigger part of me knows he won't. Jack assumes that I mean what I say if I say it. His thinking would be, why else would I say it?

"Goodnight, then. I'll wake you in the morning."

If only he'd added an endearment at the end of the sentence, honey or sweetie, it would have guaranteed good dreams.

Buried in the trash bag I filled at my home is a pair of easy-fitting black stretch pants, comfortable black shoes, and a pretty, dark brown chenille Ann Taylor sweater. Under the sweater I wear a close-fitting, white cotton T-shirt, in case the day turns warm and I need to remove the sweater. I have thrown in a pair of my favorite silver earrings with a matching bracelet. The earrings always make me feel wild and audacious. Isn't it funny how tiny carved objects hanging from your ears can do that?

There is something comforting about the idea of caring about what I wear and how I look. It's been a while since I made an effort. I put on a little green eye shadow and secure my hair in a ponytail with a barrette made of multicolored stones.

Jack, too, has made an effort. He's wearing khaki pants, soft brown suede work boots, and a pale blue work shirt. He could be the foreman of a new huge hotel or a logging multimillionaire from the Pacific Northwest. He wears casual/classy well.

Not exactly Nick and Nora Charles, but we do make a cute couple. I wonder if he notices.

"Good morning, Sammi. Did you sleep well?"

I pour myself a diet soda and drink it like there's no tomorrow. Does stress make you thirsty?

"I fell asleep when I hit the pillow and never stirred. How about you, Jack? Were you able to sleep comfortably on the couch? I feel so guilty ousting you from your bed."

"No problem. I can sleep almost anywhere. Actually, I had such vivid dreams it almost felt like I wasn't sleeping at all. Because I don't really know their personalities, I think my overactive imagination was trying to place personality traits on the faces I saw when we watched the *Today* show, if that makes any sense."

Outside, I hear birds chattering and a leaf blower buzzing. A car alarm sounds and then shuts off. I hear a woman call out, "You forgot your lunch." It feels as though I'm on the set of that old Jimmy Stewart movie, *Rear Window*. He sits with his broken leg propped up against the window and watches his neighbors through a telescope. But study the movie closely. Equally interesting is the diversity of sounds that come from the many apartments he observes.

*Rear Window* is an Alfred Hitchcock movie. The master of suspense. Hitchcock couldn't have done any better orchestrating a living nightmare than someone is doing right now, to me.

"So what did you dream, Jack? Do you remember?"

"It's not important. Are you ready?"

I'm ready. What do I need? There are no props, no gags, no special gadgets. It is going to be me launching each of them into a conversation and seeing where we land. Jack and I agreed there is no way I can rehearse. It's impossible to script out what to expect. Too many variables. And, of course, that's what makes it dangerous.

Jack locks up the house and we get into the Explorer. Jack gives me his dark sunglasses. Until I'm ready to be seen, I want to keep a low profile. We need to drive by the Chinese Theater so that I can point out Maurice. Jack will park the truck and I will stay in the truck until Jack gives me the green light that Maurice has come alone. It is possible Jack may recognize Maurice from television, but we don't want to take the chance.

Jack will then stand off to the side, like a regular tourist, getting excited over handprints and footprints of celebrities and making sure no harm comes to me. Of all the locations we've selected, this is the easiest because Jack can be in plain view. Without being conspicuous.

Maurice is early. He is waiting for me near the ticket window. Not more than twenty feet away is a city bench on which the Button Lady, Betty, is sitting, folding and unfolding her hands.

I point to Maurice. I say nothing to Jack about Button Lady. Maurice is wearing black slacks, a magenta blazer, a pale orange silk shirt, and designer sunglasses. Maurice has gone Hollywood. It would be an unthinkable outfit for Maurice in New York. But New York is three thousand miles away.

Jack turns north on Sycamore and parks the truck.

"It looks pretty quiet so it shouldn't take me long to figure out if he came alone. Don't leave the truck until I come back."

I nod. I'm not worried that anything will happen to Jack but want to say "good luck" anyway. He nods at me and walks toward the theater.

When he returns, he climbs back into the driver's seat and wrinkles his nose. I've never seen him do that before. I don't want to bombard him with questions so I exercise restraint and wait.

"I'd be very surprised if he's not alone. I walked a one-block radius in each direction. I stood a few feet away from him for a good five minutes and all I saw him do is look at his watch and check up and down the street. I think we're okay. Are you all set?"

I waited impatiently and now I would be happy for a few more minutes.

"I'm ready."

"I'll get out and walk there first. You just need to be a little behind me. Now remember, don't pay any attention to me. Focus on your conversation with Maurice."

The way Jack says Maurice, it comes out "Moe-rees." It sounds cute. I nod. I'm doing that a lot.

"When you're done," Jack continues, "walk away. I'll follow you back to the truck. If anything happens that alarms you, signal me. If he threatens you, if he pulls a weapon, anything like that."

Again, I nod. The idea of Maurice threatening me feels absurd. But then all of our suspects seem improbable and absurd. My future hinging on solving a murder seems improbable and absurd.

Being wanted by the police seems improbable and absurd.

Jack gets out and starts walking. I wait five beats and follow. I am walking on Hollywood Boulevard when I hear Maurice call out, "Oh, there you are."

Two women look up from the James Dean movie poster they are admiring in the theater store window. Button Lady lifts her head slightly. I wonder if she recognizes me. I would like to go to her and say "Betty, I want to thank you for your help the other day." I would like her to know that I remember her name. But this isn't the time.

"Hello, Maurice. You're looking very Los Angeles." I give his clothes what I hope he interprets as an admiring look. Upon reflection, I'm a little confused about why I feel inclined to kiss his butt. Why don't I just tell him that he looks ridiculous. There's a wider range of emotions wreaking havoc on my nervous system than I realized. It's not about being calm or nervous. I'm neither. I'm angry.

"Samantha, I'm so glad you agreed to meet me. Everything has been so terrible. But I don't have to tell you. Are you allowed to be walking the streets?"

Maurice isn't absurd. He's an idiot.

"Maurice, I don't want to talk about me. You wanted to see me and I'm here. What's this about?"

"Well, my darling, it's about that idea you mentioned to Carol, and now I see you've taken out a billboard, although I think it's not there anymore. In any case, I know Carol thought it was a terrible idea but . . ." Maurice either pauses for effect or to be coy. With him it's probably the same. "I don't think it's such a bad idea at all. It's bold, adventurous, very daring."

"So?" As Jack and I agreed I'm going to do minimal talking and let our suspects talk to me.

"What I thought was . . ." There it is again, that obnoxious pregnant pause. Never in my entire life have I ever been so tempted to smack someone across the face. Maurice is truly an annoying ferret.

"Yes?"

"I thought I could be your agent. I would represent you."

Mystery solved. Maurice wants to be my agent. He wants to pilfer Carol's clients and add to his new, developing roster. I can be his controversial client. Every agent should have one.

With Carol dead, it isn't exactly stealing, but it does stink of ingratitude. It may also explain why Maurice would want Carol dead. But why kill Peter and Jonathon and particularly Benjamin? Did he kill Benjamin to get me? Did he think my idea was more likely to happen and more profitable with Benjamin dead?

That makes no sense at all. If he wanted me to be his next Famous Author, why would he want me convicted for murder and put away forever? It's tough to do book tours from jail.

Maurice is not the bad guy. Well, maybe he is a bad guy, but he's not this bad guy, and I don't need to waste any more time. During the entire conversation with him, I haven't thought about or noticed Jack, but now I look. He isn't more than six feet away and though we've been talking quietly, I'm certain Jack heard the entire conversation.

"Maurice, let me give this some thought."

"Of course. I was only concerned because after I heard about the billboard, it occurred to me that you may have signed on with someone else . . ." He waits a minute, another pregnant pause. "Have you?"

"No. Let me give this a few days, all right?"

I want to tell Maurice that at the moment I'm wanted for murder and maybe we could put this off until I can be seen in public without worrying about being arrested. Maurice isn't an idiot. He's a nitwit.

He says, "Let me give you one of my cards."

"Sure. Why don't you do that?" Little Maurice, obsequious, docile assistant, hasn't been letting any grass grow under his nimble feet.

Maurice hands me his card, which is printed in pale pink. I thank him and tell him I have to go. To my retreating back, I hear him say, "Call me soon, or I'll give you a call. By the way, Samantha, you look smashing."

I remember the mocking look Maurice gave me as he and

Carol exited the Regent Beverly Wilshire. He didn't find me smashing then. Another time, another passage.

I sense rather than see Jack walk behind me. We stroll past Betty, the Button Lady. I smile at her, but she is busy scolding a woman who is trying to share the bench with her.

As I round onto Sycamore, Jack taps my shoulder, pulls up next to me, and says, "I heard it all. He's not our guy."

I feel like all the energy has been sucked out of my body. Was I counting on the killer being Maurice, or am I dreading the prospect of continuing this weeding-out process?

Jack puts his arm around my shoulder and pulls me close. It's a little off-kilter, but definitely qualifies as a hug of sorts. Did he intuitively divine that my spirits are flagging, or do I look needy?

As a famous rock star once said, you can't always get what you want. But if you try, sometimes, you can get what you need.

# CHAPTER THIRTY-EIGHT

The drive from the theater to Griffith Park Observatory doesn't take long if traffic is light. Jack has turned on the radio and an all-news station leads off with, "The investigation continues into the mysterious death of best-selling author, Benjamin Crowley. Authorities say . . ."

I flip to an oldies music station. Authorities say a lot but don't know anything. Judy Collins sweetly sings that she's looked at life from both sides now. Me, too. I turn off the radio.

"You don't mind, do you?" I ask Jack.

He shakes his head. "I thought you might want to hear the news but I understand. What's the point? Right?"

"Jack?"

He half turns toward me as he drives and gives me an inquiring look.

"You're the best. I can never thank you enough."

He does a thing where he tips his nonexistent cowboy hat as if he's Gary Cooper. "Glad to be of service, ma'am," he says in a Cooper drawl.

We are driving east on Los Feliz Boulevard and soon will make a turn north on Vermont to get to the observatory. If Sacre Coeur is the sentinel watching over Paris, I suppose one could think of the Griffith Park Observatory as the Los Angeles sentinel.

Los Feliz is on the northeastern rim of Hollywood and dates back to when the Gabriellino Indians lived in a sycamore-lined glade at the northernmost end of what is now Western Avenue. Much later, at the turn of the twentieth century, Los Feliz was developed into grand estates and architectural and botanic showplaces. Cecil B. DeMille, W. C. Fields, and Deanna Durbin, among others, had homes there.

We are early, which is good. At this hour, on a weekday, the observatory can be a quiet place. We will have plenty of time to get the best vantage point. We search for a place to observe Bicky and Dicky and keep Jack hidden. It isn't hard.

Jack and I stand against one of the walls of the observatory, and from there have a perfect view of the lot where Bicky and Dicky will park, then walk toward the observatory. A school has brought fifty or sixty children, who look to be ten years old, for a field trip to the observatory.

It is already 10:45, so we decide to stay in place rather than wander. The sisters may come early. I overhear one little girl telling her friend that she is definitely going to break up with Jason this afternoon. The other girl replies that she thinks it's a good idea because he clearly doesn't understand the first thing about having a relationship.

Certain problems are ageless. They could have been ten years old, twenty, thirty, sixty. I would have liked to give them a heads-up. It doesn't get better when you're older. No one understands the first thing, the last thing, or anything about relationships. You just jump in and hope you don't sink.

While I ponder these thoughts, I see Bicky and Dicky walking toward the entrance to the observatory. They wear matching magenta muumuus. We're having a magenta day. First Maurice's magenta jacket and now this.

I nudge Jack and murmur, "There they are."

Jack does the uncommon for Jack. He laughs. Not too loud, not too boisterous, but a definite laugh. I suppose to the unfamiliar eye, Bicky and Dicky are a comical sight. Each is holding a small pink pastry box.

Jack moves from our location and circles behind the sisters. They don't know him and he wants to be certain they are alone. No other cars have pulled into the parking area and unless someone is hiking up to the observatory, it's unlikely we have uninvited guests, but it never hurts to check.

After a few minutes Jack returns and tells me it's safe to walk toward them. As I approach, I hear Bicky saying to Dicky, "Look, there she is. Samantha."

Fortunately the only people who hear her are some loitering schoolchildren. I seriously doubt they watch the six o'clock news and will race to the phone to collect the reward money for finding one of America's Ten Most Wanted. But I'd feel more comfortable if Bicky refrained from using my name.

"Hi, Bicky. Hi, Dicky. How are you?"

Bicky starts a lengthy answer. If ever there was a rhetorical how-are-you, this is it. I cut her off. "Bicky, you telephoned and said you needed to see me. So here I am. What's up?"

Dicky says, "We wanted to explain."

"Okay. I'm here. I'm listening."

Bicky says, "We don't think you killed all those other people and Jonathon. We don't know why you're hiding but we're sure you have good reason because we always thought you were very nice. And we've tried not to read anything into the fact that you were alone with Jonathon right before he died and it was only the first time you had ever come to one of our meetings."

For Bicky and Dicky, this is about Jonathon. But if that's the case, they couldn't have killed him. What about Benjamin?

"And we thought that you and Mr. Crowley were separated, but he was always so nice to us and he sort of encouraged us to write our book."

Dicky pokes Bicky in the side. I think it is intended as gentle, but given Dicky's bulk, it's a poke that could easily leave one black and blue. I find myself wondering if Bicky's birdlike frame is covered with an assortment of black and blues from her sister's *gentle* prods.

"Truth be told," Bicky says, "we weren't completely honest on the *Today* show. Mr. Crowley never really had time to listen to what our book was about and he lost the pages we gave him to read. But he did say "write, write, write," though he may have said it only once and we may be confusing him with that UCLA professor who taught the creative writing class we took and—"

"Bicky, why did you and Dicky want to see me?"

"Well, we felt badly about suspecting that you would have harmed Jonathon." Bicky looks like she is about to cry. "And you have been nice to us and we wanted to say we were sorry about all the trouble."

Dicky pokes Bicky and clears her throat. "We saw your billboard and we want to wish you good luck with your book. And we each baked something special for you."

This speech must have been rehearsed more times than Hamlet's "to be or not to be" monologue.

The sisters hand me the little pink boxes. I don't know whether to thank them or scream. Was all of this about their guilt over suspecting me?

"We thought that if we read all of Mr. Crowley's books he would be impressed with us and maybe help," Bicky says. "But he didn't have time. And now he's dead."

That explains the day I saw Bicky racing down the streets of Beverly Hills with a copy of Benjamin's book under her arm. These women completely misjudged Benjamin. They thought the monster was a mentor.

It is time to end our meeting. "Bicky, Dicky, thank you for the goodies, but I do have to get going. Your apology, if that's what it was, is accepted."

They look at one another as if needing a signal to turn and leave. I want to make this easy for them. "I'll let you get back to work and, just for the record, I didn't kill Jonathon. As a matter of fact, I didn't kill anyone."

Dicky nods and Bicky says, "We know."

After I've said goodbye twice, Dicky silently waddles away while Bicky walks and talks. I watch Bicky start her car and slowly exit the parking lot. Who knows, maybe they will sell their book.

When I recount the conversation to Jack, I can see he's amused. "Well, that was a colossal waste of time. Shall I see what they brought," I ask, holding up my two pink boxes.

We are sitting under a tree near the observatory, and anyone passing would have thought we were a nice-looking couple having a picnic. We have a hazy view of the city below and I discover two chocolate éclairs in one box and four vanilla-lemon tortes in the other. Jack selects the éclair and I take a torte. We sit quietly, getting our sugar rush for the month.

Not far from where we are seated, a portion of the movie *Rebel Without A Cause* was filmed. Griffith Park Observatory is the site for the well-known scene where the kids congregate by the observatory wall. I think about Natalie Wood and James Dean and Sal Mineo. In the movie they were so young. All three died young and tragically.

Death is in the air. Maybe I am being melodramatic, but in spite of the heat, goosebumps spring up on my arms. We have eliminated two of our suspects and two remain. Just because I am rooting for Dr. Lana doesn't mean she's the killer.

We finish our pastries and Jack tells me a story about a stakeout in which he was involved many years ago. It is a sweet and sad story at the same time. He talks about how close he and his mom and Grant were and how she took them, as little boys, to the zoo on Saturdays and to the movies every Sunday.

She would trundle them off to the museum to see an old black-and-white classic.

Jack says he fell in love with Barbara Stanwyck and Claudette Colbert and Lana Turner. I'm not the least bit like any of those women.

We combine the remaining éclair and three tortes into one box and walk back to the truck. I love when Jack talks. But as suddenly as he starts, he stops. We drive in silence to the Wilshire Boulevard Temple.

If we were in Rome or Florence or Athens, I'd say no big deal. But by Los Angeles standards, the temple qualifies as a genuinely old and wonderful structure. It's quite lovely inside and out. The first Jewish congregation in Los Angeles worshipped at this temple in 1862. The Edgar F. Magnin Sanctuary, where I arranged to meet Dr. Lana, is a national historical landmark. The sanctuary is beautiful and peaceful with exquisite stained-glass windows. I hope it will be the site of Dr. Lana's catharsis and confession.

We park in the temple lot adjacent to the building. We are twenty minutes early, but Dr. Lana arrived even earlier. I spot her skinny bones pacing the center aisle of the sanctuary and pull Jack out of the big room.

I whisper, "She's in there already."

Jack points to the main door we entered and we walk quickly in that direction to exit. The sun is doing its best to make April feel like August. I peel off my sweater. I'm burning up. The sun, hormones, and tension make my skin feel like it's going to ignite.

Jack tugs my arm and pulls me back toward the parking lot. I wonder if my skin feels as hot to him as it does to me.

"I'm going to check the perimeter of the temple and then go into the sanctuary and see who's there, other than your Dr. Lana."

"Where do you want me to wait?" I feel like one of the

schoolgirls from the observatory.

Jack gestures toward the parking lot. "It's too hot to sit in the car. Just make yourself unobtrusive. You know what I mean."

He jogs back to the entrance of the temple but doesn't enter while I squat behind a Land Cruiser.

I can't look more ridiculous than I feel. I see Jack circling the temple. Then I lose sight of him as he rounds the end of the building. It flashes through my head that Hunter McCall never had to squat behind a car. I suddenly have a great nostalgic tug for Hunter. I plotted his death as if he was Benjamin.

Hunter McCall is my creation. He's never been the bad guy. Now that the true bad guy—his creator—is dead, wouldn't it be right to let Hunter McCall live? I don't want to kill him.

My knees are stiff as I straighten up. Big mistake. As I stand, Lana Green exits the temple and looks in my direction. Did she see me? Is she impatient or is she looking for someone who accompanied her?

She is moving her neck in a herky-jerky way, and I realize what I'm seeing. After all these years with Ren, I should be an expert. Dr. Lana is talking on a cell phone. Either it doesn't work properly in the temple, or she considered it less than appropriate to be yakking away on a cell phone in the middle of a holy place.

She hasn't seen me. She is completely involved in the phone call. I quickly return to my less than flattering squat position. Where is Jack? And as I think it, he rounds the corner and almost bumps into the dear deadly doctor. She gives Jack a rancorous look, as if an alien blob invaded her space. Jack keeps walking, successfully pretending he doesn't have a clue who she is. I assume he's going to check out the sanctuary. But the more I watch Dr. Lana chatting on the phone in her hyper-animated way, her thin arms flailing in the windless air as she emphasizes her point, the more I feel my heart sinking to my painful knees.

As unpleasant as she is, she looks like business as usual. With a horrible sinking feeling, I know she has no accomplices or police with her. Whatever her agenda, it is no doubt some self-serving project, not about harming me. I hope I'm wrong.

Jack walks out of the temple and stands behind Dr. Lana for a full minute. Then he gives me the okay sign. I realize that he's been listening to her conversation. She is oblivious to all except the person on the other end of the line. I pop up from my hiding place as if I've been on the ground tying my shoes with no laces, or looking for spare change.

Walking up the steps of the temple, directly in Dr. Lana's path, is Plant Man. What is a homeless man with a plant growing out of his head doing at the Wilshire Boulevard Temple at the exact same time as all of us?

He asks Dr. Lana for change and she brushes him away like he is a mosquito. I see Jack pull a dollar out of his pocket. Am I being redundant if I say I could fall in love with this man?

Plant Man sits down on the steps of the temple. In order to enter the temple, one will have to walk past Jack, Dr. Lana, and Plant Man. We have quite a little gathering, soon to include me. I walk out of the parking lot, stand at the foot of the steps of the temple, and say, "Lana, I hope I'm not interrupting your call, but I don't have a great deal of time."

The woman continues to talk on the phone and holds up her diamond-heavy index finger, signaling one minute. Who wears a diamond on her index finger?

She clicks off abruptly, shoves the tiny phone into her handbag, and walks down the steps to where I stand. Plant Man's plant bobs, as if Dr. Lana's movement created a bad wind. He can easily grab her tiny ankle and cause her to tumble down the steps. He doesn't. I wish—

"Samantha, you've been very secretive, though I suspect for obvious reasons. You and I have not had good communication in the past, so I'll get to the point as this is business."

I am bewildered but I like the get-to-the-point part.

"Your story has a fabulous angle for a book about the wives of powerful, rich, and famous men. It's abuse of a more insidious and—" she pauses, looking for her word "—interesting nature. I mean, even though you can be distasteful, you are sane enough to be my collaborator. So, what do you think?"

What do I think? Dr. Lana Green, whom I hate and despise, wants me to work with her on a book? Where is an airplane barf bag when you need one?

"This is far more to your advantage than mine," she continues. "You get the benefit of riding in on my coattails. My agent loves it. My publicist loves it. My editor loves it. They'll even talk to you about doing something with that book of yours that was on the billboard . . . Hunter someone is dead. What do you say?"

The problem with women like Lana Green is that there's just too much to say and, as a result, nothing ever seems to come out, and when it finally does, it's not right and it's not enough.

All I say is, "No."

"That's it. That's your entire response? You don't want to talk to anyone? You don't want details? You don't want to pencil it out? Have you thought about where your pitiful life is headed at the moment?"

On reflection, sometimes "no" says it all.

Dr. Lana is still talking. I've stopped listening. Plant Man has fallen asleep and is snoring. A droning monotone can have that effect. Jack talks over Dr. Lana and asks me if I'm ready to leave.

I say, "Yes."

Sometimes "yes" says it all.

# CHAPTER THIRTY-NINE

Did I know that the last Saturday of April is Confederate Memorial Day, celebrated by the United Daughters of the Confederacy, Los Angeles chapter, at Hollywood Forever Cemetery?

Who would have ever imagined that confederate patriots are buried in the City of the Angels? Or that they have their own commemorative stone and a regalia of costumed historians who congregate once a year to pay tribute to the fallen confederate soldiers of the Civil War?

And that day is today, the day I'm meeting my friend Ren and finding out if she killed my husband and three others and implicated me. With all due respect to the fallen soldiers of the confederacy, I feel that my business is more pressing.

The costumed historians look like they are having a blast, taking pictures, showing off their weaponry, and trading historical anecdotes. I, on the other hand, have never been more depressed in my life.

The stone, which I never noticed before, is near the entrance to the cemetery and states that it is dedicated to the memory of confederate soldiers who died—or may die—on the Pacific Coast. What were genteel southerners who wanted plantations and slavery to continue doing anywhere in the vicinity of the Hollywood sign? In my copious free time, I will research this.

Until then, Jack and I struggle to find a parking space. After we do, we walk to the tent where the memorial service has just concluded.

The stone I have never seen is noticeable today as it is surrounded by Confederate flags, cannons, muskets, and two dozen men outfitted as if ready to re-commence the conflict that my history books called the Civil War. A few of the men inform me and Jack that they prefer "The Second American Revolution" or "The War Between the States" or "The War of Secession." When they joke it is sometimes called "The Late Unpleasantness."

Jack and I are almost forty-five minutes early. We didn't plan to engage in a long discussion with the men, but it is hard not to enjoy their enthusiasm, and it is, at least for me, a welcome diversion. I don't want to think about seeing Ren at four o'clock. Even with all my suspicions lately, I never really believed Ren would do me any harm. But our other suspects are not murderers and the list is down to one person.

It's a hot day, but the men look comfortable in their uniforms. One man says that they plan for the heat by having the costumes made of cotton. Another tells me they do monthly re-enactments of Civil War battles in different locations and they've gotten used to wearing the uniforms in all kinds of weather.

The men are talkative and friendly, with interesting asides about the Civil War, or whatever name they'd rather call it. Another man points out that there are a lot of "firsts" in the Civil War, like the bugle hymn "Taps" and photographs of the battles and a president assassinated. When he mentions the war as a first for the use of telescopic sights for rifles, we hear from yet another man, who wants to make sure we don't walk away without knowing about weaponry.

I now have more information than I will ever need or want. Jack looks mildly interested. I stop listening and try to imagine my meeting with Ren. What will she say? What can she say?

Finally, I hear Jack say, "We need to get over to a gravesite, but thank you for the very interesting education about the weapons of the war."

He and I walk east on the path I know will bend south and then lead us to the Cathedral Mausoleum. Jack lets me lead. We want to get there early so I can show him where he can hide and where others may be hidden. Will Ren call the police? Would she turn in her best friend?

On our walk, I point out to Jack my favorite trees. There must be no less than fifteen different types of trees in the cemetery, but these two are distinctive. The larger is a tall palm. In its shade, a smaller, different kind of tree has grown, and that tree's thick roots have twisted and wrapped themselves around the trunk of the palm tree in such a manner that they are inextricably wed. I tell Jack that I think it's a kind of marital bliss that can only be accomplished in nature.

Jack doesn't comment on what is my cynicism or romanticism, depending on how you look at it. He likes the trees, too. He says they remind him of wrestlers in a permanent lock hold. His imagery is interesting, but I prefer a more romantic, heterosexual image. I guess I'm not so cynical that I've lost all hope.

In front of the Cathedral Mausoleum is a lovely pond. In the center of the pond is a small island on which there is a white cement mausoleum about the size of a two-car garage. It must be the most expensive burial spot in the cemetery. There's a small bridge at the northwest portion of the pond that one can cross to get to the tiny island. Spring has really arrived with a blast of heat and sun. As we troop toward the Cathedral Mausoleum, the walk is peaceful, breezeless, and quiet, except for the murmuring buzz of the insects. Buds and new growth have their own distinct fresh smell.

As we round the bend to the pond and mausoleum, the

sounds of doves and ducks hit us. It's like stepping from a monastery into a discothèque. In all my walks I have never seen so many birds or heard them so resoundingly. Doves are perched on the large cement crypts that dot the path up to the huge Cathedral Mausoleum building. Scores of ducks are strolling on the grass between and on top of the small gravesites. One dove is peculiarly perched on a sprinkler valve as if he is the appointed lookout. I hope he will look out for me, as well.

None of the birds fly away as we walk down the path. They continue to coo and quack and stroll over the stones and grass as if they know we are the intruders and this is their domain.

I watch Jack's face. He is looking everywhere. I know he is wisely more preoccupied with checking out the area than pondering the idyllic tranquility of this final resting ground. I'm looking, too, but I don't see anyone.

We stop in front of the Cathedral Mausoleum, William Desmond Taylor's resting place, and I ask Jack what he thinks.

"Unlike the rest of the cemetery, this location has a number of places where someone could be hiding," he says. "We don't have time to search behind every large crypt and tree."

He is looking at the more than twelve crypts, each the size of a large tool shed, that are on all sides of the mausoleum and around the pond.

I'm not sure if Jack is being accusatory or observant. I picked the location. When I selected it, I was just trying to make it easy for Ren to find me. I didn't remember or think about the vast number of spots a person could hide. Even inside the mausoleum there is no shortage of hiding places. There are four aisles of crypts on each side of the north/south aisle.

There are two private burial sanctuaries, each the size of a small kitchen. They have doors that close and can secrete one or more. In front of the mausoleum are huge pillars and inside the building are large Greek-looking statues, though I don't think anyone can realistically hide behind the statues.

Jack wants to check out the interior of the Cathedral Mausoleum. He selects one of the many large crypts outside the mausoleum and plants me there to await his return. "Don't move until I come back," he says.

Where would I go?

I tell him about the two private sanctuaries where someone could easily hide. I tell him that William Desmond Taylor is in the second aisle on the west side, crypt number 594. I don't know why I tell him this. I figure he's already heard so much about Bill, he may be curious.

The interior of the mausoleum is small and he is back in less than a few minutes. "I checked both sanctuaries and they were empty. I walked to your friend Bill's site and someone left a single white carnation in his vase."

I find it touching that Bill had another visitor. It makes me happy and sad. But I'm already sad for a lot of reasons.

"The building is empty except for a woman at one of the gravesites on the east side," Jack continues. "I didn't ask, but she volunteered that she was looking at the grave of Barbara La Marr. Do you know who that is?"

La Marr is a more obscure celebrity at Hollywood Forever, but by now I know all the famous and not so famous deceased who rest in the Cathedral Mausoleum.

"She was the silent screen sex 'goddess' who they labeled 'the girl who was too beautiful.' "

Jack looks unhappy. "Well, she's still in there and I don't mean Barbara La Marr. I don't understand how a person can spend more than ten seconds looking at a metal plaque with a few words. I don't like it. I know it's not likely she's a problem, but it's pretty odd that someone would be here."

Not surprisingly, I feel a bit defensive. "It's not that odd. People do visit cemeteries."

Jack gives me a look that's hard to read. I should switch gears. "What do you think we should do?"

"I'm not sure. She looked harmless. But that doesn't mean anything."

Jack the cop is talking.

"Maybe it's Ren and she's early and she wandered in there."

Jack shakes his head. "No. I saw your friend on TV. This is a blonde, not a redhead."

"What does she look like?"

"I don't know. Attractive. Lots of makeup. Very put together. In my opinion, not the type you'd expect to see spending a whole lot of time hanging around a mausoleum."

Unlike me, who does just that.

Before we can further discuss the blonde, I see Ren walking down the path. She looks great, though a little tired. She's dressed in brown silk slacks with a cream-colored short-sleeve blouse. She looks like she jumped out of an action movie, where the heroine has fallen down a mountain, blown up a munitions warehouse, and jumped from one rooftop to another, with not a hair out of place, makeup perfect, and clothes just pressed. She's wearing sensible shoes that I bet cost no less than $465. She isn't carrying a handbag. I point that out to Jack.

He shakes his head and whispers, "It's a good sign since she doesn't have a weapon on her. I can tell. No bulges anywhere. Or it's a bad sign, meaning she doesn't need anything because her backup is nearby. I guess we'll soon know."

I give Jack a smile that is braver than I feel. "Here goes. It was the best of times, it was the worst of times. We'll soon know."

When I see Ren look down for a moment, I walk out onto the pathway. As she looks up, it must seem like I appeared out of thin air. Like a spaceship dropped me right in front of her.

"Oh my God, Sam!" Ren rushes over and hugs me.

I see what looks like genuine tears. But a hard knot has formed in my belly and I'm not even tempted to break down. I want answers. I won't let myself get swept up in the avalanche of emotions that come so easily at moments like this. Business first. At this moment, Ren is guilty until she proves her innocence. When one is wanted by the police, the democratic process has too many flaws.

We walk a few paces and sit down on the steps of the mausoleum.

Ren can't get the words out fast enough. "I'm so glad you were able to see me because I have so much I need to tell you. Explain to you. But even more importantly, are you all right? What can I do to help?"

Everything about her screams "genuine," but that isn't good enough.

"Ren, you know I didn't kill Benjamin or anyone else, don't you?"

"Of course I do."

"Well then, who did?"

Again, Ren looks at me like I descended from an alien planet. "How should I know, Sam? I have no idea."

"I don't know if I believe you. I don't think I do." Now we can have fireworks or whatever surprises she has planned for me.

"I don't blame you for not believing me," she says unexpectedly. "That's why I wanted to see you. There have been entirely too many secrets. And everything is getting too stressful. Sam, I've met someone. I'm leaving Stephen."

I was right. The different look, the different aroma, the different food, the long periods of no phone calls, the secretiveness. Ren is having an affair.

"If it was just an affair, I would have told you," she continues. "But it's much more complicated."

*How much more complicated can it be?* I want to ask, but I remain silent.

"I needed to keep everything secret, not because of me but because of him."

"Because he's married?" It seems like a logical guess.

"No. I wish it was that simple. He's divorced. It's horribly complicated."

"Ren, I don't understand. Just tell me."

"His ex-wife is dangerous. She's unbalanced and ruthless. They have a thirteen-year-old son. His father . . . Rory . . . that's his name, Rory Mason . . . has custody, but she gets to visit. It's not good enough. She wants money, she wants their son, she wants everything. He's convinced she'll kidnap their son . . . his name is Taylor . . . and Rory's in violation of all kinds of court orders because he's been hiding Taylor from her. Rory says she's capable of violence. There isn't one judge who really got it. They were manipulated by her. Laura Mason is smart and pretty and fooled all the psychiatrists. Because Rory doesn't want her to find Taylor, they live a reclusive life . . ." Ren pauses. "That's not completely true. They're in hiding. I know it sounds crazy, but it's necessary."

My mom didn't raise a really dumb child, just a mildly dumb one. How could I have not seen this when it was right under my nose? Or should I say right next door? I look at Ren and the old warmth returns full force. "He lives in the Boo house with his son?"

"Yes." She looks shocked. "How did you know?"

"There were a hundred clues from before, but how about when you told a police officer recently that it was your house and that Taylor was *your* son?"

The blood seems to drain from her face. "How could you know about that?"

For the first time since seeing her, I smile. "Guess who that police officer was?"

"You?"

I nod.

"How did I not recognize you? What were you doing there?" She stops then answers her own question. "You needed to get into your house and you couldn't do it as yourself."

Ren's mom didn't raise a completely dumb child, either. We look at one another and hug. I'm bubbling. It's unexpected news and I'm happy for my friend. "I have so much to tell *you*, Ren. And I have so many questions. I want to know when you first met and how you met and what he's like."

For one brief moment I am enjoying her happiness and forgetting about my problems.

"And the gunshot noise," I add. "What was that about?"

Ren laughs. "A chemistry experiment. Rory is home-tutoring Taylor."

Listen to me, rattling on with girl talk as if my life is normal. Back to business. "But Ren, before anything, I have to figure out who did these murders, and now that I know it's not you, we've eliminated all of our suspects."

"Me? You suspected me? And who's 'we'?"

A cold hard object pushes hard against my upper back and neck. Goosebumps blossom full force down my spine and Ren's mouth is open. She looks paralyzed. I have a lump in my throat the size of a golf ball. The hard object moves. This isn't good. I hear breathing that isn't me or Ren. Then a cough. Then gum cracking.

I turn from my sitting position and see a blonde woman pointing a revolver at Ren and me, depending on which way her hand swings. She keeps sticking the barrel in my neck, then moving around. She has to have come from the interior of the mausoleum and she fits the description Jack gave me. She is blonde, lots of makeup, and though he said attractive, she's quite beautiful. Too beautiful to be holding a gun on me. Too beautiful to look as angry as she does.

And then the girl who is too beautiful smacks me solidly in the face with her cold, hard gun.

# CHAPTER FORTY

I'm dazed but still conscious. I know where Jack is hidden, though I can't see him. I know he can see and hear us. He is close but it's like a million miles away. He can't help us without one of us getting hurt.

I'm bleeding. The blonde is laughing cruelly. Ren and I show no reaction.

She stops laughing and gives both of us a look of hatred. She says, "Now I know exactly what they mean when they say you can kill two birds with one stone."

As if acknowledging the reference to birds, the doves and ducks start yammering at an increased volume. The faint sound of grass moving like a footstep makes the blonde turn abruptly and point her gun in a random manner.

It's a lone duck pecking at the grass, as if he expected to find a small fish hidden in the blades. The blonde shoos him away and he rejoins his flock near the pond.

"As you probably figured out by now, Samantha, I've wanted you dead for a while. Or indicted for murder. Dead or in jail forever. It made very little difference to me. But now this. Such an unexpected and fantastic double header."

I speak quietly, hoping my voice will calm her. "I have no idea who you are. I have no idea why you're doing this."

"Of course you don't. But you will. First, I want to thank your friend, Adrienne Martel." She pronounces Ren's name as if she swallowed something distasteful.

Ren looks startled and scared. "How do you know me?"

"That's another story. We'll get to that. What is more interesting is that you know my son and that I now know where to find Taylor. Imagine that. All this time he was right there, next door to the Crowleys and the Martels."

Ren looks as if someone knocked the wind out of her. "Oh my God, what are you saying? You're Taylor's mother? You're Laura Mason?"

The blonde points the gun at Ren. The sun makes her bright red lip gloss shine in a way that gives her mouth an evil and sensuous look. "How did you meet my son?"

Ren doesn't answer. She is stunned.

"I'm not going to ask you twice and I would love to hurt you."

"I didn't meet him," Ren says, her voice shaky. "My son figured out that a man and boy were living in the house next door. Blake spoke to Taylor once through a window and they exchanged email addresses. Then they corresponded for a month before I found out. I walked into his room while they were chatting, or whatever it's called, on the computer."

"Don't stop. What did your son tell you about Taylor?"

"Blake told me Taylor's father didn't know they were friends either, and that for some reason they don't leave their home."

I listen to Ren as intently as the blonde. I know Jack is listening and watching, too. Her story is revealing but of no help in understanding why she has killed four people and why she is after me.

She is determined to get her own questions answered. She mimics Ren and says, "For some reason they don't leave their home." She snorts and points the gun at Ren, then back at me. "When did you meet Rory?" She says his name with a sneer.

I can understand Ren's reluctance to answer. This woman is, no doubt, ready to make Rory her target as well. She steps closer to Ren and presses the gun against Ren's chest. "I asked you when you met Rory?"

"A month ago."

"Details!"

"The boys wanted to meet in person, so they planned an after-dark rendezvous in Taylor's backyard. I joined Blake and while the kids talked, I walked through the back door of the house and into the kitchen, where Rory was drinking a cup of coffee."

"And the two of you fell in love." The blonde isn't angry. She's raging. Her face has whitened. Ren doesn't answer. Her hand instinctively goes to her pocket for cigarettes. The blonde clicks the gun and I jump. Ren pulls her hand back, clearly rethinking the idea of having a smoke.

I'm feeling neither bold nor brave, but I need to deflect the attention from Ren. The way the blonde is looking, she may pull the trigger regardless of how ill advised it is to fire a gun in a public setting. A public setting that doesn't seem very public. Except for the ducks and doves and hidden Jack, there isn't a soul in sight. Souls six feet under don't count. They can be of no assistance.

"I think I should be able to ask a few questions." I swallow hard as I visualize a golf ball cruising down my esophagus. There is blood from my head wound trickling down my face and tickling my nose.

"You do, do you?" The blonde mocks me.

I try to appear undaunted. "The way I understand what you've said, you didn't come here expecting to find your son. You expected to find me. I don't know your son and I didn't know where he was living, so I don't see the connection."

"You're a regular genius, honey. There is no connection. Finding Taylor was a bonus, like I said. And the way things have gone in the past couple of weeks, I'm long overdue for a bonus.

I loved your billboard, by the way. Benjamin hid your book so well, I couldn't find it before I left his studio." She grins wickedly. "Nothing changes the fact that I need *you* out of the way. Permanently."

I'm genuinely confused. Even though I'm scared to death, I still can't connect the dots. "I don't understand. What do we have in common?"

The blonde's face twists in an unattractive way. "Not *what*, honey. Who. Let me make it simple, Samantha. I'm Benjamin's beneficiary on the life insurance and I intend to collect."

Ren says, "No, you're not. You're out of luck. You've done this for nothing. Samantha is the beneficiary."

"No, my dear. I am. If Samantha dies or is incarcerated for her husband's murder, the money designated for the primary beneficiary goes to the contingent beneficiary. Me."

I gasp. "Laura? Are you *that* Laura? *The* Laura?" I am slowly putting together the pieces.

The blonde doesn't reply. I didn't make the connection when Ren said Laura Mason. Laura is a common name. I heard it for the first time from Paul. Little nerdy Paul, who had seen it before anyone. A girl he wouldn't want to come up against in a dark alley, he'd said.

Or a public cemetery.

"You tried to get Jack to kill me. You tried to get me arrested for murder. And then you killed Benjamin. Why did you kill your lover?"

"When Jack didn't kill you, I couldn't do it. I'd be too obvious a suspect when the cops saw the insurance. So I had to have you kill Benjamin. That made sense." She says the last sentence in a little girl's voice.

So there it is. The oldest motive in the book. Money.

Ren looks confused. "Who's Jack?"

Laura takes a step closer to Ren and is startled by a bird

swooping down and cawing as if he intends to pluck one of us off the ground.

Jack's head moves. I see it. He saw the bird and how it distracted Laura. He has a fraction of a second to react and he does. He flies out from behind the crypt, tackles Laura, knocks her to the ground as her gun goes flying. It lands in front of a duck. Even knowing Jack was there, I am surprised. When I look at Ren, I can see she is thrilled and surprised as well. I pick up the gun and hold it. I've never held a gun before. This is something I'm going to learn more about in the future. I watch Jack, who is being cautious and wants to keep the situation under control. Laura isn't a professional, but she is crazy.

Jack says, "Put your hands on top of your head and sit on the ground." Without rope, handcuffs, or any of the handy police accoutrements that would have made detaining her easier, it's the best Jack can do. I hand the gun to him and he tucks it in his pants.

Jack saved our lives. I can't figure out which makes me happier—still being alive or seeing Jack as my hero. Either way, the guy has a hug coming. Almost shyly I turn to Ren and say, "This is Jack Sharrow and he's the best. He saved my life."

"Both our lives, it would seem. So this is the 'we.' " Ren gives Jack an approving raised eyebrow, gives me an appreciative wink, and goes for a cigarette. She offers one to Jack and doubles her approving look when he accepts.

"We still have a lot of unanswered questions," Jack says, looking at Laura. "I want to know how you came to involve me. How come you knew so much about me and my brother?"

"I don't have to answer your questions."

Jack looks angry. Scary angry. "No. But you will."

"You were one of many police officers who came to my house when I filed complaints against my former husband for refusing me visitation with my son. Then one time I called and asked for you. I was told you were no longer on the force. I figured that meant something went wrong because you were too young to retire. So I did a little investigating. I thought you might come in handy one day. It's always good to know the weaknesses of others. It gives you a good leg up for the future."

"So you followed Samantha and knew her routine and where she'd be. And you phoned me and hoped I would think Samantha was you when I saw her at the cemetery. You wanted me to kill her."

"Yeah."

"But that doesn't explain how you knew she'd be here today. No one knew except—"

Jack and I both look at Ren.

She lets out a muffled cry. "I didn't tell anyone. I wouldn't tell anyone. Sam, believe me."

I can't help it. It still doesn't add up and Ren is the only one who knew about our meeting today. "You were the one who told me I was the beneficiary on the life insurance."

"You were, Sam. Even she told you." Ren points at Laura. "I didn't look at the contingent beneficiary. I didn't even know about that."

Jack looks at me and Ren. "Someone told Ms. Mason that Samantha would be here and there is no one else who knew, Ms. Martel."

Ren looks desperately unhappy. "I didn't tell anyone. I didn't—" She stops abruptly.

"What is it, Ren?" I want to believe her.

"I told Blake, but he's fifteen years old and doesn't have a bad bone in his body." Ren grabs my arm. "Believe me. He was upset about us not being able to tell you about Taylor and Rory. Then Benjamin cornered him in the library one day and was pumping him, asking questions about you and making him uncomfortable. Blake adores you. Then Blake saw you and didn't know what to say and—"

"Ren, we have to figure this out. I'm not accusing Blake of anything, but he must have told someone. There has to be some logical connection back to her." I point at Laura.

"Of course there's a logical connection. There always is."

The voice saying those words doesn't belong to any of us.

Just north of where we are standing, the pond extends like a rectangular pool and in the center of that pool is a large, marble, solid arch. And behind that arch hides Stephen Martel, Ren's loving, boring, not very attractive, dishonest husband—the life insurance broker.

He is holding a gun aimed directly at Jack's back.

"Place your gun on the ground, Mr. Sharrow. Very slowly."

Ren doesn't look surprised. She doesn't even look disturbed. That's how it is when you have no expectations. I'm astonished.

Ren's face expresses only contempt and disgust for her husband and the father of her child. I say, "You want to hear something funny, Ren? I always thought you were happy. I was jealous of you."

She ignores me and stares at Stephen. "Well, I'm happy now."

Laura gets up and retrieves her gun from Jack's belt. Her arrogance has a strange and scary sexual vibe. She is over the top.

"We seem to have a situation here." Stephen Martel has never been known for his snappy repartee.

With the exception of Stephen, it is a good bet that everyone is wondering how the graying Stephen is going to keep a vicious, high-maintenance Laura happy. The initial attraction has to have evaporated, once Stephen gave her the only thing he possessed that could interest her—the information that she needed to know. That she was Benjamin's backup beneficiary on a large life insurance policy.

"Blake told you where I went?" Ren asks the question as if we're in the last minutes of a *Murder She Wrote* and Jessica

Fletcher is struggling to get the few missing pieces of the puzzle in place.

"Of course. He's my son, too, though you often forget. He told me that he wasn't supposed to tell anyone, but I told him 'no one' didn't mean me." Stephen smiles.

Laura looks at me. "None of this works until she's dead."

Jack is watching and listening. He seems to be listening to something else. Ren's phone starts chirping. It startles everyone.

Laura snarls, "Stephen, we can't stand here like idiots all day. Do something."

The command takes Stephen by surprise. He furrows his brow and says, "Let me think a minute."

"We don't have a minute. Kill her."

I shrink my body against the crypt, but I'm as easy a target to hit as Stephen's own leg, if he'd been inclined to shoot himself. He lifts the gun and puts his finger on the trigger.

I attempt to speak in a normal tone. "Stephen, you can't do this. I've known you almost twenty years. I'm your son's godmother. I've done nothing wrong. Stephen, Benjamin was your friend."

"Was, Samantha. And not a very good one, which is why I gave him the idea to put Laura's name on the policy and why I went to her and told her we should kill him. Benjamin wasn't the only one who knew how to make money. And Benjamin wasn't the only one entitled to some fun."

Stephen is the instigator. In Laura he has a soul mate of sorts. Soul mates in hell. He is the brains and she is the psychopath. Maybe they're both psychopaths.

A noise distracts us. Crossing the bridge from the small island to the cemetery are two men headed in our direction. Laura and Stephen put their guns by their thighs and wait to see who the men are and where they are going.

It is Jack's brother, Grant, and the homeless man who always asks for $1.83. They are coming, unarmed, wearing their Our Gang jackets and #1 caps, goofy-looking, and to our rescue. The homeless man wears his sneakers with no front and his toes flip-flop when he walks. Grant carries a small rock. He looks earnest and young and completely incapable of handling our situation.

Jack does the only thing that makes sense. He yells, "Grant, get help! We're in trouble!"

Trouble comes out muffled because Stephen hits Jack hard with the butt of the gun. Jack falls down on his knees, collapses to the ground, and loses consciousness. I rush over to him and Laura shoves me away.

"We can kill all three of them and be gone long before those idiots come back with help. Come on, Stephen. Shoot them."

"But if we kill them," he says, "we can't lay the blame on Samantha."

That sounds reasonable to me, but Laura says, "I'll think of something later," and I realize *she* doesn't want to shoot us. If the police connect the dots, she can play innocent bystander. And there'd be no one to prove otherwise. No one alive, that is.

Another thought occurs. If Stephen does kill Ren, Jack, and me, he'd better watch his own back.

"Stephen, if you kill Ren, Jack, and me, you'd better watch your own—"

"Shut up!" Laura glares at me.

Stephen now looks odd, untroubled, almost catatonic. Maybe the horror of it all has gotten to him.

Maybe he, too, is hopelessly insane. He raises his gun and points it at Ren. She doesn't blink. She doesn't cry. Her voice has lost every ounce of nervousness as she says, "You're all I ever thought you were, and less. I hate you."

Laura screams at Stephen, "Kill the other one, you idiot!"

Ren's words bother Stephen more than anything that has

transpired. He wipes his brow with his jacket sleeve, hesitates a beat, and points his gun. I can't tell if it's pointed at me or Ren.

Then I hear a bugle.

The bugle sounds again, but closer, and then I hear the drum of footsteps rushing in our direction. Stephen and Laura are already facing the pond. Ren and I turn in that direction. Jack is slowly rising from the ground. And Robert E. Lee's Confederate Army stands only fifteen feet away, ready for battle.

Twenty soldiers with their rifles, handguns and muskets drawn, face our small group. A strange-looking man, bearded like Rip Van Winkle, walks forward, stares directly at Stephen Martel and Laura Mason, and announces in a resounding baritone, "In the name of the Confederate Army and on behalf of the Great South, we demand that you surrender your arms."

My late unpleasantness is over.

# Epilogue

Harrowing life adventures can give you new perspectives.

After much confusion, talk, tears, and legalities, the dust finally settled.

I sold the Chagall and Matisse but kept the small Picasso. I deserved a small reward for what I'd been through.

I gave Bea the listing on my house. It was time to leave the house, Beverly Hills, and my old life.

I didn't make an appointment with Jupiter but I did go to a popular discount salon and for twelve dollars got my hair cut short. The days of frantically taming my hair were over. A new look was one step to a new beginning.

I cut bunches of roses from my rosebushes and brought them to my friends, William Desmond Taylor and Bugsy Siegel. I told the boys I would be back to visit soon and often.

Jack had a mild concussion. The cut on my forehead required six stitches. The plastic surgeon said there would be a tiny scar, but he could do something about it. I told him not to bother. I think scars are a good way to make us always remember. I know that's supposed to be figurative, not literal, but I wear my scar proudly. Anyway, it hardly shows.

There was a simple explanation for the Peter Perkal article in Jack's glove compartment. Perkal was the victim of one of Grant's cons. One of Peter's bank deposits had gone into Grant's account, and Peter had been threatening Grant with legal action.

Jack had been collecting information about Peter for months, hoping he would find something that might dissuade Peter from going after Grant.

I decided that I no longer needed to kill Hunter McCall, so I started writing a new book. It's romantic, it's funny, it's sad and silly. Just as I hope my life will be someday.

A New York publisher bought Bicky and Dicky's book. There's talk they may sell the story of their family to the History Channel. And I heard Maurice is representing them. Go figure.

Dr. Lana Green still talks about me as if we're old confidantes. She now takes credit for giving me the confidence to vindicate myself. I truly hate that woman.

I talked for many hours with Ren and found out a lot of things I hadn't known. We had both been married to creeps. We had both been unhappy. We'd both felt trapped. And we'd both been completely unaware of the other's pain and unhappiness. We resolved to have no more secrets.

We learned that Stephen Martel had planned and plotted everything down to the last detail. He had met Laura through Benjamin and recognized in her the same opportunistic qualities he possessed. Only she was capable of violence and Stephen delegated those tasks to her. They complemented one another well. It had only taken the idea of money, big money, to seduce Laura away from Benjamin.

Stephen thought he was getting the girl and the money. He really was crazy.

Benjamin ended up being the victim in a story he thought he was writing. But then, Benjamin was never good at understanding his characters. Splendid irony!

The coincidence of Rory's ex-wife and Benjamin's lover and Stephen's co-conspirator all being the same person is not nearly as improbable as it sounds. This is Hollywood. Always count on those small degrees of separation.

I've spent some time with Rory, Ren, Blake, and Taylor. They're great together. Ren even says she may try to stop smoking. I'm not holding my breath.

Ren is going to sell her house. We both think it's a real kick that the Boo house will be Ren's new home. But, as I said, this is Hollywood.

Surprise endings are de rigueur.

It turns out that Grant was at the cemetery because he had decided to carry through his threat and stalk Jack. Sibling retribution saved our lives.

Grant and his merry band of homeless pranksters have found a productive, profitable, and *legal* undertaking. With all the publicity our story generated, a movie studio executive offered Grant a job. He has pulled his homeless group together and he uses them as extras in various movies that are filmed all over the city.

At first we thought it was a joke, but apparently the city is going to give financial assistance. As our daily newspaper writes it, Grant is a budding entrepreneur and the studio executive is a modern-day Robin Hood. The irony of this has not been lost on any of us. This is Hollywood. Land of irony.

I phoned Jack and offered to take him out for a nice dinner. I told him it was a small gesture to say thank you. He surprised me. He asked if I had ever visited the Los Angeles Zoo. He didn't wait for my response and told me he would prefer to do that, if I didn't mind. I told him fine. His exact words were, "I'd like us to visit the Monkey House. There's something I want to tell you and I don't think you'll understand unless I tell you there."

It would be nice if he fell in love with me, but I know I shouldn't count on it. So if the Monkey House is where he wants to go, who am I to quibble? It's his day. He's the writer, director, and leading man, so he gets to pick the setting. That's how it's done, here in Hollywood.

# ABOUT THE AUTHOR

**Susan Goldstein** practices family law in Los Angeles, California. The many years she has spent in the legal arena have provided her with a unique view of the often humorous, highly emotional, and occasionally murderous aspects of divorce. She is the co-author of *The Smart Divorce* and has lived in Hollywood, California, for twenty-five years.